A cold dread seeped into Alessa's bones.

This was how it had started with Aidan. Personal favors that seemed innocuous, part of the job, even. But the mistake she'd made with Aidan was that she'd let him get too close. Forgotten the fact that she was an enlisted soldier and he was a commissioned officer, which meant they couldn't even be friends. She wouldn't do that with Luke.

Luke stood and she followed suit, getting ready to salute him the way she would any other superior officer. But he extended his hand and she automatically took it.

"We wear civilian clothes in this unit. No saluting. From now on, we're colleagues, perhaps even friends."

She looked into his ocean-blue eyes. *I can't be friends with you. That would be dangerous.* Her career couldn't withstand one more rumor of an improper relationship with a superior officer.

Dear Reader,

There are no words to describe the extraordinary sacrifice given by those who serve in the armed forces. It's not just the physical danger they face on our behalf, but the considerable sacrifice of their families and loved ones. This book is about the tough choices service members often face in their personal lives. While workplace romance is mainstream for most people, it is not for military personnel. For good reason, relationships during active duty are off-limits for soldiers, who can face serious consequences for falling in love with the wrong person.

This book is also about the heroines of the military. I know a lot of tough women. As a former paramedic, I appreciate how difficult it can be for a woman in a male-dominated field, and the crushing pressure to constantly prove that you can do the job well. Alessa Parrino is in the impossible situation of choosing between the one thing she's needed all her life (love) and the only thing she's ever had (the army).

I hope you enjoy Alessa's journey; it's one that many of us face when choosing between what our hearts desire and what our circumstances allow.

To get free book extras, visit my website, sophiasasson.com. I love hearing from readers, so please find me on Twitter (@SophiaSasson) or Facebook (SophiaSassonAuthor) or email me at readers@sophiasasson.com.

Enjoy!

Sophia Sasson

HEARTWARMING

The Sergeant's Temptation

—

Sophia Sasson

HARLEQUIN® HEARTWARMING™

Recycling programs
for this product may
not exist in your area.

ISBN-13: 978-0-373-36848-8

The Sergeant's Temptation

Copyright © 2017 by Sophia Sasson

Printed in U.S.A.

www.Harlequin.com

Sophia Sasson puts her childhood habit of daydreaming to good use by writing stories she hopes will give you hope and make you laugh, cry and possibly snort tea from your nose. She was born in Bombay, India, and has lived in the Canary Islands, Spain and Toronto, Canada. Currently she calls the madness of Washington, DC, home. She's the author of the Welcome to Bellhaven and the State of the Union series. She loves to read, travel to exotic locations in the name of research, bake, explore water sports and watch foreign movies. Hearing from readers makes her day. Contact her through sophiasasson.com.

Books by Sophia Sasson

Harlequin Heartwarming

State of the Union

The Senator's Daughter
Mending the Doctor's Heart

Welcome to Bellhaven

First Comes Marriage

Please visit Harlequin.com to check out all of Sophia Sasson's books.

To those who serve our country in the military. Words cannot express the gratitude we owe you.

Acknowledgments

This book, and the entire State of the Union series, would not happen without my awesome editor Claire Caldwell. Thank you for our brainstorming sessions.

A huge thank-you to my husband, who puts up with me disappearing into the writing abyss. And my critique partner, Jayne Evans, who deals with my writing crises.

Most of all, thank you to my readers. Your reviews, emails and letters keep me writing.

CHAPTER ONE

"I'LL TAKE HER."

Luke Williams couldn't get his eyes off the petite soldier who was fighting a man more than twice her size. It was better than any mixed martial arts match he'd ever seen on TV. He was standing outside the Plexiglas window of a ten-foot by ten-foot cube that had been designed to train soldiers in hand-to-hand combat. Except Sergeant Alessa Parrino didn't need any training; she was literally kicking his best man to the floor. This one wasn't made from the typical army mold.

"Oh, no you won't, Lieutenant."

Luke turned to his commanding officer, Colonel Michael McBride. "I thought the last unit member was my call."

"It is. You're just not hiring *her*."

Luke bit the inside of his cheek, keeping his voice neutral and friendly. "You have a concern, sir?"

The colonel raised his bushy gray eyebrows. "Have you read her file?"

Luke knew why the colonel was asking if Luke really wanted Alessa Parrino for his unit.

"Why did you let her apply and go through the test?"

"So I could check the box that we gave equal opportunity for this unit. You know how it is these days."

"A woman could be an asset for us." Luke said evenly. He'd worked with McBride long enough to realize the old man still wasn't used to the idea that the army was letting women into special ops.

"I don't see how. You get injured on the field, that hundred-and-thirty-pound girl isn't gonna carry your two hundred and twenty pounds to safety."

Luke watched Parrino extend her hand to the fallen soldier to help him up. *Bad move.* Rodgers was one of his dirtiest fighters; that was why Luke had used him for this exercise. All the other unit members had been handpicked by Luke's predecessor. Luke wanted the open position to be filled by someone of his choosing, a member who would be loyal to him. He needed someone on the inside to help him with what he planned.

Rodgers took Parrino's hand and predictably used her weaker position to pull downward while sliding his leg across the floor to kick her legs out from under her. *Classic. Can't believe she fell for it.*

"Don't go easy on her 'cause she's a girl," the colonel hooted even though the sparring soldiers couldn't hear him through the cube.

Luke resisted the urge to make a smart-aleck comment. He was on thin ice as it was. Parrino jumped a millisecond before Rodgers's leg would have connected and used the downward momentum her rival had created to bend her arm and bring her elbow down on the other soldier's solar plexus.

Nice!

Both Luke and Colonel McBride flinched at the look of sheer agony on Rodgers's face.

Luke slapped the Plexiglas wall, opening the door. "All right, Parrino, you're done." The last thing he needed was for one of his men to end up in the hospital. The unit was less than a month away from being fully operational. That meant he'd get to take his men and fly to an undisclosed location, far away from Colonel Pain-in-the-Neck, who would stay here at Fort Belvoir in Virginia, kissing up to the Pentagon.

Parrino released her grip on the soldier's throat and stood. Her eyes still alert for another attack, she walked toward Luke and stepped outside. She stood in front of Luke and the colonel and saluted. Barely five foot four, Parrino had short dark hair pulled neatly into a pony-tail, golden-brown eyes and cream-colored skin tinged pink around her cheeks and nose. Her breathing was even and her expression relaxed. A shiny forehead was the only indication that she'd broken a sweat.

"Well done, Parrino." Luke acknowledged.

She nodded curtly. They stared at her, and to her credit, her face remained impassive, back straight with a stance worthy of a recruitment poster. Luke tilted his head toward his office. "Wait there." He didn't offer her water or a chance to go to the bathroom; he needed to see her mettle.

"Rodgers, you're done. Go get cleaned up." The man would never live down this exercise. It was the first one he'd lost, but the unit members wouldn't let him forget the fact that he'd been taken down by a woman half his size.

As soon as Rodgers was out of earshot, the colonel placed a hand on Luke's shoulder. He wanted more than anything to smack it away. "Williams, I think it's a bad idea to take the girl. She's trouble with a capital *T*."

"Parrino's the only qualified candidate I've seen."

"What you talkin' about? There's a stack of good soldiers on your desk."

Luke had gone through all the applications

in the folders on his desk and auditioned ten other guys, all of whom Rodgers had wiped out. The colonel knew this; he'd been there for every test. Not that he was micromanaging Luke. No, the colonel was there to "lend support." Luke was supposed to have the authority to hire whomever he wanted. Technically.

That was the point of this unit, Ethan's brainchild. Luke's twin brother had convinced the brass that the only way to deal with their current problem was to create a nimble unit that could operate without the usual hierarchy. Each of the unit members had been hired for a particular skill set and they worked as a team, regardless of their army rank. The whole idea was *not* to work the usual way, so their moves wouldn't be predictable. None of the soldiers who had been handpicked by Ethan had known each other, served together or had any commanding officers in common. They were a good group of men. But they were his brother's men.

"Sir, we need a woman on the team. Men and women are regularly separated in the Sandbox, and I don't want to be in a situation where we don't have eyes where we need them."

"Have you thought about the influence she'll have on your men, your unit?" He motioned toward Rodgers, who was staring at Parrino through the glass doors of Luke's office.

Luke raised a brow, though he understood full well where the colonel was going. "Oh, I'll tell them I told Rodgers to go easy on her so they don't give him a hard time." It was a cheeky comment, but the colonel took it at face value.

"That's not what I mean. Unit cohesion is everything, and given her history, I worry she'll be a distraction. She has trouble with boundaries."

Look who's talking. The only boundaries McBride respected were the ones that suited him.

Luke resisted the urge to roll his eyes. He didn't have a good grasp on how to manage the colonel. *How would Ethan handle this?* Now more than ever he wished he'd kept in touch with his twin brother. They'd been inseparable until they graduated West Point. A rift had grown between them after they both began active duty. The last few times they'd spoken, it had been to argue over Luke leaving the army. Ethan had taken command of this unit a year ago, but Luke had hardly paid attention. He'd been too focused on getting out. The news of Ethan's death four months ago changed everything.

"Sir, no one knows for sure what happened, and she wasn't disciplined."

"Yeah, but her commanding officer still had to face an Article 134. That man will never get promoted. All it takes is the hint of impropriety between a soldier and a commanding officer, and you..." The colonel wiggled his eyebrows and pinned Luke with steel-gray eyes. "Son, I have great respect for your father—we've served in combat together—but I have to say that given your reputation, I wasn't entirely comfortable giving you command of this unit."

That's a shocker. The uptight colonel was as old-school as they came, and Luke was far from a model officer. But McBride also wanted to get his first star, and going up against Luke's four-star general father was not the way to do that. That said, Luke was on a short leash. He had command of the unit on a trial basis. A big screwup and he was out.

That couldn't happen.

Luke gave him a hard look. "Sir, this unit meant a lot to my brother, and I plan to make it a success. For his sake."

"Then I suggest you think carefully. This is your first major decision as unit commander. Pick your battles. Would your brother have wanted her?"

Luke didn't have to think about what Ethan would've done. There was a reason why his brother had made captain while Luke was still first lieutenant. Luke hadn't earned command of this unit. His father had pulled some strings, and if he hadn't, Luke would be the last man in contention for the job. The colonel knew it, and so did Luke's men. Every decision he made would be judged, and he would be blamed if anything went south.

"Sir, I know *my* reputation precedes me as well, which is why I'm more willing to give Sergeant Parrino a chance. The army has a way of blowing rumors out of proportion."

"All rumors have a basis. Now, you're a smart boy—" the colonel drawled "—you know what's at stake here." He patted Luke's shoulder in a fatherly gesture that was anything but. "I'll leave it with you. I'm sure you'll make the right choice."

As soon as I know what the right choice is.

"Yes, sir." The colonel walked away and Luke was left starting after him. He didn't need to be reminded of the stakes. The army was Ethan and his father's thing. Not his. He hadn't cared about climbing the ladder. He was supposed to be out by now, starting a new life. Then Ethan had died. Well-known for his shenanigans, Luke would have to work twice as hard to prove he was capable of commanding the unit. Without it, he had no chance of finding out what really happened to his brother.

ALESSA TOOK SEVERAL deep breaths so she'd be prepared to be neutral and deferential when Luke Williams—*excuse me, Lieutenant Williams*—returned to tell her she couldn't have the job. She'd seen it all over the old colonel's face when she'd pinned her opponent to the ground. He wasn't the first officer to give her that look of disbelief and disgust. She was a woman; how dare she show herself to be stronger and more capable than a man? It was just as well. The unit was a long shot. She'd known that coming in.

The wall clock told her she'd been waiting for well over an hour. She shifted on her feet, trying not to think about the fact that her bladder was about to explode. Forty-eight hours ago, she'd been handed papers saying she would ship out in twenty-four hours with no explanation as to where she was going. Yesterday she'd boarded a military transport and it wasn't until she'd been delivered to Fort Belvoir close to midnight that she'd been told to be ready to demonstrate her competence for the unit commander. She'd submitted her application six months ago and hadn't heard anything.

Her "assessment" for this job had started this morning with a five-mile run, followed by a tactical exercise requiring her to focus and stay quick on her feet, and then the close-combat fight. It had been seven hours since she'd been given the opportunity to use the bathroom.

She catalogued everything in the office, trying to paint her own picture of Lieutenant Williams. It was hard not to remember everything she'd heard about the man, but she knew firsthand that talk did not equate to reality. There wasn't much to see, however. The office was as generic as a grocery store aisle. Standard-issue desk, a common computer and cheap ballpoint pens. There was a bottle of water beside the guest chair. Tempting, but Alessa guessed it was part of the test. Having spent more than her fair share of time in the desert, she knew how to deal with thirst.

"Sergeant Parrino."

She moved to stand at attention.

"At ease, soldier. Have a seat."

He took a seat across from her, and she allowed herself to get her first good look at him. She'd seen his picture in the post newspaper, standing next to the general when the story about his brother broke. His eyes had drawn her in; they were so intense, so full of determination. They weren't the eyes of the entitled, carefree playboy she'd heard about.

"Tell me why you want to be a part of this unit."

Because I need to get away from my current post before I destroy more lives.

"I want the opportunity to serve, sir."

"What exactly do you know about this unit, Sergeant?"

"Not much. Just that it's highly irregular because it's special ops but isn't using Delta or other Special Forces. In fact, they were purposely excluded."

He raised a brow and she suppressed a smile. She had done her homework, called in every favor she had to get information on both the unit and the man running it.

"Glad you know the difference between special ops and Special Forces. I'm aware that you tried out for Delta   this won't be your ticket in."

Forcing herself to sit still, she met his gaze. "I'm aware of that, sir. Having been through SFAS, I'm familiar with the process." Special Forces Assessment and Selection was the pathway to Delta and other Special Forces, and she had been hoping this unit might be a way in. She leaned forward. He was gearing up to tell her she hadn't made the cut.

"Sir, when I went through SFAS, I passed the physical portion of the test with a perfect score.

I was disqualified because I'd been a sergeant for five years and two days."

He pressed his lips together and hope bloomed in her chest. It was a silly rule, that five years in the same position disqualified someone from Special Forces. She should've been promoted two years ago, but after the *incident*, there had always been an excuse for why she wasn't fit to be upgraded to staff sergeant. *Next year, Parrino. Let some time pass.* This unit was the only way she would get herself out of the career hole she'd dug herself into.

"I'm thirty-five years old and the upper limit for Special Forces is thirty-six. I am special ops material, and this is my only chance at it." Staring at him, she silently challenged him to disagree. She'd bet a month's pay that the guy she'd just fought was the best of the unit. He had been good, and there were a few times where he'd almost had her. Almost. It had been a while since she'd had to bring up the image of her father to get the better of a man in a physical fight, but she'd done it. She'd had to. Alessa Parrino didn't get second chances.

He sat back in his seat and his eyes flicked to a folder on his desk. She knew what was in that file and could see his gears churning. Part of her training was to get into her opponent's head, and she was sure Luke Williams was weighing the risk of bringing her baggage into his unit.

She placed her elbows on the desk. "Sir, have you ever done the right thing even when it was against the rules?" She knew the answer to that question. Luke was notorious in the army circles. A general father and an identical twin brother with a stellar reputation while his was less than perfect was fodder for gossip. He was the evil twin, the one tarnishing his father's reputation.

She had served with his brother when she was a private first class and Ethan Williams was a second lieutenant. Officers and enlisted didn't mix, but she always took stock of the commanding officers on post and her assessment of Ethan Williams was that he was a rising star. His good looks had been hard to ignore and the fact that he had an identical twin who was an outrageous flirt had been a common source of discussion in the female barracks. As had Luke Williams's penchant for bending the rules. She had done so much research, she felt she knew him personally. *Remember he's a superior officer.* The last thing she needed was to get friendly with him.

"Sergeant, I get the feeling you've done your homework on me, and you know full well what's in your file. So how about you give me some facts I haven't already read about."

She dug her fingernails into her palms. "Sir, I have nothing to hide. What would you like to know?"

"Your file doesn't have much on your childhood. Tell me about your parents."

She swallowed, trying to open her closed throat. She didn't have to answer any of his questions. It was none of his business what her childhood was like. It wasn't any of the army's business.

"My parents were Italian immigrants— they came over newly married. I have a younger sister. Just a typical family." Somehow she'd managed to make her voice sound normal. Maybe it was the years of practice with that line.

He narrowed his eyes. "How often do you see them?"

She forced herself to meet his eyes. Most people tried to control the pitch of their voice when they lied, but it was shifting eyes that gave them away. "As often as I can." It was best to go with half-truths.

"When was the last time?" His startling blue eyes bored into her and she blinked. When she'd first seen his picture, she'd found herself unable to look away. In person she wanted nothing more than to avoid eye contact.

"Sir, I'm the most qualified person for this position, and if you're hesitating because of what's in that file, let me assure you—"

"Sergeant, I'm going to give you some advice."

She closed her mouth, making a concerted effort to keep her expression neutral. Ever since *the incident,* every commissioned officer she'd met had felt the need to lecture her on appropriate behavior, as if she were a truant toddler. Never mind the fact that she'd already been in more combat than most West Point graduates would ever see. She composed herself so she wouldn't gag when Luke gave her the tired old speech about how she could have an illustrious career if she kept her nose clean and made sure she didn't engage in any more inappropriate behavior with a superior officer.

"If you haven't done anything wrong, don't sound apologetic."

This is new. She sat up straighter.

"If there's nothing concerning in my file, then why aren't you selecting me?"

He raised a brow, his blue eyes sparking with a hint of gray. "I haven't said that I'm not."

Her pulse kicked up a notch until she saw his Adam's apple bob. The job wasn't hers. Not yet.

"Let me tell you why I'm right for this position."

His lips twitched.

"First, I just beat the best man on your unit. Second, if you're going to operate in the Middle East or Asia, you'll need a woman to get into places men can't. And third, I'm smaller than everyone else in your unit. I can get into tight places, like a duct, a crawlspace or a vent. You need me."

"You missed something."

She leaned forward. He picked up her file and waved it. "You've beat every single one of my men in the aptitude tests."

That little fact she hadn't known but would store away for later. He stood and she followed suit. He extended his hand and she was surprised to find it callused. From what she'd heard, she'd expected a man used to giving orders, not doing the hard work himself.

"Sergeant, you are the most qualified for this unit…"

She tried hard not to smile. Finally, an officer who wasn't afraid of her reputation, who was going to do the right thing and give her what she rightfully deserved.

"…but I can't give you the job."

CHAPTER TWO

HER MOUTH DROPPED open and Luke couldn't help but smirk. Sergeant Parrino was cool as a cucumber. This was the first genuine expression he'd seen on her face. She wanted this. Bad. And she deserved to have it. It sickened him to give in to the old colonel, but he didn't have a choice. They were so close to shipping out on their first assignment. Rodgers was already working on the logistics. No matter how much he wanted to give her a proper position, he couldn't defy the colonel. As loath as Luke was to admit it, he was being watched and needed to appease the brass if he wanted to keep command of the unit. Right now, he had to focus on preparing for the mission.

Wait...

"Sergeant, before you go, what're your current duties?"

If she was surprised at the non sequitur, she didn't show it. She explained the work she was doing in Kuwait and an idea formed in his head. A win-win for both of them.

"There's another opening on the unit."

Her eyes widened with expectation.

"Logistics."

Predictably, her face fell. But before she could tell him that wasn't the job she'd applied for, he motioned her back toward the chair.

"I know it's not what you want, but hear me out. Take a seat."

She sat, her face already recomposed into a blank expression. *Unflappable.* There weren't many individuals he would describe that way since he was an expert at pushing people's buttons. The assessment had been designed by Ethan and when Luke had first read the protocol, he'd lamented his brother's sadistic nature. It required twenty-four hours of travel the day before the in-person tests. When Rodgers had been selected, he'd been located three hours away, but Ethan had put him on a plane and sent him to California and back twice. Ethan's rationale had been characteristically thoughtful: after all, they might be forced to fly to the other side of the world and hit the ground running. He'd wanted soldiers who could handle it, and Luke couldn't disagree with that. Parrino was the first soldier Luke had found standing in his office at the end of the day. The rest of them had been plopped into the seat gulping water.

"The position is going to be more than logistics. I can't give you the details yet, but trust me on this."

She blinked at him with a maddeningly blank look.

"What do you mean by more than logistics? Are you going to have me spy inside the team?"

Add "perceptive" to the list of qualifications. He tilted his head. "I wouldn't put it that way. There's work to do where information needs to be compartmentalized, and I need someone I can trust." It was a nicer way of saying "off the books."

"But if my official designation is logistics, it does nothing to get me promoted. In fact, most will see it as a step backward, like I'm being punished."

"Initially, yes, but at the end of your tour with this unit, I will reveal the true nature of the assignment. Barring any performance issues, I will recommend you for promotion." *Provided Colonel Blowhard keeps me on as unit command.*

"And what if something happens to you?"

What if I die like Ethan? She didn't have to say it out loud. He was all too aware of the risks. Then it occurred to him: he'd be putting her life in danger, too. He shook it off. She was a soldier, she had signed up to take risks, and he'd give her a full briefing. If she wanted out at that point, he'd let her go.

She won't want out. He could see it in her eyes despite her bland expression. She was looking for adventure, a way to fill whatever hole there was in her life.

"As unit command, there are any number of things that only I'm privy to. There are files my commanding officer will receive should something happen to me. Details of your operations will be in those files."

"They'll be the first ones Colonel McBride burns."

Luke couldn't help but smile. He and Sergeant Parrino were going to get along well. She had no history with the colonel, but she'd gotten a good measure of the man in just a few minutes. That's what he needed, someone with judgment who could take care of herself.

"That's a risk you'll have to accept. Look, what do you have to lose? Besides, part of your job will be to keep me safe, so how about we call it added incentive?"

Her brow went up slightly and he swore a smile was tugging on the corners of her mouth.

"What's the assignment?"

"Not so fast. To become a member of the unit, you need to sign some additional confidentiality agreements. These are beyond the army standard. I need to let you know that it's serious business. If you talk in your sleep and your boyfriend gets details of our missions, you won't be court-martialed and put through the ringer—big, bad men will come in the middle of the night and ship you straight to Gitmo."

She reached out and plucked one of the pens from the holder on his desk. Clicking it, she tilted her chin. "I don't talk in my sleep and I don't have a boyfriend. I've faced worse than Gitmo. Where do I sign?"

What horrors are you hiding in your past? He wanted to know more, but she'd told him all she would for now. Turning to the computer, he pulled up the paperwork. Several minutes later, he plucked the forms off the printer and handed them to her.

"I suggest you read these carefully. There's a bathroom behind that door if you need it." He was done testing her. She was the toughest soldier he knew, but there was something about her that was bothering him, and he couldn't place his finger on it.

He stopped at the door. "Parrino, I don't care about what's in your file. But this is the kind of assignment that needs complete focus. No distractions. Before you transfer over, I'm going to require you to take a one-week leave. You can have more if you need it. In that time, you deal with whatever ghosts you have in your past. Once the unit is operational, you're totally mine."

ALESSA TOOK A breath after he left. It was hard to remain calm when he looked at her with those intense blue eyes.

She signed the papers in less than five minutes. She read them quickly, but it didn't matter what they said. Her life already belonged to the army. There were no other options for her. She didn't have a college degree, had enlisted the day she graduated from high school, so she wouldn't have to spend another day at home. This unit was the only way to make sure she didn't get squeezed out.

Expecting Lieutenant Williams back any second, she used the restroom and took a long drink of water from the faucet. She washed her face and used a paper towel to dry it. The physical exertion she'd gone through was nothing compared to the sheer relief of not having to return to Kuwait. The papers she'd signed said her transfer was effective immediately. Maybe with her gone, Aidan Connors could finally move on with his life. After *the incident*, she'd thought things would die down in a few months and both of them could forget about it. But that hadn't happened. They were based at Camp

Arifjan in Kuwait. It was a relatively small in-
stallation with no life off the camp. The story
had lingered on, grown additional arms and
legs and wrapped around her and Aidan until
neither one of them could escape it. She'd been
warned about Williams and could see why. He
had a way of pulling you in, making you feel
like he was on your side. Just like Aidan.

Returning to her seat, she waited, curious
to hear what secret stuff Williams had for her.
Truth be told, she would've taken the logistics job even without the added intrigue. Since
the incident, she'd been relegated to desk assignments that included mounds of paperwork.
She'd lost track of how many transfers she'd
applied for and been denied.

The lieutenant returned with two steaming
cups of coffee in his hand. He placed one in
front of her and pushed the bottle of water toward her. She picked up the coffee, eager for
the caffeine.

"Before we get started, I need to know everything about you."

Keeping her face neutral, she spread her
hands. "I don't think there's anything the army
doesn't know about me. My file even documents the birthmark I have on my hip."

"It also documents bones that you broke as
a child."

Her mouth went dry but she nodded, smiling disarmingly.

"It's a lot of bones for a little girl to break" he said carefully.

"What can I say; I was always a tomboy."

But Luke wasn't buying it. Brows knotted, he leaned forward. "I need to know who did it to you." His voice was hard and Alessa took a sip of her coffee, letting it burn down her throat, trying to loosen the frog lodged in it. There was only one other person she'd told. After years of serving together and becoming good friends. *And that didn't turn out so well.* She hardly knew Williams. Could she trust him?

"This is just between us—it doesn't go in the file. In order for this job to work, we need to trust each other. Right now, I need to know you can tell me the truth and you need to believe that the information won't end up in your file."

She searched his eyes for signs of malice but all he gave her was an intense, serious look that was completely inconsistent with his golden-blond hair and Ken-doll handsomeness.

"If you can't trust me, this won't work."

She needed this transfer. *I just have to say enough to appease him.* But then she made the mistake of looking at him, and something told her she wouldn't get away with a lie. "My father. He was a drunk and a hitter."

He nodded as if it was the answer he expected. For a second, Alessa wondered whether he'd already known and was still testing her. He took a sip of his coffee and she noticed that his other hand was clenched in a fist.

"When did he stop hitting you?" His voice held the slight tremble of suppressed anger and Alessa's heart warmed. When she'd told Aidan, he had been sympathetic and coddling. It hadn't been the response she'd wanted.

"When I started hitting him back."

"That's why you got a black belt in karate."

"And tae kwon do."

"Is the rest of your family safe?"

It was the first time someone had asked the question and Alessa wasn't sure how to answer. More than anything she wished it could be a simple *yes*. "My sister is. She's finally decided to go to law school. I'm paying her way as much as I can so she doesn't have to move home. My mother refuses to leave. I've tried to get her out." That was the simplest response she could give.

"Would you like to pay your father a visit?"

The menace in his voice was oddly comforting, and she longed to tell him that was exactly what she wanted. It wasn't as if she hadn't thought about it herself, but it wasn't her place to save her mother. She had tried several times, given her mother all the resources she needed to get out, but the woman refused. She was a devout Catholic and didn't want to leave her husband. Alessa was tired of going home and cataloguing new bruises. It had been a year since she'd seen her mother. Five since she'd laid eyes on her father. He was getting older and weaker. That's what her mother said, anyway, but his heart was just as dark.

Shaking her head, she locked eyes with him. "My family has been messed up for a long time. It's not a new issue for me. I don't need to deal with it right now—or ever, for that matter. I'm good to go. I can start tomorrow."

"You're not good until you have a permanent solution. I can help you."

She placed a hand on the table. "Lieutenant, I appreciate the offer but you need to understand that this is my personal business." His eyes hardened so she softened her tone. "Relationships are complicated. I don't understand why my mother stays with my father, but I've come to accept the fact that she'd rather die than leave him."

He flinched and she realized she'd hit a nerve. *Didn't his mother commit suicide?* She remembered that fact from the news coverage of his brother's death.

"You asked me to trust you. You're going to

have to trust me that this is not an issue. I don't need time to go deal with it. What I really need is to get to work." Work was the only thing that kept her sane. She needed the order in her life.

He opened his mouth, then closed it. Desperate to move on, Alessa filled the silence. "Your turn to tell me something I don't know, perhaps starting with why you need me to be your spy."

Leaning back, he wove his hands into his hair. The creaking of his chair was the only sound in the room for several moments.

"If this is going to work, we need to trust each other," she repeated quietly, as much for her own sake as his.

Finally, he unlocked his hands and placed them on the table.

"My brother Ethan isn't dead. Someone in the army is holding him captive and I need your help to find him."

CHAPTER THREE

IT WAS MADDENING. After his explosive announce-ment, Lieutenant Williams had been called away and Alessa had been assigned to a bed and in-structed to get some sleep and report for duty at 0700. At least he'd relented on the one-week leave. Exhaustion eventually won over curios-ity and she managed to get some good rest on a top bunk with a threadbare mattress.

She woke early and joined a group of sol-diers on a predawn run. It was early spring, and after years in Kuwait she enjoyed the feel of cool, dewy air that smelled of flowers and grass rather than dirt and exhaust fumes. Reveille played around 0600. After ending her run, she went back to the barracks and took a shower and changed. She loved the routine, no matter where in the world she was.

"Sergeant Parrino."

Rodgers was standing at the entrance to the warehouse she'd been instructed to report to. She almost didn't recognize him because he wasn't in army fatigues but was wearing jeans and a dark brown T-shirt that matched his hair and eyes.

A wave of disappointment hit her. She'd been expecting to see Lieutenant Williams. *To find out why he thinks his brother is still alive.* There was absolutely no other reason.

"Welcome to the unit. I'll be giving you the tour and explaining the assignment."

She nodded. "Thank you for going easy on me yesterday, Sergeant." Rodgers was three years younger than her but the same rank. Experience had taught her that men didn't like to be beaten by a woman and it was advantageous to put them at ease. A little trick she'd learned from her mother.

"I didn't go easy on you. In fact, I gave it my best. You won fair and square, and I don't mind admitting it."

This is a first. "I appreciate that, Sergeant."

"Call me Dylan or Rodgers. We're equals. In fact, Luke isn't into formalities—he wants us to call each other by first or last names. The point of this unit is to *not* follow our traditional training."

"And why is that?" Despite her preparation for the assessment, she knew very little about the unit or its mission. Lieutenant Williams, *Luke*, had given her nothing. The papers she'd signed didn't even have a designation for the unit.

"We are like secret internal investigators for the army," Rodgers explained. "There have been some issues with treason, but we can't seem to get to the root of the problem because we're fighting an enemy within, one who knows how we work. There might even be some Special Forces involvement, which is why none of the unit members are Delta. Ethan started this no-rank business—he didn't want the enemy to know how we operate, so first thing he wanted us to do was stop thinking like army grunts."

Alessa couldn't help but smile. She'd fit in perfectly.

"Did Ethan hire you?"

He nodded. "I was one of the first, so I've pretty much done all the jobs on this unit. You're the sixth, but I understand you're filling the logistics position." He shot her a quizzical glance.

"Yes I am, Sergeant—I mean, Rodgers."

"That makes no sense to me."

She raised a brow. "Me neither. But it was either this or nothing at all."

He shrugged. "My guess is it was Colonel McBride. Luke can't stand up to him the way Ethan did."

Aren't you just a fountain of information. "How come?"

"He's still feeling his way. Only got the gig because of General Williams. McBride wanted to put his own man in, so he's looking for a reason to get rid of Luke. This unit was Ethan's baby."

"What's your impression of Lieutenant…of Luke as a leader?"

Rodgers shrugged. "It's too early to tell. He's not his brother, that's for sure, and that's been hard on the unit. He looks just like Ethan, talks like him, but he's a different man."

"How so?"

"He's not regulation army."

"Didn't you just say it's not supposed to be?"

"Yeah, but he's not an army man. The rest of us are here because we love the military, and we believe in the mission of this unit. Before Ethan died, he was lamenting the fact that Luke was quitting. So why take over his brother's unit?"

"Because he wants to complete Ethan's mission?"

Rodgers shook his head. "They weren't tight like that. Anyhow, I've said too much to the newbie. Part of the training… We've been encouraged to fight our instincts. Do what doesn't come naturally and be more transparent—whatever that means."

He led her through a maze of boxes and random equipment, then opened a door to the area they'd been in yesterday. Luke wasn't in his office. Rodgers stopped outside a door marked Men and went inside. Alessa followed.

"Heads-up." Rodgers yelled, and Alessa averted her gaze as four men in various stages of undress quickly pulled on clothes and slapped on towels.

"This is Alessa Parrino." He turned to her. "What do you prefer to be called?"

"Parrino is fine."

"You the one who kicked his baby bottom yesterday?" one of the men asked.

Rodgers took it in stride. "Yep, so I'd watch myself if I were you guys. She's mightier than she looks."

Each of the men stood in turn and introduced himself. The tall African American man showing off a set of perfect abs over low-slung jeans was Boots. The baby-faced man with freckles on his nose and a mop of curly red hair was Steele, the dark-haired, dark-eyed man with a pockmarked face was Dan, and the skinny man with the easy smile was Dimples. They each gave her a hard handshake with a warm welcome in their eyes. She also noted that they were all around her age.

"There's no women's locker room. You're welcome to use ours or use the bathroom in Luke's office while we're here."

"What, Luke doesn't have a nickname?"

The men looked at each other. "Not one he knows about."

Alessa put a hand on her hip. "Out with it. Remember, I'm the one who'll be planning where you stay and what you eat."

The men exchanged another round of glances.

"All right, then, roach-infested motels and MREs it is," Alessa said, crossing her arms.

Rodgers held up his hand. "It's Fabio."

Alessa laughed and the men joined in. "That's perfect for him." While Luke's golden locks were cropped short, he had the kind of swoon-worthy looks that could grace the covers of romance novels. With his playboy reputation, the name fit.

"What do you guys think of Colonel McBride?" If the collective nose-scrunching and eye-rolling was anything to go on, they felt the same way about the colonel as she did.

"That guy really needs to retire. But the only way he's leaving the army is if he's six feet under," Steele muttered. They all nodded their agreement. These were good men, and Alessa felt a frisson of excitement roll through her. This was what she loved about the army, the camaraderie and feeling of being part of a team. "Do you have a nickname for him?" she asked.

"Nothing that's stuck." Dimples spoke for the group.

"I've got one." Alessa smiled. "Black Tag."

There was a beat, then the room filled with roaring laughter. In disaster triage, medics and doctors were taught to tag people according to the severity of their illnesses or injuries. Red tags for those who needed urgent care, black tags for those who couldn't be saved or were already dead.

"That's just perfect. Something goes down, that old coot is the first one I'm leaving behind." Rodgers hooted.

And just like that, Alessa was one of them. No matter how "un-army" Luke wanted the unit to be, nothing changed the fact that Luke was their immediate commanding officer and the enlisted would band together.

Rodgers took her to a cubicle and motioned for her to sit. He handed her a piece of paper. "Here's your computer login and password. Unit ships out in a month. The stack of files there is the equipment and transport we need, and a list of lodging options. I'll be in the training pit with the other guys—come get me if you have a question."

"Let me know if you need any help. Training, that is." She wiggled her brows and Rodgers laughed.

"Guess I deserve that." He turned, then stopped and looked back at her. "I am sorry Black Tag screwed you. You should be in the pit with us. The guys know it, too. Once we get in the field, things will be different."

He wouldn't say more, but Alessa smiled. If the men respected her, they would let her help on ops. Being in theatre was very different than being on post. At her rank, in combat, she commanded a small squad of men and women. On post she fetched coffee.

All day, she kept an eye on Luke's office, but it remained empty. The men ordered pizza for lunch and invited her to eat with them in the pit, which was their term for the warehouse-like space with the Plexiglas box in the center. The ten by ten foot box had been set up for training exercises, and it was where she had fought Rodgers. She didn't ask where Luke was and none of them commented on his absence. They talked easily about Fort Belvoir and gave her tips on what to avoid if she ate at the mess hall.

It had been a while since she'd been one of the guys, and Alessa felt less anxious about the transfer. Even if she was stuck doing grunt work, it was worth it to be away from Aidan and get her career back on track.

"So how did each of you end up on the unit?" Alessa asked through a mouthful of pepperoni pizza. It wasn't as good as her mom's home-made version, but far better than anything cooked up in a mess hall.

Rodgers answered first. "Back in the Sand-box, I worked with General Williams. When Ethan started the unit, the general called and asked me to apply. I was going through a di-vorce and it was a nice distraction."

"I'm sorry to hear that," Alessa said qui-etly. Though Rodgers said it nonchalantly, she sensed the divorce hadn't been so easy on him.

He shrugged. "Army life is hard on spouses."

Alessa looked around and saw several of the men nodding in more than just congenial agree-ment. Steele spoke up. "I've been through two divorces—the first when I enlisted after 9/11 and my high school sweetheart decided she wasn't going to support me, and the second after three back-to-back tours. My second wife decided she wanted someone who was home for more than a weekend a year. She wanted kids and was tired of waiting on me. By the time I applied for this unit, I was a free bird."

Alessa swallowed. On the few occasions she talked to her mother, she was diligently reminded that her window to have children was rapidly closing and if she ever wanted anything more than a bunk bed in a barrack, she needed to find a husband. She usually tuned her mother out, but ever since Aidan, each conversation had pinged her heart in a way the admonition never had before.

"Maybe you should marry another soldier," Alessa said lightly.

They all shook their heads and turned to Dan, who rolled his eyes. "You're going to make me tell her, aren't you?"

Dimples slapped him on the back and Dan smiled at Alessa.

"When I was a young private buck, I fell head over heels for a wide-eyed doe, also a private. It was love in the headlights and we were married within weeks. Then we got deployed to the same desert and I loved it and she didn't. Got her leg blown off and decided I wasn't good enough for her anymore." Dan's casual shrug and broad smile did little to hide the raw pain in his eyes. A heavy silence fell over the room and Dan's too-bright smile dropped.

Boots finally broke the somber mood. "Well, I've never been married."

"That's 'cause there's no woman out there that can stand the smell of your feet," Dimples teased.

In response, Boots lifted his foot and shoved it toward Dimples, who smacked it away. Alessa laughed along with the guys, enjoying the good-natured ribbing.

"We're all here because we love the army," Boots said more seriously. "I had a girl back home but I broke up with her when I enlisted."

"Don't listen to any of them. I've been happily married for twelve years and have three adorable children." Dimples smiled proudly. "My girl gets that country comes first." He pulled out his phone and turned the screen to show her. "That's Emmy with my three brats. Army life is good for them. She's got a house on post, daycare for the baby and school for the older two. We've got medical and dental, and she's got a support system when I get deployed. It's a good deal."

The rest of the men went quiet and Alessa got the feeling that they were all trying to figure out whether Dimples was just lucky or whether they had it wrong.

"We all came for Ethan," Steele said. "He recruited us in one way or another. We believed in him, in the work of this unit."

"And now?" Alessa prompted.

"We're here to complete Ethan's work," Dan said simply. "All of us were on the mission where we lost him, and we're gonna make sure we make it right."

The men nodded solemnly and Alessa's heart squeezed. How was she going to spy on them for Luke? They were good guys, each sincere in his desire to serve. There was no way one of these men was a traitor.

When they were done eating, she stepped out of the pit and watched the unit members run through a home invasion scenario. She'd already finished the day's work. Having been assigned to logistics for six months after *the incident*, she was already familiar with all the army systems. It was mind-numbing drudgery. But she would get to travel with the unit. They were going to Pakistan for a month, and she'd been asked to set up a safe house close to the Afghan border and organize all their travel and meals.

"It'll be different once we get out of here."

He'd snuck up on her. She stood at attention. Unlike yesterday, when he'd been dressed in fatigues just like her, Luke was dressed in jeans and a polo shirt.

"Sir?"

"Call me Luke. I'm sure the guys gave you the lowdown. We keep the formalities around Colonel McBride, but inside the unit, there's no rank."

"Except for you."

"Someone has to be in charge. But the guys are involved in all major decisions."

"Except the one to hire me. Or use me as a spy."

He pressed his mouth into a thin line but then his lips turned upward and he grinned broadly. "Parrino, you're going to keep me in line, and I like it."

Better watch this one. He was one of those guys who flirted without even thinking about it. *Fabio.* Except *his* transgressions hadn't halted his career as they had hers.

"Are you going to fill me in?"

He motioned toward his office and closed the door behind them. After she was seated, he pushed a file across the desk. "The safe house the team was using blew up. Ethan walked right into it. The rest of the team was out on surveillance and he returned to check something out. Dimples and Rodgers came to the house when Ethan stopped responding and found it burnt to the ground. They pulled out Ethan's charred body. Forensics identified him from DNA and dental records."

"So why do you think he's still alive?"

"I'll get to that. First, I want you to consider how the safe house was compromised."

"Surely someone has already looked into that." There was no way the guys in the unit would have accepted that it was Ethan's body otherwise.

"This unit doesn't really exist. We're technically paper pushers tasked with archiving old army records. The official story is that Ethan died in a training accident. So only the unit members have been studying the details, and we've found nothing. The guys only believed it after the DNA results came back. But the safe house could only have been compromised by someone on the inside. We suspect someone in the army set him up."

She flipped through the file. There were pictures of the burnt house and Ethan's body. It wasn't recognizable. Reading through the operational details, it was obvious the unit had been set up. But how? The only people who knew of the operation were the unit members. Even Colonel Black Tag didn't have all the details.

"So I just set up the safe house in Pakistan. I'm the only one who knows where we're going, but I used army assets to find it. If someone on the inside knows we're going there, it wouldn't take them long to use the same resources I did and by process of elimination, identify our safe house."

Before he opened his mouth, she held up her hand. "I need to find a new one, not using army assets."

"Good, you're a quick study. As hard as it is, don't do things the army way."

Easier said than done. The army way was all she knew.

"Okay, so someone on the inside knew you were going there. Possibly a member of the unit." Even as she said the words, she couldn't see any of those guys betraying them. They were a team. They'd been together for six months, and while they hadn't fully accepted Luke as their commander, they believed in the unit. She'd seen that in the way they handled themselves during the exercise. Each member was top notch.

"I'd be surprised if it's one of my guys, but I'm not eliminating that possibility. You weren't a part of the unit when they lost Ethan, which is why you're the only one I'm reading in on the next part."

"Why you think your brother is still alive."

He slid another folder toward her. It was the autopsy report. She scanned it, not knowing what he wanted her to find. The DNA test seemed pretty conclusive.

"Page 7, the skeletal scan."

She flipped to that page, then looked at him questioningly.

"It shows his ribs are intact. He fractured his ribs when we were kids."

So that was why he'd picked up on her broken bones.

"Maybe the coroner missed it."

"He didn't. I showed the original X-rays to another doctor. No broken ribs."

"Maybe you're mistaken about the break."

He shook his head. "We were thirteen and spending the summer with a cousin overseas. Ethan got trampled by a sheep. When we stopped laughing, we figured out Ethan was in real pain and took him to the hospital. The fractures were obvious on the X-rays, even to me. He was in bed and I had to take care of him for the better part of the summer."

She sat back in her chair. There had to be a more reasonable explanation.

"I've spent two months thinking about this and the only possibility is the dead body wasn't Ethan."

"The DNA tests."

"Were based on matches in our database. Someone could have switched the records. Same with the dental scans."

Realization dawned on her. "The broken ribs—you weren't on post. You went to a private hospital so it wouldn't be in the army records."

He clicked his fingers and pointed them at her. "Even my father didn't know about the broken ribs. I need to get to the bottom of what happened with Ethan. Call it the twin intuition thing, but I feel it in my bones—he's not dead."

Alessa's sister, Julia, was three years younger than her but while they were growing up, Alessa could always sense when Julia was in danger. She couldn't even imagine what it was like to have an identical twin. If Luke believed Ethan was alive, then chances were good that he was.

"How can I help?"

"Right now, learn your job. Rodgers has been doing logistics, so he'll talk you through the mistakes you made on today's assignment. Get friendly with the guys, be a member of the unit. If you hear something that seems suspicious, let me know."

A cold dread seeped into her bones. That's how it had started with Aidan. Personal favors that seemed innocuous, part of the job even. But the mistake she'd made with Aidan was that she'd let him get too close. Forgotten the fact that she was an enlisted soldier and he was a commissioned officer, which meant they couldn't even be friends. She wouldn't do that with Luke.

Luke stood and she followed suit, getting ready to salute him, the way she would any other superior officer, but he extended his hand and she automatically took it.

"We wear civilian clothes to shed the army

way. No saluting. From now on, we're colleagues, perhaps even friends."

She looked into his ocean blue eyes. *I can't be friends with you. That would be dangerous.* Her career couldn't withstand one more rumor of an improper relationship with a superior officer.

CHAPTER FOUR

THREE DAYS INTO the unit and Alessa didn't
know whether she'd made the best or worst
decision of her army career. Now that she had
to do things the un-army way, the logistics job
was much harder than she'd expected. It was
easy to click through some databases and fill
out paperwork, but a whole other task to rely
on general internet searches and online contacts
to set up the most basic arrangements. There
wasn't exactly an Expedia for safe houses and
covert air transportation.

It was a challenge she welcomed, but it also
left her little time to train with the team. She'd
been stuck behind a desk for the better part
of three days. The guys stopped by to see her
and that made it even harder. They were kind-
hearted men who genuinely respected her, and
no matter how many times she told herself she
would prove them innocent, she felt disingenu-
ous in her attempts to bond.

Tapping at the keys, she reconfirmed yet another one of the details for the team's upcoming

trip. Every logistic mattered. They were going into unfriendly territory without the cover of the army. If she overlooked even one minor point, she could jeopardize the team's safety.

"You've been sitting behind a desk way too long."

Alessa turned to find Luke leaning over her shoulder. He smelled of soap and coffee and looked entirely too fresh for the late afternoon.

"You're right. Want to give me a field designation and hire someone else for logistics?" She was surprised that she managed to make her voice sound normal despite the fact that her tongue was stuck to the roof of her mouth.

He eyed her monitor, then placed his hand over hers on the computer mouse and clicked to see the itinerary she'd been working on. He moved his hand before she could snatch back her own. She had barely processed the invasion when he pointed to the document he'd pulled up and asked her about their travel plans.

She answered his questions, miraculously focusing on the content of the inquiry and not on the lack of personal space between them. The heat from his body made her shift in her seat. This mission was too important for her to be distracted, and Luke was a superior officer. *Pull yourself together, Parrino.*

He pointed out some issues in her plans and

she bit her lip to keep from screaming in frustration. Luke wasn't wrong; he was catching some fine points she should have thought about.

"It's a good start. Keep at it and you'll get it," he said encouragingly. Alessa nodded blandly but all she wanted to do was pull her hair out. With the things he'd pointed out, she still had a lot of work ahead of her, which meant she'd be behind the desk for a while. At least in Kuwait she got to go out on patrol once a day even when she was on primary desk duty.

"Why don't you take a break and come do some exercises with the team? We're in the pit."

If Luke hadn't been standing so close, she would've jumped up immediately.

"Thank you, I'd like that," she said serenely.

He placed a hand on her shoulder and she flinched involuntarily. He immediately pulled back. She stood and followed him across the warehouse, but he stopped before reaching the pit. "I'm sorry, I didn't meant to touch... I mean..." He took a breath and she shuffled on her feet. "I didn't mean to make you uncomfortable," he said finally.

"I like boundaries," she said simply. Alessa shouldn't have been bothered by his proximity. Personal space was a luxury you didn't get in battle. She was used to the closeness of men, riding in trucks, staying in tight quarters. She and Luke were an officer and a soldier, nothing more. She wouldn't have bristled if Rodgers had put a hand on her shoulder. She'd had full body contact with Rodgers when they were fighting and hardly noticed. In fact, she'd seen all of the team, minus Luke, in various stages of undress and it hadn't bothered her at all. *All the more reason to keep my distance from him.* The last thing she needed was another Aidan situation.

When they stepped into the pit, Luke divided everyone into teams and paired Alessa with Steele. They would be practicing close-quarters combat. Alessa and Steele were the first team, so she only had a few minutes to warm up. Each pair would fight in the pit while everyone else watched from the outside to give them tips afterward. It felt like being in a fishbowl, but that was also part of the training. To focus on the fight despite distractions. She got into the exercise with gusto. It felt good to get rid of her pent-up energy and she quickly had Steele on the ground.

"Told you, man, she's small but mighty." Rodgers said in a gloating tone as they stepped out of the Plexiglas cube so the next team could take a turn.

"Okay, I want each of you to figure out how your partner got the better of you, then switch partners. It's important to know your own weakness, acknowledge what your partner exploited," Luke instructed. The guys had told Alessa that unlike Ethan, Luke spent a lot of time in running exercises himself.

They worked at the exercise for the better part of two hours until Alessa had pretty much kicked all of the men to the ground.

"C'mon guys," Luke yelled. "I want at least one of you to find Parrino's weak spot. Get inside her head."

"She's made of titanium," Dimples quipped, his characteristic smile lopsided as he grabbed the side of his head that Alessa had slammed into the wall.

"Everyone has a weak spot, guys, and you need to find hers," Luke said firmly.

"Oh, yeah? If you think it's that easy, why don't you do it?" Rodgers shot back. Alessa sensed that Rodgers had been a little hesitant on their second fight and she'd told him his fear was what made him an easy target. He'd been afraid of her based on their previous encounter, which made him tentative, and that hesitation would be the death of him in a real combat situation. She didn't have the strength that the men did, so she got the better of them through lightning-fast moves.

"Yeah, *Lieutenant*, why don't you show us grunts how it's done," Dimples jeered.

Alessa looked at Luke and smiled at the panic evident in his eyes. It would be fun to kick his rear end to the ground, put him in his place. She cracked her knuckles.

"What, you afraid to get whooped by a girl?" she taunted.

He narrowed his eyes, then gestured to Alessa. Luke stepped onto the rubber mat and held the door while Alessa stepped across the threshold, unable to contain the smirk on her face. Luke closed the door behind him.

He stepped toward her. The guys wouldn't be able to hear them with the door closed but he kept his voice low.

"Are you sure you want to do this?" he asked.

Of course not. Her stomach fluttered as she studied the stormy blues of his eyes. Fighting with someone meant close body contact. His proximity at the computer had been enough to supercharge her senses. Was she really ready for that again? He raised his brows, giving her a way out. All she had to say was no. She wasn't required to do this training. After all, she was only the logistics person. Fighting him was a bad idea. *A very bad idea.*

"It's on," she said, chin raised.

His eyes darkened and he stepped back from her, his jaw set. There were no rules in this exercise. The idea was to take down your opponent by any means necessary using your bare hands. The rest of the team was watching intently behind the Plexiglas. Her gaze was laser focused on Luke.

Alessa's martial arts training had drummed into her the importance of looking into the opponent's eyes to anticipate his next move. It usually worked for her, but not this time. Looking into Luke's eyes was like watching the swirls of a tornado. *Get it together!*

He wouldn't make the first move. In a disciplined fight, offense was not always the best defense. If she moved first, it would give him time to react. He would get to decide whether to evade, block or retaliate. He'd be the one with the choices and she would give away her preferred fight mode. The movies often showed two adversaries circling each other ready to pounce, but neither of them did that. They stared at each other for what seemed like hours but was in fact mere seconds.

Luke wasn't going to budge. Alessa had to make her move. She led with a kick, hoping to throw him off balance, but he was expecting it and blocked her deftly. She anticipated a counter punch, but it never came. She successfully twisted away from him and they were back in the face-off.

He'd had the perfect opportunity to at least

get a jab into her, and he hadn't taken it. Why? While it was understood that they wouldn't seriously injure each other in these exercises, everyone expected to walk away sore and bruised, including Alessa. The bruises would remind them of their weak spots so they could protect them better next time. Luke should have taken at least one punch.

Most people thought fighting was about power and speed. And it was. But it was also about messing with the opponent's head. Faking left and going right was the simplistic version of that.

She inched closer to him. "You'll regret pulling that punch," she said, then jabbed at him with her fists. She was at a significant disadvantage. Her arms were shorter than his, and just as she expected, he blocked her with ease. But counting on the fact that he wouldn't make an aggressive move, she turned and slammed her body against his, pushing him hard into the wall.

She heard his moan a millisecond after the thud of his body against the solid Plexiglas.

"Alessa, I don't want to do this." The way he said her name, the apology in his tone, sent warmth through her heart. It was her downfall, the momentary distraction. She was already at a disadvantage trying to hold down his large body with her smaller one. Before she knew it, Luke had spun her around and pinned her arms to her back. He held her close, his grip firm. Focusing on the rise and fall of his chest, she calculated her next move. She wasn't going to let him get inside her head again.

In a normal fight, he could put a knee to her back and push her to the mat, but instead he leaned closer to whisper in her ear.

"You underestimate me. Maybe I was just making you comfortable to get the better of you." If the words were meant to be menacing, they were badly delivered. His breath was ragged in her ear, his voice thick and throaty. *Is he also having trouble concentrating?* She shook off the thought. He was trying to distract her.

She kicked behind her, catching Luke in the knee. Hard enough that he grunted and loosened his grip just a fraction, which was all she needed to free herself from his grasp. She whipped around to face him in their now-familiar standoff.

His eyes smoldered. Her entire body burned. *I could end this now, say I'm not feeling well.* Fighting Luke was a kind of torture she didn't need. It didn't matter what he did or did not feel for her. There was at least a flirtation between them and the entire team was watching. Try as she might, she couldn't focus on the fight and the guys would know it. She needed to be above reproach to counteract everything that had happened in Kuwait. The guys had all been in the pit with her; they knew she didn't fight this sloppily.

Time to focus. Whenever she was in over her head in a fight, she thought about her father. It was a good tactic to bring in a rush of anger that helped her overcome any pain or doubt. The trick had never failed her. But now, all she could think about was the way he was looking at her. No man had ever looked at her that way. More importantly, no man had ever made her feel the way Luke was right now. Like she mattered. Like he cared. *Shake it off Alessa, it's not real.* But she couldn't.

A bang on the Plexiglas made them both flinch. Rodgers held up his hands in a gesture of confusion. They'd been standing there without doing anything for several minutes. Alessa took a breath. She had to get through this; if the guys thought there was anything other than a professional relationship between her and Luke, her career was over.

I need to end this. Rodgers was still miming, and while Luke's attention was on the other man, she charged at him with everything she had. She crashed into him as she intended, but he twisted away. Before she could deliver her final blow, he pivoted and crouched at the same time. He knocked her off her feet. She landed on the padded floor but not before she managed to sweep her leg under his. She turned immediately, intending to get up before he regained his balance but he was too quick. He rolled over top of her to keep her down.

His face was less than an inch away from hers, their noses nearly touching. His blue eyes drew her in and she found herself unable to look away. Even though she knew it was crazy, she felt as if a riptide was pulling her into the depths of his soul.

They were both frozen, unsure of what to do with such intimate contact. "We're ending this." Luke said softly. He shifted his weight with a clear intention to let her up.

As soon as she had room to move, she shoved against his chest and his grunt told her she'd successfully knocked the wind out of him. It was a provocation. His eyes flashed at her, a clear warning that she was playing with fire. But Alessa wasn't going to let up. Never in her life had she been so aware of every nerve in her body. She wasn't ready to let go of whatever it was that was igniting her from the inside.

She was still in a vulnerable position and this time he didn't go easy on her. He returned her jab and attempted to pin her back down but she was quicker, managing to twist away from him while delivering a few kicks. Luke had asked them to train with their shoes off, partly to avoid serious injuries but also because shoes add an inch or so to the foot. If they got used to kicking with bare feet, the extra shoe length in real combat would maximize their contact with an opponent. Alessa had trained barefooted in martial arts gyms, breaking boards with her hands and feet. She knew all about aiming past the target to maximize her blow and she used this training to the fullest. Luke moaned after a particularly vicious jab that she managed to land on his solar plexus. When she paused to make sure she hadn't gone too far, Luke came at her within a second and she forgot all about her concern. Now that they were in the throes of the fight and he'd stopped handling her delicately, she was enjoying their encounter. Luke was good. Better than the rest of the team, even Rodgers.

He managed to get her against the wall. "What are you doing, Alessa?" he snarled, his breaths coming fast and heavy, blowing warm air against her ear.

What am I doing? He had given her plenty of chances to get out of this; why wasn't she taking them?

"I want us to finish this exercise," she squeezed through a closed throat. He had her pressed tight against the Plexiglas and her lungs were starting to burn. As if realizing that, he eased up just a little, enough that she could take a full breath but not so she could get the upper hand.

"You want to finish the exercise, you got it."

He twisted her arm behind her back. Alessa knew what he was trying to do. He would pin her to the floor so she couldn't get up. Like a wrestling match, it would effectively end the exercise.

Taking a breath, she twisted her shoulder, wrenching her arm tighter against him. Luke swore under his breath. There was only one way he could keep her down and that was to put a knee in her back and slam her head into the floor. It was a vicious move and she needed to find out whether he'd use it on her. She knew without a doubt the other guys wouldn't hesitate to be rough with her.

"Why are you so stubborn?" he asked through gritted teeth as she continued to struggle against him. Her shoulder and arm burned, but she didn't care. Pain was something she understood, something she could deal with. The feelings Luke was bringing out in her were something she could not.

He placed a hand between her shoulder blades. Rather than knee her back, he was going to force her down with his hand. It was a kinder, gentler way, but just as effective, so she wrenched her shoulder as hard as she could against his hand.

Something popped in her shoulder and a searing pain traversed her arm. She cried out, then collapsed.

CHAPTER FIVE

LUKE KNEW THAT the floor was padded and Alessa wouldn't be seriously hurt if she fell, but he couldn't stop himself from catching her. He gestured to the team and they came rushing through the door. Rodgers had some basic medic training.

"She dislocated her shoulder," he said immediately. While Luke was no medic, the protruding knob on her shoulder was clear as day. Her face twisted in pain as she clutched her arm, and his chest burned. *What was I thinking?* He'd known from the moment he stepped into the ring that this would end badly. When Rodgers first asked him to fight Alessa, he should've declined. She wasn't one of the guys, and treating her like one had gotten her injured.

Luke yelled for someone to get the medic kit. While Rodgers ran to get it, Luke bent his head so only Alessa could hear. "I'm sorry, Parrino, I didn't mean to do that."

"You found my weak spot," she croaked, and he felt a punch to his gut. Alessa had dislocated her shoulder twice before—it was in her file—which meant her shoulder was more prone to a repeat injury. And yet, he'd mercilessly yanked her arm.

What had he been trying to do? Show the guys he was better than them or prove to himself that Alessa was nothing more than another soldier? *Good job, Luke. Fail on both counts.*

Rodgers went about immobilizing her arm with a sling.

"You can let go of her now," he told Luke not-so-tactfully. Luke was still cradling Alessa, and she seemed to realize it at the same moment. She sat up on her own, grunting as she did.

"If we were in the field, I'd set it for you," Rodgers said, "but we have the luxury of a clinic on post. I'm going to give you a pain-killer to tide you over." He handed her a pill and Dimples followed with a bottle of water, which she chugged down.

Luke stood back while Rodgers and Dimples helped Alessa up and out of the pit. She tried to shrug them off, but they wouldn't have it. They even helped her get on her shoes, ignoring her protests. Dan and Boots had gone to fetch a car. Luke felt useless, but he followed along, unsure of what to do.

At the jeep that Dan had commandeered,

Rodgers held up a hand. "We only have room for four. Dan is driving, Dimples and I will go with Alessa."

Luke scowled at him. "Dimples can stay here. I'll go with you."

"Don't you think you've done enough?" Rodgers said unkindly.

It was no way to talk to a superior officer, but Luke was the one who had been training them to do just that. To treat him like they were a private security firm, not the disciplined soldiers of the army. He had encouraged his men to question orders and call him on his bullshit, which was exactly what Rodgers was doing now. Luke had no reason to go to the hospital with Alessa.

"Listen, there might be some administrative hassle with the unit designation. I don't want there to be a problem," Luke tried.

Rodgers narrowed his eyes but didn't say anything. Luke got the distinct impression that the other man could see right through him but was choosing not to say anything. They got into the jeep, Alessa in the back with Rodgers while Luke rode in the passenger seat. He would much rather have been with her, but Rodgers hadn't given him a chance. Luke knew that Rodgers was single and irrationally wondered whether the man had feelings for Alessa. He seemed to be overly protective of her. *And you're not?*

He snuck a glance at Alessa. She was holding her right arm to her chest, her face composed, but he didn't miss the slight flare of her nostrils or the tinge of pink on her cheeks and throat. She was in pain. His stomach churned, the adrenaline burning off. In its place was the sickening feeling of self-loathing. He'd physically hurt a woman. And not just any woman. Alessa. Of course, he hadn't meant to hurt her; in fact, he'd been very careful not to. Things had happened so quickly... Had he lost focus and missed that she was turning her body? Had he twisted her arm a fraction too hard? None of this would have happened if he'd been a stronger man and just refused to fight her.

In that moment when the team was goading him, he'd been ready to step away, to take the guys' ribbing, but then he'd looked at Alessa and the fervor in her eyes had lit him up. He'd wanted nothing more than to prove to himself and his team that he deserved to be their commander, and that Alessa was nothing more than a soldier to him. So he'd stepped into the pit, and he'd hurt her. Possibly badly. Under normal circumstances, a dislocated shoulder was not a permanent injury, but with the previous trauma she'd endured, what if he had effectively ended her career? His mouth soured. *I'm supposed to put my unit's needs before my own. What kind of leader will I be?*

They took her to the community hospital on base. The emergency room wasn't busy, and Alessa was whisked into the treatment area. Luke, Rodgers and Dan were firmly told to stay in the waiting room. Dan volunteered to go find coffee for the men.

"What was that all about?" Rodgers didn't waste any time once Dan was out of earshot. When Ethan died, Rodgers had been the de facto unit commander. By rank, Dimples was the most senior, but Rodgers had been with the team the longest and so he had been the one to get the team back home after their mission literally blew up. He'd been the one to hold the team together while Colonel McBride jockeyed for position and the team's future hung in the balance. If it hadn't been for Rodgers, Luke wouldn't have a team to command; he was the heart and soul of the unit. So Rodgers was not a person to lie to. He would see right through Luke, and Luke needed Rodgers on his side to help him keep the unit together.

"I didn't want to fight her."

"Because she's a girl or because you have feelings for her?"

Luke bit the inside of his cheek. *It isn't be-*

cause she's a woman, and it isn't because I have feelings for her. I don't. I can't.

"The colonel didn't want me to hire her. That's why I put her in logistics. I didn't want her getting injured and the colonel asking questions about why she was training." It was a partial truth.

"Don't you have a high opinion of yourself? She was holding back with you, and vice versa."

Luke had sensed that, too. He'd seen Alessa fight and she was rough and fast, but with him she'd been way too hesitant.

Rodgers leaned forward. "Neither of you can afford a scandal. Maybe we're just seeing things between you and Parrino 'cause you've got a reputation and it makes for good gossip between men. But it almost feels like you two are hiding something."

We are. Luke didn't want to have this conversation, but he couldn't have the team suspect Alessa was spying on them. One way or another, a unit member was involved in Ethan's disappearance and Luke needed the guys to trust Alessa. It was almost better for them to believe the worst of him. "You're right, I've been treating her differently. Maybe because she is a good-looking woman. But I promise you there is nothing romantic between us, nor will there be. I'll make sure of it."

Rodgers nodded. "Good." Then he took a breath. "As much as it pains me to say this, if she'll be a distraction, I suggest you take her off the team, or at least keep her stateside for the next mission. We can't screw this one up again."

Luke pressed his lips together but said nothing. Rodgers was right. If he couldn't even complete a simple exercise with Alessa, how would they ever work well in the field? The unit was already fractured; he couldn't make it more divided by favoring a member. Not to mention that Rodgers was right in saying Alessa could ill afford another rumor. Luke was well aware of his own reputation and if the colonel even caught whiff of what had happened in the pit today, he wouldn't hesitate to use it against Luke.

"It won't be a problem." Luke said with more confidence than he felt. Dan returned with steaming cups of coffee and they all sat in silence.

It didn't take long for the doctor to set Alessa's shoulder. Luke didn't trust her to heed the doctor's warning, so he pulled the man aside to ask him what her prognosis was.

"She asked that I not discuss her medical issues with you," the doctor said.

He was a short, bald man in his sixties and he pushed his glasses up the bridge of his nose. Luke towered over him but the man did not seem to notice.

"I know this is her third dislocation, and I'm asking as her commanding officer whether she's fit for duty."

"Her chart says she's logistics. She needs to wear the rotator cuff brace for at least two weeks, so she's fit for whatever work she can do with her left hand. No heavy lifting for six weeks."

"Will she regain full use of that arm?"

"I don't see why not, as long as she follows my directions. Though I warn you— as I warned her—that next time she may separate her shoulder entirely and in that case, there is no guarantee what kind of nerve damage she might have." The doctor peered at Luke. "I suggest you keep her to light desk duty." He was an army doctor and completely used to soldiers wanting to get back to physical activity as soon as possible. "No training," he reiterated.

Alessa wouldn't even look at him, and after asking how she was doing in a perfunctory way, Luke told Dan and Rodgers to take her back to her barracks to rest. He could walk back and use the time to clear his head.

"I'm fine. I need to go back and fix the travel issues you found earlier," she insisted.

"The doctor said you need to rest for two weeks."

"He said I need to keep the brace on for two weeks max. I am perfectly capable of using my left hand to operate a keyboard and mouse."

"I'm ordering you to return to your barracks for the day," he said firmly.

"With all due respect, *sir*, you've asked us to think and operate independently and to question orders if they don't seem right. I disagree with yours right now."

Luke didn't miss the smirk on Rodgers's face, nor the matching one on Dan's.

"You are correct that that is how I want the unit to operate. However, in this circumstance, my order stands."

She looked like she was going to say more but then thought better of it and responded with an unenthusiastic, "Yes, sir."

He motioned to Dan to hand over the keys to the jeep they had borrowed. "On second thought, I'm going to drive you myself." The guys could walk back or get another ride.

"Will you also tuck me in?"

"If I must," he retorted.

Dan and Rodgers exchanged a glance and Luke glared at them. "Rodgers, get one of the guys to pick you and Dan up. I need you to round up the team. We're going out for target practice. I'll meet you there."

Rodgers nodded, though disapproval was clear in the man's eyes.

Alessa signed her discharge papers, then Luke held the door open for her as they exited the emergency room.

Once they reached the parking area, he watched her struggle to get into the car. Having the use of just one arm, and her non-dominant one at that, could not be easy. He extended his arm to help her but she ignored him, obviously unwilling to have any contact with him.

"I'm sorry," he said turning to her as soon as they were seated.

"You should be," she shot back while she fumbled with her seat belt. She glared at him. "This is all your fault."

Meeting her gaze, he nodded solemnly. She had every right to blame him.

"I know. I am so sorry, I never should have fought you." He reached over, pulled the seat belt and clicked it into place. She slapped his arm with her left hand.

"No, you should be sorry for *not* fighting me. What was that in the pit? You couldn't decide whether you were going to let me win or force me to lose?"

She was right. He had let himself get into a situation and then hadn't been able to decide how to handle it. He'd started by thinking he would let her take some jabs at him and then call a truce, but the more she pushed, the more the fight had spun out of control.

"The whole thing was a mistake. I didn't mean to hurt you."

"This wouldn't have happened if you'd gone through the exercise like you were supposed to, and fought properly. Tell me something..." She turned in her seat and though she tried to hide it, she winced in pain. "If I'd been Rodgers or Steele or one of the other guys, would you have fought the way you did?"

He didn't bother responding because it was a rhetorical question. They both knew the answer was a clear no. He started the jeep and put it in reverse. The next question was inevitable and he didn't have an answer, even for himself.

"Either you went easy on me because I'm a woman or you don't think I can cut it on this unit, or—"

Or I have inappropriate feelings for a soldier in my command.

"You're not an official member of the team," he interrupted. "An injury is what I was trying to avoid. If Colonel McBride finds out about this, I'll have a lot of explaining to do."

"If that were true, you wouldn't have let me fight the rest of the guys. Unless you are *so* arrogant that you're assuming you would've gotten the best of me."

She was right, and he'd have to come up with a better excuse than Colonel McBride to explain his bizarre behavior.

"I did get the better of you. I was trying to spare you the humiliation." He kept his tone light.

"I can take care of myself," she said tightly.

The words were on his lips to reassure her but he focused on pulling up to her barracks unit. He leaned over and released her seat belt, earning another glare. Before he could get around to her door, she had it open and had stepped down, her eyes warning him not to help her.

She turned to him before going through the front door. His stomach twisted at the shine in her eyes.

"I don't know what you're playing at, but the army is all I have, it's all I've ever had. Please don't ruin it for me."

CHAPTER SIX

ALESSA'S SHOULDER WAS killing her, but she couldn't take the painkillers the doctor had prescribed. She tried going for her morning run but gave up after the first two miles. The sun wasn't even up when she arrived at her desk. If Luke thought he could marginalize her, he had another think coming. She'd have all the corrections he had suggested yesterday done by the time he came in. Only she'd underestimated how hard it would be to type and operate a mouse with her left hand. When she'd dislocated her shoulder before, she'd been in middle school and then high school.

What was wrong with her? She'd been so desperate to get the upper hand on Luke, she'd twisted her body beyond the safe zone. The man brought out an irrational side of her that she wasn't used to. The self-discipline she'd worked so hard to attain seemed to melt away when he was around.

One assignment, then I'll request a transfer. Even as she thought it, she hated the idea.

She loved the guys in the unit. They respected and accepted her, something that wasn't easy to find in the army. Which made spying on them that much harder. And then it hit her. If Luke was right about his brother being alive, he wouldn't necessarily remain unit commander. From what the guys had told her, he'd only gotten the job because his father had insisted on it. But if Ethan was alive, and they found him, wouldn't he return to take command of the unit?

More incentive to find him and prove that the guys weren't involved. Another reason Alessa wanted to complete her assignment was so she could have time to study the satellite maps from the area where Ethan had supposedly been killed. She wasn't skilled at reading satellite imagery, so it would take her some time to learn. Once again, she marveled at what a great opportunity working on the unit was. Normal army assignments were remarkably monotonous; you did the same job over and over again.

A few hours later, she had finished her logistics work and had turned to her spy assignment. "What're you working on?"

She jumped in her seat and turned to find Rodgers peering over her shoulder. "Just studying the satellite maps to get familiar with the area. I've served on the border, but never in Pakistan."

Rodgers nodded and went over some of the landmarks with her, including the safe house where Ethan had been killed. He didn't once question why she was so interested in the imagery, trusting her half-truth.

"Are you okay with going back there?" She asked carefully.

Rodgers shrugged. "I need to be. Our mission was simple—grab and interrogate Azizi to find out who the army leak was. We never even got to Azizi, though the guys and I talked about finishing the mission since it was important enough to get Ethan killed. But McBride ordered us back. It's time to get it done."

"Did Ethan know something you didn't?" Rodgers narrowed his eyes at her, so she quickly explained. "I'm trying to make sure I cover our bases so we stay safe. Luke briefed me on the mission and I've read the files, but you were there."

Rodgers took a breath. "I try not to get defensive about it, but it's hard not to question every move we made. Ethan was really open with us, kept us in the loop on all details, no hierarchy. Then when we got on the ground, he was listening to surveillance tapes and heard something he didn't want to share with us. He insisted on following a lead by himself. Refused to let us get involved. It was the first time he pulled rank on us and we didn't know what to do, so we let him go. I thought about following him, then decided against it."

Alessa had read most of this in the after-action reports, but those reports were missing the emotion she sensed in Rodgers. He seemed to be genuinely struggling with the events of that mission.

"It's not your fault. You were following orders."

"Which is exactly what I'm not supposed to do in this unit." He smiled sheepishly.

"It's hard being in the unit, isn't it? You're supposed to question orders but follow them anyway?"

He shrugged. "If you're talking about Luke, I think he's still trying to find his way, figure out what he's supposed to do with us."

"Have you figured out what to do with him?"

Rodgers laughed. "No, and I think he's having a particularly hard time with you."

"Is it because I'm a woman?"

"No, I think it's because you're cute."

She froze. Rodgers's tone was teasing and flippant, but she sensed a deeper concern.

"What are you implying?"

He sighed. "Listen, Luke has a reputation.

I think being a ladies' man comes naturally to him. This mission is dangerous. Whoever killed Ethan is going to come after us. We all need to be totally focused. We can't have Luke distracted."

The subtle warning in his tone made her stomach twist.

"Yesterday wasn't my fault. I was fully prepared to fight him."

"Yes you were, but you were slow on your feet. I've fought you, remember. Twice. You have sonic speed, but seeing you and Luke fight was like watching a slow-motion video. It wasn't all him."

"Nothing is going on between us."

"I believe you, but to make sure it stays that way, it might be a good idea for you to sit this mission out."

Her eyes widened. "This mission is my chance to prove I have what it takes. I'm not sitting it out."

Rodgers shifted on his feet. "Obviously it's not my call. You're better than anyone on the team, me included. You'd be an asset on the mission. As long as you can keep things professional with Luke."

Her cheeks burned. The unit was a fresh start for her. The last thing she needed was another scandal. Especially one so similar to *the incident*.

"I haven't done anything to invite Luke's attention."

"I know. I'm not mentioning it again. Let's move past it."

She nodded, her mouth dry. Nothing ever stayed in the past. Rodgers would be watching her and Luke closely. Alessa would have to put some good distance between her and Luke. She was technically on detail to the unit until her transfer paperwork came through, which meant that she'd have to return to Kuwait and to Aidan if she didn't go on the mission. That could not happen.

The rest of the day went quickly and by the end of it, Alessa was operating a little more fluently with her left hand. She had emailed the final logistics arrangements to Luke several hours ago. The less physical contact she had with him, the better. The team had left for the day, but not after every single man had stopped by to check on her. Everyone except Luke, which was just fine by her.

She shut down her computer, secured her ID card, and neatly stacked the papers on her desk.

"How's the arm?"

She hadn't heard him approach. Taking a

breath, she steeled herself and turned. "It's fine, thank you for asking."

He eyed her arm, his gaze lingering on the brace that held it against her chest. "I have some notes for you on your arrangements. I'll email them later tonight."

She nodded. *Why is he here?* He could have just emailed her in the first place.

"I wanted to tell you in person…"

Her stomach hardened.

"…you can't come on the mission."

CHAPTER SEVEN

"THE DOCTOR SAID I need to be in a sling for two weeks. We don't ship out for another four," Alessa said evenly. She put her good arm behind her back so he couldn't see her make a fist.

"He also said you need to take it easy for six weeks or more." Luke shifted on his feet, unwilling to look her in the eye.

"Technically I'm logistics so I'll be sitting in the safe house monitoring your operations. That's the definition of easy."

"C'mon, Parrino. You designed our entrance strategy into Pakistan. We're going to be crossing the border illegally from Afghanistan. That's not only dangerous, it'll be physically taxing."

"If I'd dislocated my shoulder in the field, Rodgers would have set it and we would've moved on. I wouldn't even have this brace."

"We're not in the field—you know it's different."

How is it different?

"I can handle it."

He met her gaze, his blue eyes intense. There was so much he wasn't saying.

"I can't take the risk. We don't know what we're facing, and I need each unit member in prime condition."

She wasn't going to win this one, so she decided to change tack.

"You need me to find Ethan. I've been looking at the satellite imagery from the last mission." He raised a brow and stepped toward her. Smiling, she booted her computer. "I found an image of the safe house from two years before the ambush."

"What good does that do?" Luke frowned.

She held up her hand. "Just wait."

He tapped his foot as she inserted her access card and punched in her pin. She resisted the urge to look at him. He was keeping his distance this time, close enough to see the screen but not as close as he had stood yesterday. Still, she felt the heat coming off his body and tamped down on the irrational feeling that she wanted him closer.

"Okay, this is the picture of the safe house from the unit's files, shortly after the attack."

He nodded impatiently. She knew he'd probably studied this picture for hours so she didn't dwell on it. "Look at this area right here." She pointed to the southwest corner of the property where the house had stood, then quickly switched the picture.

"Now look at that same corner two years ago."

Luke leaned forward, placed a hand on her desk and inched his face toward the screen. "Oh, my God."

She nodded excitedly, pleased that he felt the same way she did about the finding. It had been a long shot, going back through the prior satellite images, but her instinct had led her there and it had been the right call.

"That depression in the ground..." He turned to look at her and she realized how close his face was to her own. She could see the blond stubble on his cheeks and wondered what it would feel like against her skin. The harsh overhead light glinted off his hair, giving it a coppery glow.

He cleared his throat and straightened. "I've been having a hard time figuring out how Ethan would have escaped. Satellite imagery clearly shows him entering the house seconds before the blast and nothing afterward, but if that depression..."

"...is a tunnel, it explains how he might have escaped." She spun her chair to face him.

"Or been taken."

"Either way, it's plausible that he wasn't in

the house when the bomb went off." She held his gaze, and as if sensing what was coming, he broke eye contact. "Luke, you need to focus on the mission. I can concentrate on tracking down the leads related to Ethan. I won't be a burden."

He rolled his shoulders and sighed. She had him. Almost.

"When we're on the ground, you can't disappear to go check out that property and confirm that depression is a tunnel," she continued. "But I can. Who knows what else we may find. You need me."

His eyes connected with hers and warmth filled her heart. *Why is he looking at me this way?* She could see the *no* forming, the downward turn of his lips, the plea in his eyes. A rational argument wasn't going to win him over. This wasn't about her injury or her usefulness in the field.

"If you keep me off the mission, there will be more rumors about me. About us. Whatever your real reason, I hope it's worth ruining my career for." It wasn't a fair jab, but she had no choice. This was too important. If a rumor circulated that she'd been asked to sit on the bench because of her relationship with the commander, she'd never live it down. She couldn't spend the rest of her life as a sergeant. A promotion was long overdue, and she'd never get it without being part of something big. Finding Ethan alive was big.

He rubbed the back of his neck and his shoulders dropped. The fluorescent light highlighted the bags under his eyes as he sighed. Her words may have hit him harder than the punch she'd delivered to his solar plexus.

"I need your word that the second your shoulder bothers you, you'll tell me."

Fat chance. She smiled sweetly. "Thank you. I won't let you down." No good soldier ever told a commanding officer the truth about the extent of their injuries.

He narrowed his eyes but nodded and left. Alessa let out a breath and sank back in the chair. She had convinced Luke that they should work together, but could they?

Last year when things had evolved with Aidan, she'd convinced herself that it was love. But even a kiss with Aidan hadn't made her glow from the inside out like even a look from Luke did. She closed her eyes. It had to be the excitement of working in the unit, the departure from routine. It was time to focus on the assignment at hand. She couldn't let another man be the downfall of her career.

"How come you get to be the husband?" Luke's teasing tone came off with a hint of jealousy and Alessa smiled inwardly.

Rodgers took it in stride. "'Cause I'm the better-looking one."

"Can't believe you made me the boozing foreign correspondent who flirts with all the women," Luke whined.

"I needed you to have cover for when you disappear or don't answer your door. If you're a boozer, you're prone to be sleeping it off. And being a womanizer gives both of us cover if you need to talk to me in public or if for some reason I need to come to your apartment. Remember, my husband, Rodgers, doesn't really take care of me, if you know what I mean."

The men laughed and Rodgers pretended to look hurt.

"Are you sure that our explanation for this many foreigners arriving at the same time will fly?" Steele asked. His mop of curly red hair was scraped back into a ponytail.

They were in the training warehouse they called the "pit," sitting around in a circle, eating dinner and going over the final details for their mission. The last few weeks had flown by. The team had pulled together, putting in eighteen-hour days to get ready. Alessa had never worked this hard in her life, and she loved it.

They had ordered pizza, Chinese and subs. They hoped to only be out of country for two weeks but had planned on six just in case. They had all served in the Sandbox before and knew that while there was good food to be had overseas, there was nothing like greasy pizza, Chinese and salty deli meats.

Alessa grabbed a box of noodles and used a pair of chopsticks to spoon some onto her Styrofoam plate.

"In that area, the only new arrivals are refugees. That's why Rodgers and I are from Azerbaijan. Since we don't speak the language, none of us can be Afghani or Pakistani. That's why Luke and Boots are Canadian foreign correspondents and the rest of you are from Syria. That way only three new apartments are being rented. We won't arrive together since we're using separate border crossings, and I did get us on different floors. I'll make a big show of talking about how nice the Canadians are."

Alessa had picked an apartment building for them to stay in. It hadn't been easy finding a safe house without army resources.

Dimples snorted at the remark and Alessa tried not to get irritated at him. "I know it's a stereotype, but we don't have a lot of time to create backstories, and the reason stereotypes exist is because lots of people believe them. We have to behave in ways people expect based on who we say we are."

"I still say we should've used a single safe house," Dan said quietly.

Alessa took a breath. Once the commander approved a plan and issued orders, she wasn't used to people continuing to discuss and question. But that was the whole point of the unit. She and Luke spoke at the same time and she paused before he waved for her to continue.

"I didn't find any houses that I could verify. I can check out more possibilities once we're on the ground." Alessa knew she sounded snippy, but she had spent days vetting all the options and the apartment building was the best choice.

"None of you can complain. I've got to share with Boots. Man, in the summer heat, the whole apartment will be smelling like toe fungus in a minute." Luke's tone was light. He was sitting cross-legged and reached for another slice of pepperoni pizza.

"I've got news for you." Alessa took a bite of her noodles. "The whole apartment probably smells like a rat died in there last year. Boots is going to be your air freshener." She pointed to the phones sitting beside the men. Non-army-issued smartphones that she had gotten them for communications and to download briefing materials. The phones were encrypted and required each man's thumbprint and a password to access any information. Even if someone forced their thumb, they would still need the password. A team member under duress could also enter a panic password that would make his captors think he had unlocked the phone while sending his location and a distress signal to the rest of the team. Getting these phones had taken some doing. The unit had a spending account, but purchasing required using army resources so she'd bought standard-issue supplies and equipment, sanitized them, then sold the items on the black market to get cash to buy the phones from an underground network. Her first illegal act. Selling government property. Authorized by Luke. Technically, she had cover, but she really hoped this was all legitimate.

"Okay, one last time, we have to get serious about our covers. Look at the personality sheets coded in green on your briefing materials. We can't all behave the same way, so I've given you all personalities. For example, I will be the gossipy Azerbaijani woman who shares a little too much about her husband's shortcomings."

Rodgers made a sound of protest at that. "You better keep it limited to professional things," he muttered.

Alessa rolled her eyes at him and Luke

laughed. The sound wrapped around her and she fought to keep her eyes pinned to her plate of noodles. One look at him and she wouldn't be able to stop staring.

Since the fight and her injury, she had managed to sneak in some training. Her shoulder still hurt, which made her train even harder. She wasn't going to let the team down. Thankfully, Luke's time had been taken up with administrative tasks, so she'd seen very little of him. Nearly all of their recent communications had been through email and this was just fine with her. Perhaps the closeness she'd felt to Luke was just because of the explosive secret they shared about Ethan and things would be businesslike from here on out.

"Hey, at least you don't have to see his ugly mug every day." Steele motioned toward Dimples, who gave him a wide grin. "Parrino, you did a great job with these covers, but I'm not sure I can pull off being this guy's brother. I mean, look at him—men ain't supposed to have dimples." Steele made a face.

The guys laughed. "You're brothers in a spiritual sense, not biologically connected." Alessa clarified, even though she knew they understood. The details were too important to assume anything. "And remember that Dan is also a spiritual brother."

"Parrino, can you go over the covers again? I don't think I quite understand even after you've given us color-coded sheets, sent it out in email, downloaded them to our phones and explained it three times." Rodgers said.

The guys laughed and Alessa flicked a piece of broccoli at Rodgers. It was good-natured fun and she didn't mind at all. It meant she was truly part of the team.

"Take it easy on her, guys, she's just trying to do her job."

He did not *just say that.* Alessa glared at Luke. Rodgers exchanged glances with Boots, and Dan smirked.

As if realizing his mistake, Luke cleared his throat. "Got to switch to a serious topic for a minute. Have you all taken care of your personal business?"

The guys fell silent. Rodgers was the first to speak. "Ethan made us go round and say what's what in case something happens. So the rest of us make sure our families are okay."

Luke sat up straighter. "What did Ethan say that last time you did this?"

Rodgers took a breath and looked at Boots and Steele. The men nodded. Rodgers turned back to Luke. "Ethan said if something happened to him, you'd take care of everything that needed taking care of and we didn't have to worry about his affairs. He told us to make sure the unit continued without him."

Luke picked up his soda can and took a big swig, but Alessa didn't miss the shine in his eyes.

"I'll start," Rodgers said, saving Luke from having to respond. "My wife already got half of everything in the divorce, so I don't have much in the bank and no real assets. Talked to her yesterday and told her I was deploying. She told me it's getting serious with the new guy in her life and she wants to move on. Asked me not to call her anymore. So no need to notify her if something happens."

Boots was sitting next to Rodgers and slapped him on the back. "Well, I've got my will squared away. My sister and her son get everything if something happens to me. I talked to her today. My nephew started chemo a month ago—it's hard on them, but they're getting through it. If something happens to me, make sure the army processes my death benefits fast. I get the feeling his treatments are gonna be more than what my sister's insurance will cover."

Everyone nodded and Alessa got the feeling that if something did happen to Boots, everyone on the team would bankrupt themselves to make sure his nephew got the treatments he needed.

"My will's good, too," Dimples said. "Talked to the kids today. Mickey is gonna join the chess club, God help him. I'm gonna see if I can pay for karate lessons for that kid. I mean, what fourth grader wants to join chess? Isabel is giving her mother a hard time." He shook his head. "The girl's in sixth grade and Emmy says it's a daily struggle with clothes, shoes, cellphone… She even wants to start wearing makeup. The good news is that Lizzy is finally potty-trained." His voice was full of pride, as if he were announcing that one of his kids had won the Nobel Prize, but none of the guys teased. They sat and listened and Dimples didn't bother to hide the tears welling in his eyes. "If something happens to me, Emmy's gonna need a hand. I love that woman, but she doesn't know how to change the oil in her car or fix the garbage disposal when it gets jammed. And she doesn't know how to teach a ten-year-old boy to deal with bullies at school. She's gonna need all that."

Once again everyone nodded, including Alessa. The team was a family and they were going to take care of each other no matter what.

It was Alessa's turn, and suddenly all eyes were on her. She swallowed. What was she supposed to say? "I have a will. My sister gets what little I have in my bank account. Julia can take care of herself, but I guess I would appreciate someone checking in on my mom. Make sure she's okay." Alessa could feel Luke's eyes on her, but she wasn't going to say more.

"Don't worry, I'll make sure she's okay." Luke said, his voice thick. The group fell silent and Alessa focused on scooping up noodles with her chopsticks to avoid looking at any of them.

"Y'all don't have to worry about me," Steele drawled. "The second wife got what the first one didn't. Can't buy any of you a cup of coffee with what's in my bank account. What I do have, I'm giving to the Wounded Warrior Project."

"What about your parents or siblings?" Alessa asked.

Steele laughed mirthlessly. "Mom was a crack addict who didn't know who my dad was. She overdosed when I was ten. I bounced around foster care until I turned eighteen, then I enlisted."

Alessa wanted to say more but it was clear Steele was done talking and the guys already knew the story. Dan was next. "My dad left me a hunting lodge when he died. That's the only real thing I got. Mom doesn't want it, so I'm leaving it to my ex-wife, Clarissa. My death benefits go to my mom. She's getting up there in age and is probably going to need them for nursing home care if I'm not around."

"Man, why you gonna leave the lodge to your ex? You've got a brother right here who loves hunting and fishing." Steele thumped his chest.

Dan smiled. "She loves that place." What he didn't add but was clear in his face was *and I still love her.*

All eyes turned to Luke, including her own. He chewed on a piece of pizza. His blue eyes clouded over, the small laugh lines by his mouth becoming more pronounced as he spoke. "My death benefits and assets will go to various charities. Dad will handle my financial affairs. I need you guys to find out what happened to Ethan."

It was the white elephant in the room. A weight descended on all of them. "We got you covered." Rodgers said softly. "That's on all of our lists."

Luke's eyes met Alessa's and she understood what he meant without him needing to say it. He wasn't ready to share his suspicions with the guys.

Steele stood and brushed the crumbs off his pants. "Okay, now that we've all Kumbaya'd together, it's time to get real." Steele left the pit and the guys all grinned. Again, Alessa's eyes found Luke's. Clearly they were about to witness another unit tradition.

Steele returned a minute later holding a stack of clear plastic cups and a fancy crystal decanter.

Luke's eyes widened. "Please tell me that is not Colonel McBride's."

Steele grinned, his face transformed into that of a mischievous little boy. "Okay, I won't tell you that. What I will tell you is that this is a Glenlivet twenty-one-year-old archive." Rodgers took the plastic cups and handed them out while Steele lifted the top off the decanter and took a whiff of the scotch inside. "Full malt, hints of chocolate, citrus, vanilla and smoke." He poured a good-sized portion into his glass and took a sip, closed his eyes and swallowed after a few seconds. He opened his eyes. "Perfection."

There were several chuckles in the group. Rodgers took the bottle from him. "If you're done making love to the scotch, maybe we can all have a sip." Once everyone had some in their cups, Rodgers raised his arm. "Here's to the soldier who fights and loves—may he never lack for either."

They raised their cups and tapped them against each other.

Alessa caught Luke's gaze and she read her thoughts in his eyes.

If I screw up, a lot of lives will be ruined.

CHAPTER EIGHT

THE PLAN WAS to take a military jet into Afghanistan, then cross the border in teams of two and three. The official plane manifest showed no passengers on board. The pilot and copilot were used to this, assuming this was a black ops unit. Still, Alessa didn't want to take a chance flying them directly into Pakistan, so they would walk into the country through illegal border crossings. Each unit member wore local Pashtun clothing under their camouflage ACUs; a long tunic *kameez* and harem-like pants called *salwar*. For her part, she would add a head-to-toe burka.

Alessa had been raised Catholic but she wasn't practicing. Now she said a small prayer for the team. She'd signed up for the army because it was disciplined and regimented. She knew what she had to do and how to do it. While the extraordinariness of the unit excited her, it also scared her. What if she made the wrong choice and got one of the guys killed? While logistics was considered the kiss of death for most soldiers, it was mission-critical. Soldiers needed a safe place to stay, somewhere they could sleep at night so when they put their lives in danger, they could do so with a clear head and well-rested body. And logistics for this kind of unit was not exactly normal army logistics. Something as simple as how they got into Pakistan, a country they would have normally flown or helicoptered into, was going to be a death-defying exercise.

She had worked with Rodgers on the plan to split up and enter the country in different locations. While Rodgers worked on the routes, she had come up with the supplies they'd need. Crossing the border from Afghanistan into Pakistan made the Mexico–US border look like child's play. She'd agonized over every decision with Rodgers, who despite having four operations with the unit under his belt was still tentative.

"Okay, ten minutes to wheels down." Luke announced after checking the altimeter. Without another word, they all unharnessed their belts and stretched before finding their designated crate and climbing into it. They were going be carried out in crates that were supposed to be full of MREs and stacked in a warehouse. The crates did have MREs inside; just enough for each of them to throw over themselves in case someone pried open the lid. Alessa and Rodgers nailed the boxes shut on their team members.

"Okay, Luke, you go in before Rodgers and I close up." Alessa had rigged one of the crates so she and Rodgers could get in and nail it shut from the inside. It required one person to hold the lid down by running their fingers in between the slats while the other person secured it with a nail gun. Alessa was the only one whose fingers were small enough to go between the slats, which was why she and Rodgers had to share.

"I'm going in your crate." Luke said firmly. Before she could protest, he motioned to Rodgers, who reluctantly got into the box meant for Luke. Alessa stared open mouthed as Luke nailed Rodgers in. She had spent hours meticulously calculating the size of each crate and team member to make sure everyone fit and would have enough air given all sorts of stacking scenarios. And Luke had just made a snap decision. He was six inches taller than Rodgers and his backpack was exactly two inches wider and one pound heavier. *What's wrong with him?*

Luke was already in their box and waving impatiently at her. *I don't really have a choice.* The plane was descending; they didn't have time to argue. She got into the crate, taking as little space as possible, trying her best to leave enough room so Luke wouldn't have to touch her.

She and Luke were face-to-face, on their knees with barely half an inch of space between them. Not seeming to notice their close proximity, Luke gestured for her to pull the lid over their heads. Alessa reached up, trying not to pay attention that doing so brought their chests into contact. Sucking in a breath, she stuck her fingers between the slats and tugged the lid until it fell into place. Luke deftly secured it with the battery-operated mini pneumatic nail gun she'd handed him. While he might not have appreciated that little detail, she'd spent several hours scouring websites and home improvement stores to find a gun that would leave enough clearance to use it inside the crate and still have nails long enough to secure the lid, but not so long that it would be difficult to open.

She, not Luke, had agonized over all these details, and yet he had made the quick decision that it would be okay to switch boxes on her. She had even measured Rodgers's arm length to make sure he could operate the gun. What if Luke hadn't been able to do it? Was the entire mission going to be this haphazard?

The plane dropped suddenly as the pilot descended toward Bagram Airfield. Given that they were flying into what was still a war zone, the pilots tended to stay high and drop as close to the airfield as possible to maximize the amount of time they were out of range of hand-held surface-to-air missiles. Despite her best attempts at keeping her back pressed against the side of the crate, Alessa tumbled forward into Luke. Her breath stuck as she registered his arms around her, his lips close to her cheek. She didn't like him being so comfortable in her personal space. Pushing against him, she slammed against the other side of the crate and pulled her legs up to her chest.

"You okay?" Luke's voice was so soft that she barely heard him.

"Yes," she squeaked out, feeling sheepish at the overreaction. Having served for almost seventeen years, she was used to being in close quarters with men. She had been in transport trucks where she was practically sitting on a strange man's lap, in trenches and alleyways where she was pressed so close against her colleagues she couldn't tell where her body stopped and theirs began. The bulky roughness of the ACUs helped create a barrier in her mind. Not that the physical proximity didn't take getting used to, but she was no stranger to these types of situations. She had learned to accept and deal with them. Even in cases where fellow soldiers weren't as gentlemanly as they should be. So why was it so difficult with Luke?

"Why did you switch crates?"

Normally she would never question a superior officer, but Luke had made it clear it was a unit expectation, so for once she didn't have to bite her tongue.

"I thought it might be a good time for us to talk about the mission."

It was a good point, one she had thought of when she'd planned this part but had immediately dismissed the idea when she'd realized that they could be stuck in the creates for hours. Bagram wasn't exactly known for its efficiency; they could be waiting forever for someone to offload the crates.

"I'm all ears," she said easily. Truth be told, it had been grating on her that she didn't know exactly what he was planning, and more importantly, what her role might be in terms of helping Luke find his brother.

"You did well analyzing those satellite photos. I looked into everyone that had ever been connected to that safe house and wouldn't you know it, our target—Azizi—was held there."

She gasped. Their current mission was to capture and interview Azizi. The man was a senior Taliban leader and the unit members suspected he might be working with a traitor in the army. If Azizi had something to do with Ethan's death, then he would expect the unit to come after him.

Ice seeped through her veins and she hugged herself tighter. Whoever had taken or killed Ethan was probably going to attack Luke, maybe even the whole team. If one of the unit men was involved, it would be even worse. It was more important than ever that everyone follow her plan. On Luke's instructions, the mini-teams only had their own travel instructions, not each other's. If one group was apprehended, they wouldn't be able to reveal the locations of the other members. She had to tell Luke that he couldn't change plans on her last-minute again. From what she'd read about him—and seen in the few hours since the start of the mission—he was impulsive.

She leaned forward, and just as she did, the plane dropped precipitously. She reached out to grab onto something but her head hit the top of the box. As the thud reverberated through her, flashes of light danced before her eyes. She felt the comforting warmth of muscled arms envelop her, squeezing her tight.

Her shoulder sparked with pain and she bit her tongue from crying out. Luke held on to her, preventing her from moving as the box shifted. Her face was buried in his chest and she moved so she could see what was going on. *That was a mistake.* Her nose was now touching Luke's, her lips a hair's breadth away from his. His hands moved down her back. He was loosening his hold, but she sat frozen on his lap, unable to look away from the slight parting of his lips, wondering if he would kiss her.

She tilted her head just a fraction so their noses were no longer touching.

"Alessa." It was the way he said her name, the whisper of warm breath across her face and neck. Something ignited inside of her and for the first time in her life, she refused to plan or think it through. She leaned forward and pressed her lips against his.

Just as their lips touched, the plane landed hard on the tarmac and both Luke and Alessa were momentarily lifted. Reflexively, Luke placed his hand above Alessa's head, cushioning the bump, while his head took the brunt of the hard knock that came.

The plane taxied for a few minutes and Alessa scrambled as far away from Luke as she could get in the small space. As if sensing her discomfort, he too seemed to fold into himself. Their eyes locked and a thousand words passed between them.

She finally said a few of them out loud. "We need to stay away from each other."

CHAPTER NINE

PREDICTABLY, THEY WERE still sitting in the crates at Bagram. At least an hour had passed since they'd landed. This was not unusual. Alessa had been quiet the entire time and Luke dared not speak or get any closer to her. Had she kissed him or had he kissed her? He couldn't tell. Luke had never had trouble holding limits with women. Yet when he had Alessa in his arms, it had taken every molecule of self-control to keep it professional. And he'd failed miserably. She was a soldier in his command. He was responsible for her safety and well-being. More importantly, he needed to be totally mission-focused. Including his brother, seven lives depended on him.

Unlike his past commands, he was solely in charge here. For other operations he'd led, there had always been a higher officer who helped him plan and monitored his moves. There was no safety net with this unit.

Ethan had designed the unit to compartmentalize information. The army leaked like a sieve, and despite Ethan's best attempts to keep the existence of the unit secret, word had already trickled out that there was a special unit rooting out traitors. But no one had any idea what their area of focus was. Not even Colonel McBride.

Like Ethan before him, Luke was supposed to find his own missions by reviewing hundreds of army operations that went sideways to look for patterns. Colonel McBride had no idea which area Luke was targeting, though he'd tried mightily to get the answer out of Luke. To keep him on his toes, Luke had intimated that they were staying on the home front. He didn't know whether the colonel believed him, but Luke didn't feel bad about lying. The unit was authorized to operate in complete secrecy in order to prevent the kind of leaks that had already happened.

But McBride wasn't stupid. While Luke hadn't shared his suspicions about Ethan being alive with anyone except Alessa, it didn't take a genius to surmise that Luke would want to know why his brother's mission had failed. Luke had struggled with the decision to go back to Pakistan, but his position as unit command was just too tenuous to risk doing another mission first. Ultimately, he'd gone with his instincts. The same instincts that had told him to kiss Alessa.

He was beginning to seriously doubt whether he should trust those instincts.

He activated his comms system. "Check in."

One by one, each of his men let him know they were fine.

After what seemed like an interminable wait but was actually just another half hour, they heard the cargo doors open. Several minutes later, a forklift connected to the box, which tipped Luke backward as the machine lifted it off the plane. Alessa hung on to her side of the crate, but gravity eventually pulled her toward him. She used her arms to keep her body off his, but there was only so much space in the crate and once again they were face-to-face, their noses a hair's width apart.

Daylight streamed through the slats of the crate coloring her eyes with soft hues of brown. Up close, he could see the light golden freckles on her nose and an image of a little girl with freckles on her cheeks filled his mind. Their girl. With Alessa's dark hair and brown eyes. *What are you thinking?* He had never considered marriage and children. Not as long as he stayed in the army. He'd seen what army life had done to his mother, and he had no desire to do that to a woman, or to himself. If he ever married, he wanted to spend his life with his partner, play ball with his children—not be out fighting wars in foreign lands.

The crate shifted again and Alessa rested her forehead on his. *Is it her shoulder?* He realized with a pang that she must be putting a lot of pressure on it to hold herself up.

He put his hands on her waist to steady her and she jolted, lifting herself away from him and settling back into her corner of the crate that had now been set down. She tried to hide it, but he saw the pain on her face. He had caused her injury because he'd let himself get distracted by her. It was time to focus on the mission, before something else went wrong.

Thump!

He and Alessa looked up. Another crate had been placed on top of theirs, boxing them in.

Luke muttered an expletive. They had clearly marked the box so it would be placed on the top of a stack to avoid this situation. He pushed against the top of the box but it wouldn't budge. He opened his backpack and extracted a small axe, then whacked at the top, but it was no use. He managed to decimate a board but the box on top of theirs was too heavy to move. Alessa sat in her corner calmly watching him, that infuriatingly blank expression on her face.

"Any more ideas?" she asked.

He scrunched back into his corner. "The team will have to move it."

Alessa nodded. There were no sounds coming from the outside, so it was fair to assume that they were in the holding bay where the crates would stay until they were processed at Bagram. She took out a pipe camera from her backpack and snaked it through, looking at the visual on her smartphone. She gave him a thumbs-up. Coast was clear; it was time to exit.

"Check in." Luke said into the comms system. The team members acknowledged that they were also out of the aircraft and were working on getting out of their crates. Alessa had nailed them shut using short nails, just enough to secure the lid but not so tight that they couldn't push them out. Luke went back to trying to muscle the box on top of them, but Alessa tapped him on the shoulder and motioned for him to sit down. He stared at her for a beat, then did as she asked. She snaked the camera out again, then took a small hammer out of her backpack. She used the claw to pull nails out of one side of their box. When she'd loosened a number of nails, she curled up, then kicked the side, which fell outward. She looked at him with a smirk and all he wanted to do was take her in his arms and kiss her. Instead, he smiled back at her and nodded.

"Well done."

"It's all up here," she said tapping her head.

He laughed, then gestured for her to crawl out of the box first. He followed. They were in an airplane hangar, a cavernous gray space with concrete floors, gray walls and a dark ceiling Luke guessed to be at least ten stories high. The hangar was full of random noises. They crouched down low behind some boxes peering around to see if there was anyone nearby.

There were personnel of all sorts in the hangar; forklifts whizzed about, soldiers and men and women dressed in maintenance coveralls walked purposefully about. The key was to blend in, to make it seemed like they belonged and hadn't just materialized out of a crate.

When no one seemed within their direct line of sight, they stood and brushed off their clothes. Alessa lifted her backpack off the floor and he noticed her eyes scrunch as she swung it onto her right shoulder. She saw him staring and smiled. *Made of steel.* Unlike any woman he'd ever met.

Not that there weren't women out there he admired. Kat Driscoll-Santiago was one of them. The congresswoman and soon-to-be senator from Virginia was a close personal friend. Another was Doctor Anna Atao, who he had encountered in Guam when he was helping Kat do a good deed.

Kat and Anna had given him hope that there was a woman out there who was, for lack of a better term, *army strong*. A woman who wouldn't waste away under the shadow of army life. Who could handle the burden of marrying a soldier. Alessa could take care of herself. He'd seen ice in her eyes when she described how her father had stopped hitting when she lashed back. She hadn't waited for someone to come rescue her, hadn't blamed her life or circumstances; she'd taken control. It was something he wished with all his heart his mother had done.

Despite her strength, Luke wondered whether he'd made the right call letting Alessa come on the mission. If she separated her shoulder, she might suffer enough nerve damage to become disabled. Especially if they couldn't get quick or specialized care here in Pakistan. All his life, Luke had done what he felt was right. He and Ethan had often disagreed about decisions that affected both their lives or the well-being of their family, and Luke had always gone with what felt right to him. But the last time he hadn't listened to Ethan, their mother had died. His instinct had failed him, and his mother. *What if I made the wrong call with Alessa?*

"We have a problem." Rodgers's voice cracked through the comms system. "Dan got made. There's a sour-looking Afghan talking to him."

Luke pressed his lips. Bagram had recently been on lockdown because of a suicide bomb attack that killed a couple of soldiers. Security had been tightened. As a NATO base, Bagram housed forces from around the world plus Afghani contractors who provided everything from food rations and basic human services to security. Luke had to make a decision; try to extricate Dan and possibly make the team's presence known or leave him. Dan would be detained and he'd create a distraction to give the team a chance to get away. Eventually Colonel McBride would rescue him, but Luke would lose him on the mission.

"Make like you belong and go get him." Alessa said.

Luke didn't hesitate. He asked for Dan's exact location, then strode over like he owned the place. "There you are. Have you found my boxes? I expected you back an hour ago." Luke nodded to the Afghan dismissively. Dan raised an eyebrow but knew how to play along. "I'm sorry, sir, I was detained." He looked accusingly at the man who was eyeing Luke's ACU. Luke glared at him, then pivoted dramatically and walked toward the exit. He heard Dan follow. The Afghan let them go. Luke heard the team chuckle in the comms system and give him verbal high fives. He smiled. *Alessa has good instincts.*

"Okay, everyone, let's gather at the PX." The Post Exchange was the army's version of a mega store. One could buy everything from a tomato to a Harley-Davidson motorcycle. There was even an Afghan market with local merchants selling the usual wares; rugs, jewelry, artisan crafts and the occasional black market items they'd managed to sneak past the guards. There was a chain burger joint and Afghan restaurants to give soldiers ethnic fare.

Luke blinked in the sunshine. The one thing that always hit him when he came to this part of the world was the dust. Taking a deep breath felt gritty, like the air was infused with sand. He took a second to orient himself and Dan stepped up beside him. It had been five years since Luke had been on Bagram and the base looked totally different. Over the last several years, they'd been demolishing buildings that had housed troops. Concrete barriers that once created a perimeter were gone from several sections, reducing the footprint of the base. It took Luke a moment to figure out where they were.

Alessa had downloaded a map of the base

with the current demolition. The old, crumbling, Soviet-era buildings were still there, as if marking time. Luke wondered if they'd been left standing as warning to the next force to use the base.

The rest of the team had almost reached the PX, so Luke walked faster. He needed to be quicker on his feet. Even a second's hesitation could get them killed. He was a good soldier; that fact he didn't question. But he'd never been a good leader, and as important as it was for him to find Ethan, was it really worth the lives of his team? Was it worth Alessa's life?

It was well past the lunch hour, but the PX was busy as usual. The smells of fried meat floated through the hot, dusty air. Luke decided to go for a popular fast food chain; it had the shortest line. The unit gathered at a communal table. Bagram was a big enough place that a group of army soldiers would not get noticed.

Everyone scarfed down their food. The faster they got off Bagram, the lower their chance of discovery.

"Change of plan," Luke said. Everyone froze midchew. "Rodgers, you'll go with Boots and be the new mini-team Delta and I'll go with Parrino and be the new mini-team Alpha. We'll coordinate in Pakistan." Luke knew he was throwing a grenade onto the lunch table.

They'd discussed these plans several times and he'd had plenty of opportunity to bring this up. Right or wrong, he was going with his gut and he sensed that he needed to be close to Alessa; to keep an eye on her and make sure she was okay. He should never have let her come on the mission, but now it was his responsibility to keep her safe.

"Luke…" Alessa's voice was tentative. "Cell signals are spotty near the border. We might not be able to communicate with the others. If I don't go with Rodgers, he won't have a plausible cover."

It was a good argument. One for which Luke had no answer. "He'll improvise," he said shortly.

"But…" Alessa wasn't going to let up, and he wasn't in the mood to argue.

"We don't have time, so this is not up for discussion. Now let's go."

Luke didn't miss the knowing glances Boots and Rodgers gave each other. Under normal circumstances, he'd have asked them what their problem was, but he knew exactly what they'd say. It wasn't the right decision. Parrino was just another team member. If Boots or Rodgers had been hurt, Luke wouldn't be changing plans like this. So why was he giving Parrino her special treatment? Maybe it was because he was responsible for her shoulder, and for bringing her on this mission against his better judgement. He needed to be the one to take care of her.

Besides, it wasn't just that she was hurt. Keeping her close to him would make it easier for them to work on finding Ethan. He knew the team didn't like what he was doing but the one good thing about the army way was battlefield orders were obeyed, even if a soldier disagreed with them. Rodgers and Boots walked off and Luke waited a minute to let them exit before he and Alessa strolled nonchalantly through Bagram as if they belonged there.

Luke had served in Iraq and Afghanistan and he'd led units through countless patrols and missions yet never had he felt his stomach twist and knot the way it did now. A few minutes ago it had felt like the right decision to make but now, walking alone with Alessa, he wasn't so sure.

Alessa grabbed his arm. "Why did you change the orders?" She whispered even though the sounds of moving machinery and equipment were so loud that he could scream at the top of his lungs and not attract any attention.

"I think your shoulder is hurting more than you let on and I want to keep an eye on you."

She shook her head. "I'm fine!"

"Let's go. We have a long way to go." Once again he thought of Ethan's brilliance in designing the test procedure for the unit. They had already been traveling for sixteen hours and easily had a twelve- to twenty-hour journey ahead of them. The assessment weeded out soldiers who wouldn't have that kind of endurance. That was Ethan; he planned things to perfection. Unlike Luke, who flew by the seat of his pants.

Under normal army procedures they would have arranged for transportation to a forward operating base on the border. That's how Ethan's missions had been run. But Alessa had taken the mandate not to use army resources pretty seriously. They all had to do several miles of walking to cross the border. Originally, he and Boots were supposed to find local transportation—which was a nice way of saying a rickshaw, donkey cart or anything with wheels—to Kabul, then take a bus to Jalalabad, then more local transportation until they got close enough to illegally cross the Khyber Pass. Now he'd be doing that with Alessa.

As they continued toward the edge of the base, Alessa stumbled. Luke grabbed her arm to steady her. Alessa shook him off. "I'm fine!"

"Are you sure?"

"I tripped on a paver, that's all."

"Khyber is dangerous, Parrino. It's not the place to be trekking through if you're less than a hundred percent." He knew he was belaboring the issue, but the way her forehead creased and the obvious frustration in her voice told him something was wrong. The woman was usually a brick wall when it came to showing emotion, so reserved that she was impossible to read. Even the guys joked that they weren't inviting her to the poker party.

"Every way is dangerous. There is no safe path across unless we go with an army transport."

That wasn't exactly true. He'd noticed this when he'd studied the mini-team routes. Alessa had chosen the hardest one for herself and Rodgers. Their route had the most walking and open exposure. That was another reason why he'd switched her to his team. He had the easiest route. He'd tried not to read too much into it other than the fact that it was also the fastest, which made sense for the team lead.

She stepped up to him and lowered her voice. "I'm okay. Really. Can we drop it and focus on the mission?"

What would Ethan do? He would tell Luke that Alessa had performed better in the unit entrance test than all his other men. The woman could handle this; that's why he'd hired her.

"Fine, let's keep moving."

It wasn't as hard to leave Bagram Airfield as it was to get in. The perimeter security was focused on keeping suicide bombers and other riffraff out. Luke and Alessa managed to sneak through without incident, taking advantage of the busy afternoon when the guards were busy with truck deliveries.

Bagram was located in a relatively rural area, though there was never a shortage of people milling about right outside the base. Some were there to gawk, some to see if someone would give them money or work. The lookie-loos stared at him and Parrino. To her credit, she didn't flinch and walked along as if this were a perfectly routine patrol.

The landscape around Bagram was mountainous with little vegetation. It took them a few minutes to find a relatively secluded area amongst some brush. They shed their ACUs and pulled cloth knapsacks from their army-issued backpacks. Underneath their ACUs, they were wearing the loose cotton pants and tunic known locally as *salwar kameez*. Alessa threw a powder blue burka on top of hers, covering her entire body, including her face. He could barely see her eyes through the mesh covering. Once they got into Pakistan, she could take the burka off and wrap a scarf around her head, but in the rural parts of Afghanistan, the burka was still prevalent and a man and woman walking together would attract a lot less attention if the woman was covered.

Stuffing their ACUs into a bag, they went in search of a fire pit. These were pretty common as the nights were about as cold as the days were hot, and they found one within fifteen minutes. After making sure no one was paying them any attention, they threw in the uniforms with their army backpacks, added some lighter fluid and lit a match. They waited until nothing was left but ashes before silently continuing their journey.

For most soldiers, burning a uniform was a deeply unpatriotic and disrespectful act. But they didn't have a choice. They had to travel light and in the event they were caught, having uniforms on them could blow their cover, or worse, terrorists could steal the ACUs and use them to get an edge in an attack. All of the unit men had protested at the necessity of this action but had ultimately seen Alessa's point and conceded it.

"I think that might have been the worst thing I've ever done." Alessa's voice was so quiet in the comms system that Luke almost missed it.

He stopped and turned but she kept on walking and he had to hurry to get a few steps ahead of her. Women here were expected to walk behind men, and as much as he despised the practice, the whole idea was not to attract attention.

"Why was it so hard for you?" he asked softly.

The whole thing had been her idea and despite the men's objections, she had held fast to the recommendation that they burn their uniforms for safety reasons.

"I am a soldier who just burned her uniform."

"Not as an act of defiance but out of necessity to protect the uniform, to make sure it isn't used against us."

"I know," she said in a small voice. He could tell she was conflicted, that it wasn't sitting well with her.

They walked for nearly two miles before they came to a small village crossroads where they knew they'd find transportation. Luke's *kameez* was heavy with sweat and sticking to him, the white cotton almost transparently wet.

While they waited for someone to pass so they could try to hitch a ride, Luke found a tree stump and patted it. "Sit." He couldn't see her eyes or her facial expression but somehow he knew she was going to protest. She hesitated but then sat down. Her backpack was underneath the burka and he heard her gulping water. The burka was like a nonbreathable bubble around her body and he immediately felt guilty that they hadn't stopped sooner for a rest. As hot as he was in the light cotton clothing, she had to be sweltering underneath all those yards of fabric. Not to mention the fact that her shoulder injury had obviously flared up.

"Before you ask, I'm fine," she said irritably.

He remained standing. If he took a seat on the tree stump, she would be forced to sit on the ground at his feet. Despite the supposed social progress in Afghanistan, the rural areas remained rigid in their treatment of women.

"Why did the uniform burning bother you so much?"

He wished he could see her eyes, read her face, but he'd have to settle for words alone.

"It's nothing."

"Tell me, Alessa."

She took so long to respond that he thought the conversation was over.

"When I was growing up, I didn't have a lot of things that were just mine. Or things that weren't broken or damaged one way or another. When I left home, it was literally with the clothes I was wearing. The uniform is the one thing that's been a constant in my life. Something with my name on it that I can be proud of. It's perfect." Her voice cracked a little and the weight of what she'd said washed over him like a tidal wave.

Luke thought of all the "things" he and Ethan treasured. Military brats often complained about the lack of permanence in their lives, the need to move from one place to another all the time. He and Ethan had had a special handmade trunk with secret compartments that their father had purchased during a short stint in Japan. The trunk had moved with them to every new post, and the twins had often hidden contraband inside.

The trunk now sat in his father's home, in the room that his mother had dubbed "the boys' room" for when he and Ethan would visit. Luke and Ethan hadn't lived with their parents for nearly twenty years—ever since they left for West Point after high school— but his mother unfailingly decorated "the boys' room" in every new house they set up. Ethan was the only one who'd really used it.

Alessa had fallen silent and he felt the overwhelming need to touch her, tell her that she deserved to have more than just a uniform to call her own. A deep, dark rage pulsed through his veins, making him wish he could punish her father for everything he had ever taken away from her.

His own father had many faults, but the

one thing he'd been very clear on teaching his boys was that there was no circumstance under which it was okay to hit a child or a woman. Luke knew men who hit women. At least five soldiers under his command had been disciplined for beating their wives. Those were just the cases he knew about. Luke considered them to be weak men who couldn't handle the stress in their lives and took it out on others. He had no use for them and had given them the harshest reprimands the army would allow.

"You still have the uniform, so to speak, but it's not the only thing you have. You also have…" *Me*. He was about to end that sentence with *me*. "The unit," he finished weakly. What was wrong with him? That would've been incredibly inappropriate. He was her superior and an officer. It was his duty was to protect her.

Especially from himself.

CHAPTER TEN

LUCK WAS NOT on their side. After waiting for
an hour on the roadside, they'd finally caught
a rusted pickup truck to Kabul. The driver had
demanded a generous fee and asked way too
many questions. Both Alessa and Luke spoke
some Pashtun but nowhere close to enough to
keep up a conversation or to pass as natively
fluent. So Luke had used grunts and nods, hoping the driver would get the hint. Alessa stayed
silent because it would've been improper for
her to talk.

The man made Alessa ride in the truck bed
while Luke was asked to keep him company
in the cab. Alessa could almost see the steam
coming out of Luke's ears but he smartly realized that he had no choice. If he made a fuss,
the man would ask even more questions and get
suspicious. As it was, they'd have to alter their
plans. A nosy driver meant he'd talk about the
strangers he'd picked up and someone could
easily follow their trail if they caught a bus
from the Kabul stop.

Bouncing uncomfortably in the back of the pickup, Alessa was almost glad to get a break from Luke. Her shoulder was throbbing and there were times when her vision wasn't entirely clear. She didn't know if it was the heat or the burka's mesh covering her eyes. She had practiced wearing the burka, worn it for two days stateside in preparation for this mission, but the temperature was much higher here and something just felt off. Sitting down and letting herself relax was a welcome respite.

She couldn't let Luke see she wasn't feeling well. How dare he change the plan on the assumption that *he* needed to take care of her? A bump on the head and healing shoulder were hardly cause for alarm. She was an experienced soldier, with far more years in active combat than Luke. After working so hard to prove to them that she qualified to be a member of the unit, a proper member, she couldn't believe Luke would undermine her like that.

The truck hit a giant pothole and her arm exploded into a million pieces as she slammed into the side of the truck. This was no rougher than a ride in a jeep or transport truck. She'd been on thousands of those. So why was her vision all fuzzy? *Must be the burka.* It would be better once they got into Pakistan and she could switch to a lighter headscarf.

She turned her back to the cab and lifted the veil covering her face, but her vision didn't clear. Taking several deep breaths, she reached into her backpack and pulled out the canteen. Normally she would take small sips throughout the day to get her body acclimated to the hot weather and conserve water but she downed more than half the canteen, figuring she was dehydrated. She could refill the canteen at the Kabul bus station. It would be a lot worse for her to pass out. Luke wouldn't make it to the safe house ahead of the others. She couldn't let the team down.

Alessa had failed at a lot of things in life; she'd barely passed high school, hadn't held down a single teenage job. Being a soldier was all she'd ever been successful at. Until *the incident*, she'd regularly been promoted and had nothing but stellar ratings in her performance appraisals. Her integrity as a soldier was all she had, the only thing she could hold on to when her father's voice snarled at her about how she was nothing, and that the best he could hope for was that she'd find a guy like him who would take care of her.

Perhaps it was that realization that had compelled her to enlist with the army. The horrifying thought that if she didn't change her life, she'd end up like her mother, a woman who had to rely on her abusive husband to feed and clothe her and her children. Alessa would never put herself in a situation where she needed a man to take care of her.

THEY WERE AT the Kabul bus station. Luke directed her to a bench.

"Don't move," he said ominously. He went to a ticket booth and elbowed his way through the small crowd gathered in front of the window.

Once he'd bought tickets, he proceeded to a roadside stand. Alessa couldn't remember if she'd ever eaten at a real Afghan restaurant off the base. The best she'd ever seen was an open kitchen inside a blown-out building with chairs and tables outside on the sidewalk.

Luke brought back two heaping plates of rice. Handing her one, he began eating with this hands, which was the traditional way. "He claims there's really meat in there." Luke said. The rice dish was known as *kabuli pulao*, and could include a combination of various meats, vegetables and nuts. Meat was expensive, but even if there was none in theirs, the hot meal was far better than the MREs they had in their backpacks.

Alessa did the best she could to shovel food into her mouth under the veil. Luke's eyes sparked with amusement as she tried and failed to get a finger-full of food into her mouth.

"Want me to feed you?" he asked cheekily.

"How about I dress up like a man and you put this on," she retorted.

He crouched down so he could meet her eyes. "Seriously, Parrino, you scared me back there. I think you passed out in the back of the truck. Tell me what's going on."

"I did not pass out! I fell asleep."

"When I woke you up, you were confused, mumbling incoherent things. Your eyes were unfocused, too."

She didn't remember any of that.

"I'm dehydrated, that's all—a problem I've corrected."

His eyes narrowed. "Parrino, you're lying to me." His gaze bored into hers and for once she was glad for the mesh over her eyes. Yet the intensity of his look warmed her. He genuinely cared about whether she was okay. The words to reassure him were on her lips—a platitude to get him off her back—but she couldn't utter them. Her tongue stuck to the roof of her mouth as her throat went completely dry.

She didn't know how to react to a man who was worried about her well-being. Aidan had been the first man who had shown any concern for her. At some level, she was sure he truly had cared about her, but ultimately, as happened with most men, his needs had come before hers. While he hadn't exactly thrown her under the bus, he hadn't gone out of his way to help her, either. Unlike Luke, who was jeopardizing the mission to assure her safety.

"Why did you switch teams?" she asked, not caring that she was skirting his question about her health.

"I was worried about you. Still am. I think you're in pain and lying about it."

"I'm in better shape than any number of soldiers currently in combat. Would you have switched places if it were Boots or Dimples or any of the guys that was hurt?"

His hesitation was all the answer she needed and she waved her hand dismissively. "I hate when people assume women are frail and weak. Look around. The men are nice and comfortable in their loose-flowing *kameez*. Let me tell you, if men had to wear this burka in the heat all day, they wouldn't last more than a couple of hours. While you were enjoying a nice cushioned seat, I was riding in the back of a truck with no shocks smelling donkey poop."

"What're you trying to convince me of, Parrino? I already know you're a great soldier. I'm not concerned because I think you're weak but because…"

He looked away. If they were in any other place, she would've gotten in his face, challenged him to explain himself. Instead, she set down the nearly full plate of rice and tried to meet his eyes.

"Because what?" she whispered.

"...because I feel responsible for you," he said finally.

What's that supposed to mean?

"Why? I'm just a soldier in your command. No one special." It was the role she had played her entire life. She was the expendable one.

"That's..." He shook his head, then picked up their plates and returned them to the food vendor, ignoring the fact that she hadn't finished eating. She knew what he was doing. Putting distance between them. It was what Aidan had done when things went wrong. In his case, he'd gone out on patrol, every day, even when it wasn't his turn, and he'd found excuses to avoid her at the small camp. It was what her mother did whenever she had a rough time with Alessa's father. The easy way to handle a difficult situation.

When he returned, he finally met her gaze. "I'm not going to pretend that I'm not treating you differently. I am. Why? I don't know. If I did, I'd stop doing it. All my life, I've followed my gut and my gut tells me to keep you close.

I dislocated your shoulder and I'm not sure if it's guilt or something else. All I know is that my concern for you has nothing to do with your abilities as a soldier. You are one of the best I have. You've proven that."

Her body warmed from the roots of her hair to the tips of her toes. Luke was a charmer, the kind of guy who always knew the right thing to say to diffuse a tense moment. She'd learned this not only from his reputation but from observing the way he interacted with everyone from the other members of the unit to the obnoxious truck driver. Yet she believed him.

"You want something to worry about? Worry about the mission. Think of how we're going to skirt the truck driver who has been watching us like a hawk since the moment he dropped us off."

He seemed relieved that she wasn't going to push him further. She knew if she did, he'd dig deeper and give as honest an answer as he could. But she wasn't ready to hear that answer.

Luke straightened and made a subtle scan of the area. She could tell he'd spotted the truck driver chatting with a small group of men by the twitch of his jaw.

"I bought a ticket for a bus tomorrow to Herat. I said something to that truck driver we got a ride from about how you had family in

Iran. He'll assume we're shady because we're trying to cross into the country illegally. The bus leaves at dawn, so we'll get a room tonight, then sneak out in the middle of the night."

"Won't we attract attention going to a hotel?"

Only tourists could afford hotel stays in Kabul. Like restaurants, they were a luxury common people who were working to put food on the table did without.

Luke grinned and despite the fake contacts, she could see the twinkle in his eyes. "I took care of that, too. The rice guy told me there's a locally-operated guest house not too far from here. We'll make a show of you being sick and check in there."

Alessa agreed, and they made their way to what turned out to be a flat-roofed structure with rubble piled beside it. The once-white walls were discolored into shades of black, gray and brown and covered in graffiti and haphazard posters advertising products and politicians. A guard stood by the door and Luke gave him a couple Afghani notes. Once inside, they were greeted by an old man with missing teeth who looked at them suspiciously until Luke pulled out more Afghani bills. Then his mouth widened into a big smile.

The man was about Alessa's height and she didn't like the way he wet his lips as he studied her. For once she was glad for the burka and the cultural appropriateness of averting her eyes while staying behind Luke and acting frail.

She followed Luke to their bedroom. Once inside, Luke considered the door, which had a flimsy lock that could be opened with a key from the outside. There was no security chain to ensure their privacy. He dragged a night-stand across the room and pushed it against the door.

"It's not going to stop anyone, but at least we'll have time to react."

Nodding, Alessa pulled off the burka. *Blessed fresh air.* Or as fresh as indoor air could be in Kabul. She looked up to see Luke avert his gaze and she suddenly realized that her *kameez* was soaked with sweat.

The bathroom was in the hallway. There was no way she was going out there alone with the creepy owner hovering. While she had no doubt that she could teach him a lesson he'd never for-get if he ever came near enough to touch her, they didn't need any incidents. Luke seemed to understand her dilemma without her having to say anything. "I'm going to look at the wall. Change in here. If you need to use the restroom, I'll come with you and stand guard."

She waited for him to turn around, then

quickly pulled off her *kameez* and replaced it with the only other one she was carrying.

"I need to wash this out," she said quietly, not even wanting to think about how she smelled given the decided odor coming from the wet shirt.

He removed the nightstand from the door and peered out. She put on the burka, then followed him to the bathroom. The toilet was a hole in the ground, and there was no running water, but an empty bucket sat nearby.

"You go outside to fill the bucket," the owner yelled from down the hall.

Alessa and Luke went into the yard, where they found a hand pump. Darkness had settled on the Hindu Kush mountains and was slowly creeping into Kabul. The hues of orange, purple and gray reflected off the dust in the air, leaving the city in an ethereal fog. It dampened the cacophony of city sounds: honking cars, whistling bicycle bells, construction noises and the hum of daily life.

While Luke pumped, Alessa washed the shirt using a bar of soap she had had the forethought to pack in their bags.

After they were done washing, she plucked a clothespin from a line, while Luke carried the toilet bucket that he'd filled for their use back to the room. She hung the wet *kameez* on one of the bars that ran across the window. Warm air blew through the room. The room was pleasant and would soon cool as the temperatures fell. The concrete construction of the houses held on to the night chill, making the daytime heat more bearable inside.

There were two chairs and a small table. Alessa took a seat, unsure of what to do next. The bed looked really inviting but she sensed that they needed to talk face-to-face. While the comms system was great for being able to quietly communicate while on the go, it was impersonal. She wanted to look into Luke's eyes.

Luke went to the dirty mirror hanging on one wall and took out his contacts. They were disposables. "I hate these things," he commented as he rubbed his eyes. Alessa watched the transformation in the mirror, unable to look away. He caught her eye and she shifted her attention to the phone she'd retrieved from her backpack.

"We should check on the locations of the guys."

He sat down across from her at the little table. Their knees touched, and she shifted her chair back. He waited a beat and did the same.

"I've been keeping my eye on them. Looks like Dan, Steele and Dimples will be the first ones there. They're already at the border."

Alessa bit her lip. That's not how things were supposed to play out. She had carefully calculated the travel times for each mini-team to make sure Luke got there first. "I'm slowing you down. You should go ahead without me." They were hard words to utter, but she had to be honest. Her pace wasn't as fast in the burka, they had to make sure she was acting appropriately for an Afghan woman. These were all little things that added up to significant delays. She could wait out the mission by posing as a tourist, then return on a military transport once the guys had Azizi.

"I would've made the same time on this route with or without you. We couldn't help the transportation issues. It's not the end of the world—the others know what they have to do to set up for the mission. They've done it before."

"Isn't it a little risky to take this on as your first mission?"

"I don't have a choice. I'm not sure how long Colonel Blowhard will keep me on as unit commander."

Alessa sat up straighter. It wasn't exactly a secret that the colonel was looking for excuses to get rid of Luke, but to hear him say it out loud was something else. Officers were taught to always display confidence to their command. To exude leadership.

"You don't think you can do the job." As soon as the statement was out of her mouth, she realized she shouldn't have said it that way.

"You're right. I don't think I can." His voice dropped so low that despite how close they sat, she could barely hear him. Her heart dropped into her stomach. No commander wanted to hear that his soldiers doubted him. *Take it back!* But she didn't want to soothe him with platitudes. Alessa was good at lying to men—had been doing it all her life—but she didn't want to lie to Luke.

"Ethan and I are identical in looks only. We think and make decisions very differently. Ethan analyzes every decision before he makes a move. I go by my gut, and…"

He didn't need to say the rest.

"Why don't you trust it?"

He blinked, then looked away from her. The sun had set while they were talking and the room was blanketed in dusky darkness. A streetlight right outside the window cast shadows on his face. He stood and flipped the light switch by the door. Nothing. There was an oil lantern on the table, and shaking it, Alessa could tell it was half full. It wouldn't give them a whole night's worth of light, but it would likely make it a few hours. She lit it with a match and the soft orange light flickered in the room. Her shoulder throbbed and her body was screaming to fall into the bed and close her eyes but she fought the urge. She wanted to resume their conversation, understand who Luke Williams was.

It seemed Luke also didn't want the conversation to end. "Two years ago my mother committed suicide."

She knew this already but it didn't stop her heart from jolting. The raw pain in his voice grated across the table. Once again she remained silent, sensing that he didn't need her making sounds of sympathy. She hadn't known his mother, couldn't say anything that would make it better for him.

He continued. "My mother was an adulterer."

The words knifed through Alessa. Her heart lodged in her throat.

"For as long as we can remember, Ethan and I covered for her. No matter where we were posted in the world, she somehow found 'friends' to help around the house, keep her company. When we were younger, they would stay the night. That stopped when my father came home from deployment early one time. Then she started disappearing in the evenings. I remember one night when a pipe burst in our house and water was dripping into my bedroom. Ethan and I were only eleven and we couldn't find her but we dared not call anyone. So we kept ladling the water into buckets until she returned early in the morning. The house was a mess."

"So your father knew?"

His face twisted and Alessa kicked herself for being so insensitive. Once when she was in middle school, she'd caught her mother being friendly with another man. The manager of the local grocery store. Seeing her mother smile genuinely when she interacted with him had made Alessa wish her mother would have an affair with the man and leave her father. It was a secret childhood dream of hers. The flirtation ended as quickly as it had begun but Alessa clung to the fantasy. Even then, she'd known that if her father found out, he'd throw her mother out of the house.

"He did. You know how it is on post. No matter how discreet you are, neighbors keep an eye on when you come and go, people talk. As my father advanced in the ranks, my mother got better at hiding it. But I always knew, and so did Ethan."

"Your father didn't care that this was happening?"

"My father couldn't stop it. He loved my mother and knew that the only way to make it stop was to divorce her or leave the army, and he wasn't willing to do either."

"Why didn't she divorce him?"

He leaned back and placed his hands on the nape of his neck. "Ethan and I talked about it. I think on some level she loved my father but was unhappy with the army life and was looking for a way to get his attention."

"Or she felt stuck and couldn't get out."

He leaned forward so suddenly, the chair scraped on the floor. *Shut your motor-mouth, Parrino.* What was wrong with her today? She couldn't seem to filter herself.

"What do you mean?" He pinned her with his dazzling blue eyes.

Swallowing, she continued. "My mom is from an old-school generation of Italian women who believe their role is to take care of the family. She barely has a middle school education and speaks English with a heavy accent. My grandparents didn't see the point in educating her. So when my parents came to America as a young couple, my father was the king of the household and she had no power over her own life. That dynamic never corrected, and the imbalance grew worse. My father keeps his control over her by convincing her that if she left, she'd have no home, no food, and no way to support herself or her children. When I was a teenager, I tried to explain social services to her, but all she heard was welfare. She's too proud to accept charity."

"So you think my mom felt she had no other options?"

"I'm not saying anything. I don't know your mom or your family situation."

He got the hundred-yard stare again. "My mom came from a good family. She married my father right out of high school, so she didn't go to college, but she was certainly smart enough to realize she had options in life."

Alessa kicked herself for saying anything at all. Luke obviously had a narrative he'd told himself about his mother and she was poking holes into it. Her family situation was nothing like his.

"The week before she killed herself, Mom called me and Ethan. She made our favorite dinner, reminisced about the good times we had as little boys, even showed us where she kept all our childhood treasures."

Alessa's chest tightened at the crack in his voice.

"She was happier than I'd seen her in years." He shook his head. "Ethan was worried, though. He was busy with something—I know now it was getting approval for this unit—and he asked me to come stay with Mom.

I didn't listen to him. I thought she was fine, that maybe she'd finally found someone she was happy with."

Alessa touched his arm. It was an inappropriate contact but they couldn't have this raw conversation and pretend they were just dots on an army matrix.

Luke hung his head. "If I'd listened to Ethan, maybe I'd have seen the signs. At the time I was so absorbed in myself. I was trying to get out of the army and just didn't want to be home and around my dad."

She opened her mouth, then closed it. Nothing she could say would make him feel any less guilty, but she didn't want to make it worse. "I've tried to get my mother to leave my father for as long as I can remember. I've offered her everything she could ever need, including spending a large chunk of my savings setting her up to go to Italy. She won't do it. Her decision is steadfast and maybe your mother's was as well."

He grabbed her hand and squeezed it tight, like a man desperate for human contact.

"Maybe. Or maybe she was feeling stuck, like you said. Dad would have fought her on a divorce. She had no money of her own, no house. When we were young, I remember her saying things would be better when we grew up. She was counting on me and Ethan to take care of her. Had I been around, I might have been able to show her a way out. My father has a way of presenting options as black or white. Like when Ethan and I were kids, there was no career path other than the army. My father did a great job convincing us of that. I can only imagine the number he did on her."

I understand that all too well. She had to constantly remind herself that just because her father believed she'd end up needing a man to take of her didn't make it true. Alessa had, and would continue to make sure that she was always in control of her destiny.

"You can play the what-if game forever, and all you'll do is live your life a little less fully."

He brought her hand to his forehead. "I don't know what I'm going to do. I don't know what the right call is."

She wanted nothing more than to run her other hand over his head, to let him know that he wasn't alone.

Instead, she tugged gently and he let go of her, his eyes shadowing into a dark blue.

"You don't have to make all the decisions alone. The unit is supposed to be collaborative, remember. Not the army way. Don't take it all on yourself."

"I'm sorry. I shouldn't have unloaded on you."

"I can handle it, Luke." She needed him to know she was strong and didn't need him taking care of her.

"I know you can. I don't worry about you."

"Right. So then why did you change the mini-team assignments?"

He gave her a crooked smile. "Okay, you got me there. I was worried about you."

"Do you think this is the first time I've had to soldier on after I've gotten injured?"

He shifted in his seat, then stilled. "That's just it. You would've continued no matter what. In fact, I fully believe that you will drop dead before you spend a second to take care of yourself. That's why I changed the assignment."

"So you could save me from myself." She didn't even try to filter the annoyance from her voice. *How dare he?*

He pushed his chair back and stood, then retrieved the battery pack from his backpack to charge his phone. He busied his hands getting it connected.

"You are a good soldier, Alessa, but as unit command, it's my job to protect my soldiers and the mission."

She took a deep breath. So they were back to being commander and soldier. At least, unlike many commanders she'd had, it was obvious that he wasn't out to get her, to prove that she couldn't do the job.

He clicked on his phone and frowned.

"What's the matter?"

"Rodgers and Boots just went dark. They were five clicks away from us not too long ago."

"You know how it is around here. They may have gone into a zone where someone is jamming satellite signals or coverage is bad." It was something they expected on this mission, which was why they had multiple rally points in Pakistan in case the safe house didn't work out and they couldn't reach each other.

"I need everything to be perfect. Once we return, Colonel McBride will scour the after-action reports and pick apart every aspect of this mission to find a way to remove me as command."

Which brought up another issue for her. If Luke was removed as command, she was likely out of her posting. Who knew where they would transfer her. Plus with her "logistics" designation, Colonel Black Tag was sure to send her to the remotest corner of the earth to push paper around.

"That's if I manage not to get myself killed," he added.

Another cheery thought.

"I thought I was supposed to make sure that doesn't happen. In my self-serving interest," she said lightly, eager to break the intense mood. The flickering shadows of the oil lamp didn't help.

He smiled. "It's not something I should be telling you, but before we left, I sent a file to my father that includes the details of this mission and your role in it. If anything happens to me, you're protected."

Oddly, she found she suddenly didn't care about her promotion. What bothered her more was the idea that Luke could actually get hurt or worse. Before she could ask the obvious question on her lips, he leaned forward.

"Yes, we can trust my father. The man is an army man through and through. He'd never do anything to hurt this country. Even so, the package won't get to him for a few days."

"Aren't you worried about yourself?"

His lips twitched. "Nothing in my life makes sense anymore. I want to find Ethan so I can get back to my life and stop living his."

"And what does your non-army life look like?"

He met her eyes, his brows knotted. "You know, Parrino, that's an excellent question."

He gave her a wide grin and she responded

in kind. It was hard not to get taken in by his boyish charm. She wondered how his many girlfriends had reacted to it.

"So what do you want me to do? How can I help?"

He gestured to the bed in the middle of the room. "Right now, I want you to get some shut-eye."

Alessa turned and eyed the mattress. The sheets were threadbare and had many mysterious stains. Dust clung to the headboard. Yet it was the most inviting sight she'd seen.

"I'll take the first watch, then we can switch," Luke said before she had a chance to speak up.

Normally she'd insist on taking the first shift. Luke tilted his head toward the bed, silently pleading with her not to argue. It would be a struggle to keep her eyes open, so why not take advantage of Luke's offer?

"Ninety minutes, then wake me up." That would give her one REM cycle. She sat on the bed. The mattress was as ratty as the sheets. As she lay down, the hard wooden slats greeted her back. She didn't care. It was better than many of the places she'd had to sleep. It didn't take long for her lids to close as she began to blissfully drift off.

It seemed only a few minutes had passed

when Luke shook her awake. She blinked until his face came into focus.

His tone was urgent. "We need to go."

CHAPTER ELEVEN

ALESSA SAT UP so suddenly that Luke barely had time to move out of the way. It was pitch dark outside. Grabbing the slightly damp *kameez*, she stuffed it into her backpack, then pulled on the burka. She checked her watch and was aghast to see that five and a half hours had passed since she'd fallen asleep. But now was not the time to get on Luke about not letting her do her share. He was loosening the bolts on one of the window bars, trying to pry it open. She went to the other side and began pulling to help him.

"I'll go first," he said.

She knew from their earlier walk around the perimeter that he would land close to the water pump. It wasn't a long drop. Once she heard the telltale squelch of his boots on the mud, Alessa wasted no time in getting herself out. The burka made the landing interesting and she found herself on her knees in the mud. Thankfully she managed to protect her right arm and shoulder. Luke was there in a flash, helping her up. She didn't bother to protest. Time was of the essence.

He held on to her left arm as they navigated the compound spanning several homes and buildings that shared the water pump. Exiting into an alleyway, Luke marched forward at a good clip and Alessa struggled to keep up. The bottom of her burka was wet with mud and clung to her ankles, making it difficult not to trip. For a country where water was scarce, she never understood why the streets were always muddy.

When they got to the street, Luke hailed a bicycle rickshaw with a beat-up seat. He instructed the kid to take them to the taxi stand.

When they arrived at the small patch of road with two rusted old cars, Luke paid the rickshaw driver in the local currency and ushered them toward the first taxi. He had to wake up the driver, and though Alessa was standing several feet away, she could smell the alcohol oozing off him. An empty bottle lay on the passenger seat. Luke haggled over the fee to take them to Jalalabad. Not negotiating would have been a red flag.

They entered the taxi and the driver started the clanking engine. It was eighty-five miles to Jalalabad. Back in the States, that was nothing, a two-hour drive at most, but here it would take three to four hours assuming they only made one gas stop and there were no checkpoints or other unexpected delays. The taxi was plan B and in hindsight, might have been better than plan A. On the bus, they could be recognized, identified and targeted by any number of people. Now they only had to deal with the one taxi driver, and he'd probably be stuck in Jalalabad for at least a day trying to find a fare to pay him for the trip back.

They rode in silence. They couldn't assume that the taxi driver didn't speak English. She'd met many Afghans who were good at not letting on that they understood. It was a defense mechanism.

Predictably, they had to stop for gas a couple hours into the drive. The driver demanded money from Luke, who once again negotiated how much of the fee he would pay, relying heavily on facial expressions and hand gestures to convey his frustration. Alessa knew Luke couldn't care less about the price but had to put on a good enough show, particularly with his less-than-passable Pashtun.

While the driver filled the car and took a smoke break, Alessa whispered into the comms system, which they had reconnected. "What's going on?"

"The truck driver that drove us to Kabul

showed up at the guest house and was asking the owner all kinds of questions. He was drunk and belligerent, saying something about how we didn't pay him. I didn't catch all of it, but thought we should get out of there before the two of them came barging in on us."

Alessa let out a breath. The truck driver's interest was concerning. He could be an insurgent who was suspicious about them, or he could be looking to rob them, or maybe he was just overly curious. None of the scenarios were good. Neither was the return of the pain raging through her shoulder. She'd gotten more than enough sleep to be functional but she wanted nothing more than to fall back asleep. *Get it together, Purrino.*

Luke was eyeing her. "You okay?"

She began to nod her head, then looked at Luke and shook it. She'd been about to placate him, but it was time to trust him. The mission was too important; the guys were counting on her and Luke. She couldn't jeopardize them for selfish pride. "My shoulder's been bugging me."

He sucked in a breath.

"You should have said something earlier."

"I can still continue, I just need to be careful."

He opened his backpack and handed her

some pills and his canteen. She pushed them away. "I need to be clear."

"It's just ibuprofen, to take the edge off. Once we get to Pakistan, we'll go to a pharmacy and get you something stronger. Right now I want you to rest."

Her heart tumbled in her chest. She'd never had anyone take care of her and it felt good not to have to play the strong, indestructible one. She leaned toward him and he wrapped an arm around her. She snuggled her face into his chest and fell asleep listening to the steady beat of his heart.

No MATTER WHAT she said, he would never forgive himself if something happened to Alessa.

It seemed this mission had been doomed from the start. Rodgers and Boots were still dark and Dan, Steele and Dimples hadn't made any progress since last night. They should have crossed the border; the cover of night was the best time. Were they hurt or captured? If Ethan were here, he would abandon the mission; that was the prudent course. Too many things were going wrong, and it was risky to continue. But this was Luke's only shot at finding his brother. He wouldn't get another chance, and even if the army's mission was a bust, he had to check out the clue Alessa had found that could bring him closer to confirming that Ethan was still alive.

Alessa's head bounced as the car hit a pot-hole and she shifted and put her head in his lap, curling up into a ball on the seat. He lifted her veil so he could see her face, then dropped it back. It seemed like an invasion of privacy somehow, but the brief glimpse of her peaceful face, her lashes casting long shadows over her cheeks, lit his heart. Ever since Nazneen had died, he hadn't felt a spark with anyone. He'd met plenty of intelligent, attractive women who had captured his attention but none who had made his heart flutter like it just had.

She's a soldier in your command. He looked out the window. Alessa was off limits. Unlike him, she was army material, the next generation of army leaders. She was the kind of woman his father would have wanted for a daughter: a soldier who believed in the army. He didn't care about himself, but even the hint of impropriety would ruin her career. Her encounter with Aidan Connors had been bad enough. Luke didn't need to add to her problems.

He had done his research on Second Lieutenant Aidan Connors and had some opinions on him that he was sure Alessa didn't share. He'd gotten his hands on the internal investigation report on the incident that had halted her career, and it was obvious to him that Alessa had been thrown under the bus. But that was the army way. Darling officers were protected and good soldiers scapegoated. Once something ended up in a personnel file, not even an act of Congress could remove it. Alessa would be haunted by it for the rest of her career.

The taxi driver hummed as he drove. Luke wanted to engage him in conversation and would have normally drawn the man out but his cover was thin given his lack of language skills. He hid his terrible accent by coughing and grunting like a chain smoker, but the less he communicated, the lower the chance of being caught.

Luke studied the inside of the taxi. There were pictures pasted where sun visors should have been at the front of the cab. The driver caught him staring and smiled.

"My family. In India now, I goodbye them before the Americans come so they live." The man spoke to Luke in halting English and smiled reassuringly.

Luke nodded. There was no point in pretending; the man had obviously figured them out.

"My heart is crying for them. But I am happy."

Luke knew exactly what the man meant. All he hoped and wished for was to find Ethan alive. No matter his differences with his brother, Luke felt a void without his twin, like a piece of his soul was missing. Once he knew his brother was alive and safe, he'd be happy.

He directed the cab driver to drop them at the Jalalabad bus depot. The sun was rising and early morning commuters were already crowded in front of the station. Merchants were setting up tables to sell their wares to both passengers and locals who came here just to shop. Some buses were already full with new arrivals jockeying for space on the roofs, where thin handrails created the illusion of a safe place to sit.

The sky was a colorful mixture of orange and purple. The thick cloud of dust that always hung in the air had settled overnight, replaced by a cool, morning dew. Luke shook Alessa awake, and she rubbed her eyes through the veil.

It was less than seventy miles to their destination, the safe house close to Peshawar, and there were buses that serviced that route. It was a tempting option, but a bus meant an official border checkpoint. Given the volume of illegal crossings into Pakistan, authorities and insurgents were on the lookout for those who could be asked to pay "taxes" to cross. While money was not a problem, sometimes Americans got kidnapped for ransom. In all cases, the situation was dangerous at best, deadly at worst.

They exited the taxi and blended in with the throngs of people.

"You looking for a guide?" Alessa asked.

"Yes," he said into the comms system.

There were plenty of entrepreneurs who made it their business to get people across the border illegally. Men and women who knew the terrain and could get them through certain unofficial checkpoints. For just as many of those, there were insurgents who found those with means who were desperate to leave the country and kidnapped or robbed them. Luke and Alessa had to find the former and stay away from the latter.

"Black turban, brown vest." Luke whispered into the comms. Thanks to the burka, Alessa could more easily study someone without drawing too much attention. The man Luke was interested in stood away from the ticket counter, shuffling on his feet. He kept muttering things to passersby. One family stopped to talk to him, then walked away.

"No good. He's wearing a Rolex."

Luke swore quietly. "I should've seen that." Missing little details could make the difference between life and death. What was wrong with him? Why couldn't he focus?

"I have the advantage of being able to stare at them longer." Alessa reminded him. A Rolex meant the guy wasn't exactly the kind of person who was working hard shuttling someone through dangerous passes. No way a valuable watch would survive one of the checkpoints.

"How about the guy standing by the telephone booth?" Alessa suggested.

Like the black turban guy, he was standing around muttering under his breath. As Luke watched, a couple approached him. The woman was obviously pregnant. They chatted for a while, then exchanged something while thcy each looked around nervously.

"Okay, let's go," Luke instructed.

They walked past the telephone booth guy, who predictably tried to get Luke's attention.

Here we go. If I'm wrong about this guy, he'll be the death of us.

CHAPTER TWELVE

ALESSA COULD HEAR their conversation through the comms system. After chatting for a few minutes in broken English, it was clear the guy could get them across the Khyber Pass. He had a car that would get them most of the way, then they would have to walk about six miles. His detailed description of the route and modes of transportation made Alessa feel more comfortable that the guy was trustworthy. She tuned out as Luke haggled over the price, studying the other couple the guide had been talking to. They were speaking quietly a few feet away. Alessa could see the woman gesturing under her burka, her movements muted by the tented cloth.

Luke stepped away from the guide and toward her. The walk across the Khyber wasn't going to be easy, and Alessa could see the worry in Luke's now-brown eyes. But he had the good sense not to ask her if she was okay, which she was. The nap in the taxi and back at the guest house in Kabul had refreshed her. Maybe that was all she had needed all along.

Older soldiers had warned her to sleep when she could because as she got into her late thirties, she would no longer be able to go for days without rest. Was she really getting that old? The thought tightened her chest.

When she was in high school and the class had done the baby exercise where they had to take care of an egg for a few days, she'd thought a lot about whether she would want children. At the time, she'd concluded that the world was too unkind a place to introduce a new life. But as her fellow soldiers married and tacked up pictures of their kids on their bunk beds, she'd wondered whether she'd be happy doing this all her life without something else to hold on to.

Nearly all the soldiers she knew who were her age had someone to go home to, a family who served as their motivation to get through the day and stay alive. Even the single guys in the unit had people who cared for them. She looked at Luke and for a fleeting second wondered what it would be like to know that someone else cared about her, would be there to welcome her home when she returned from deployment.

"His name is Ali," Luke said, pulling her attention.

"We all set?"

Luke nodded. "He wants to leave right away. We're going to have company," he said, raising a brow in the direction of the other couple.

Ali motioned for them all to join him. Alessa wasn't sure whether crossing with more people would hurt or help them. If they got caught, it would certainly obscure their intentions to be traveling with others, but they now had two additional people—one of them pregnant—to get across a dangerous crossing.

As if reading her mind, Luke whispered, "Let's hope they change their minds once we get to Khyber."

Alessa had never crossed the Khyber on foot, but she had patrolled the area and been on routine transports through the pass, overseeing supply trucks shuttling between Pakistan and Afghanistan. Though there was never anything routine about Khyber. Insurgent attacks were common, as was interference by both the Pakistani government and the Khyber Agency, the tribal government that ran a fraction of the pass near the Pakistan border.

Ali instructed Luke to buy a shawl and sweater from one of the children who was walking around selling those items. Luke had a sweater in his backpack but he followed Ali's advice. Locally bought clothing would make them stand out less. From this point on, they'd be going up in elevation to cross the Hindu Kush mountains, and both day and nighttime temperatures would be cold.

The other couple didn't speak Pashtun but they did speak English and so did Ali, so it was decided that would be the language of their group. The pregnant woman, Amine, quickly sidled up to Alessa, glad to have a compatriot. She was dressed in a near-identical burka. The man with her was not her husband but her brother, Reza.

"How far along are you?" Alessa inquired as the men broke off to go buy water and food for the journey.

"Six months," Amine said, touching her belly.

Alessa's stomach turned. The woman was pretty far along, and while still three months away from giving birth, traveling would be difficult.

"I know what you are thinking," she said softly in her musically accented voice. "I should not be traveling, but we had no choice. Reza wanted me to get my baby to safety."

She didn't have to say anything more.

"I do not know you, but I must ask something," Amine continued.

Alessa couldn't see more than the shadows

of the woman's eyes, but her voice was laden with desperation.

"Are you okay?" Alessa asked.

The woman nodded. "If something happens to me along the way, you must tell my brother to leave and go on without me. He won't, but…"

She didn't have to finish the sentence. Alessa reached out her hand and Amine extended hers and clasped Alessa's. It was a gesture Alessa had seen other women do but had never done herself. Now it felt like the most natural thing in the world and she found herself oddly comforted by the squeeze of the other woman's hand. It was a silent promise that they would get through the coming adventure together.

Growing up, Alessa had often been socially withdrawn, unable to relate to the other children in school who obsessed over boys and whether their mothers would let them wear slinky clothing. She loathed those girls who said they hated their fathers because they wouldn't buy them the latest hit CD or a new car. She had wanted nothing more than to scream at them, to tell them they were lucky they didn't have to come to school wearing long sleeves on a hundred-degree day to hide the bruises on their arms.

However, she sensed that Amine's life had been just as dark as hers, if not more. They held on to each other until the men approached, then retreated inside their burkas with a nod of solidarity.

"Stay alert." It was an unnecessary warning from Luke. They had just hired a human smuggler and were travelling with two strangers; she wasn't about to let down her guard. Still, she instinctively trusted Amine and Reza.

Luke crouched down, ostensibly to put his new purchases into his backpack, and muttered into the comms system, "Reza is getting his sister away from an abusive husband." Alessa tensed. If Amine was escaping her marriage, they had the added complication of family members possibly coming after them. That was the last thing they needed and she could tell by the clipped way in which Luke had relayed the news that he felt the same.

Ali motioned to all of them to follow him and they wove through the crowds around the bus station. The smell of sweat and exhaust fumes was stifling, and despite the cooler morning temperatures, Alessa found it hard to breath as they made their way to the periphery. Overloaded buses coughed their way through the crowds who didn't seem to notice the black smoke.

Alessa longed to lift the veil that clung to her face. She stumbled as someone pushed past her and Luke's strong arms went around her. Her initial instinct was to push him away, but then she felt the strength of his body against hers and it felt good to have someone to lean against; for just one moment to feel like she didn't have to do it all on her own.

The crowd was packed so tightly that hardly anyone noticed Luke's arm around her. There were few women in the crowd, so it was easy to spot Amine's blue figure ahead of them. Alessa worried about how she was getting through. It couldn't be easy for a pregnant woman with the pushing and jostling.

They finally broke through the masses, but the air was still stale under Alessa's veil. She lifted the cloth a fraction and fanned her face, but stopped when she noticed an old man staring at her. Luke stepped away from her, as if feeling the glare of that old man on him. They made their way to Ali's truck, an old pickup with no doors and panels of so many different colors that the truck looked like it had been constructed from spare junkyard parts. It probably had been.

Without discussion, they squeezed Reza and Amine into the passenger seat and Luke and Alessa took the truck bed. Ali wasted no time getting out of the bus depot. Luke and Alessa marveled at his ability to maneuver around the crowds and other double- and triple-parked vehicles. Jalalabad was awake and in full swing as Ali pulled onto the main road and navigated the traffic, joining the other horn-happy drivers expressing their frustration through noise pollution.

The sounds pounded through her head, making it hard to see, to breathe or to think.

"It's quite the place isn't it?"

Alessa lifted her veil, desperate for a breath of air.

"Are you okay?"

She was about to say yes, then it all went dark.

CHAPTER THIRTEEN

LUKE HAD COVERED Alessa's body with his own. The car didn't slow but increased its breakneck speed, now bumping over sidewalks and even the median in the road. Luke risked lifting his head just enough to peer over the side but saw nothing other than the usual mix of rickshaws, cars, trucks, buses and pedestrians on the road.

"Get off me, Luke, I'm suffocating in this thing," Alessa shouted from underneath him. He sat back and Alessa straightened herself, lifting the top of the burka off her head some more and sucking in some breaths.

"There are a lot of guns in this area," she said softly. He could process that. Now. Gunfire was not that unusual in the area. "It was too far away to get us," she said. Again, he knew she was right, but in the moment he'd heard the sound, the only thing he could think about was protecting Alessa, making sure the shots wouldn't hit her.

Alessa leaned forward just as Ali jumped another curb to bypass a slow-moving bicyclist and he wrapped his arms around her as she fell into his lap.

"I seem to be making a habit of this," she said awkwardly as she fought to regain her balance in the unsteady truck.

She pushed aside pieces of wood, metal brackets and other junk to make a space next to him, then sat down with a sigh. Their sides touched, and he liked the feel of her so close to him…and the fact that she wanted to sit so close.

They finally left Jalalabad and the ride became smoother as Ali bumped over the potholes in the country road.

Alessa leaned her head into his and he instinctively put his arm around her. She didn't resist, so he pulled her closer, warmth settling into his chest. He leaned back, and for the first time since they'd left Fort Belvoir, he allowed himself to relax a fraction. Something about having Alessa beside him calmed the constant churn of his stomach.

"You can do this, Luke," she whispered. They had their comms system turned on so they didn't have to yell over the clanking engine.

He wished he could believe her. He reached into his pocket and powered on his phone. Alessa shifted so she could see his screen. They checked the GPS locations of the rest of the team. "I don't understand why Boots and Rodgers are dark still."

"Do you want to try and contact them?"

He shook his head. If they'd gone dark in order to avoid surveillance, calling them might give their location away. The emergency protocol that allowed Luke to remotely activate their phones was for the sole purpose of locating them if everything went wrong and they had to go in to retrieve their team members. It wasn't time to panic. Yet. Dan, Steele and Dimples looked like they'd started moving again and were across the border.

Alessa filled him in on her conversation with Amine.

"That jives with what Reza told me. He said she was married to an old tribal leader to pay off a debt their father owed. Her husband was pretty abusive, so Reza decided to defy the family and smuggle her away."

"He's not going to get far in Pakistan, especially at the border. If Amine's husband has connections with the Taliban, they'll catch him in no time."

"I told him that and suggested they keep moving to India. Reza is an architect and managed to make a little bit of money through development contracts. That's what he's using to get his sister out."

"He told you his whole life story in the few minutes you guys were shopping?" Alessa's voice held amusement.

"I guess for better or worse, the four of us are on this journey together. He doesn't totally trust Ali, either. Figures it would be good if we were aligned. He also guessed that we are not local and outright asked me whether I was American, Canadian or European."

"I'm not surprised," Alessa said. And neither was Luke when Reza had asked. Most of the people they'd encountered probably hadn't believed their cover either, but so far no one had questioned them—likely because of the wad of Afghani notes Luke kept in his pocket.

"Life is so tentative here," Luke mused. "Reza made it sound like he didn't fully believe he could make it across the border but wanted to die trying."

"Amine was the same way." Alessa's voice was soft, her head a warm weight on his arm. "But her I understand. When you live under the threat of violence every day, you almost hope that death will come knocking soon."

The blood in his veins turned to ice, his stomach twisting painfully. "Is that what it was like for you growing up?"

She didn't answer, but she didn't need to. He could feel it in the way her body slumped.

"You know, last year I was helping a friend in Guam and I met this doctor—her name is Anna. She had lost her infant son and couldn't find a way to grieve for him, so she went around the world working one disaster after another, hoping to forget what happened to her."

"Is that what you think I'm doing in the army?" Alessa pulled away from him and he turned to face her, grateful that she'd lifted the veil and he could look directly into her soft brown eyes.

"I think you want very much to find happiness but you don't know how to move past what's happened to you."

Her eyes widened and he winced at the tears starting to form in them. Since when had he become a therapist?

He expected her to shut down, tell him this whole conversation was none of his business, which it wasn't. He had no right to get into her personal life.

"I was going to say that my personal life is none of your concern, but that seems petty right now when I look at Reza and Amine sitting in the front seat, and the fact that a stray bullet could hit us at any second."

That was one thing about coming to a place

like Afghanistan; the country had a way of reminding him just how much he took for granted on a daily basis.

"So what about you? Since you're lecturing me about finding happiness, how do you make the most of your life?" Alessa asked.

He laughed. "What you do mean?"

"Well for starters, do you have a girlfriend or someone special?" Alessa tried to keep her face nonchalant but the slight lean of her body and quirk of her mouth told him it was more than a passing curiosity.

He smiled, then pinned her with a steady gaze. "I don't have a girlfriend. I would have told you carly on if I did."

Her cheeks colored and he smiled.

"That's surprising," she said cheekily.

"Not everything you hear about me is true. You should know that the army has a way of exaggerating."

She smiled slowly and his heart gave that kick again. "This is true."

"How about you? Anyone special in your life?"

She shook her head. "It's hard in the army. You know how it is, being stationed in all kinds of places. The only people I meet are other soldiers."

"Have you ever been in love with anyone?" he asked.

She froze, then shook her head. "Maybe I thought I was, but I don't think I've really been in love."

He wondered if she was talking about Aidan Connors. The way she'd stood up for him implied that she'd had feelings for him. His chest burned at the thought of Alessa being with someone like Aidan. The man was a total user; that was obvious from the way his file read. A quick rise through the army without the commendations that should have come with such promotions, glowing recommendations from senior officers. He was the kind of guy who irritated Luke. Rather than put in the time and bravery needed to rise in the army, he brown-nosed his way to the top. He was a younger version of Colonel McBride. He had preyed on Alessa, and when his nefarious plan had backfired, he'd scapegoated her.

"What about you? Ever truly been in love?"

A painful tightness engulfed his chest. He nodded, then looked away from her. Silence settled between them, letting in the sound of the truck's noisy engine and splat of the wheels against the poorly maintained gravel road. "Her name was Nazneen. She was an Iraqi girl from one of the villages we patrolled, but she spoke

English. In fact, she was a teacher and had set up an informal education program for the village girls." The countryside flashed before him but his mind retreated to that little one-room school Nazneen had built of mud and straw so the girls could be in a room without distractions.

"Nazneen was something else. Every time I came out on patrol, she extracted something from me in exchange for information. All of the villagers did that, but she didn't ask for money or food like most of them did. She asked for books. For the kids she taught."

He remembered vividly how her eyes would shine as he'd hand her the notebooks where kids could practice writing letters. She would clutch them to her chest like they were bars of gold and give him a smile so brilliant, he would think of nothing else for the rest of the day.

"How did she die?" Alessa asked so softly that he only heard her through the comms system.

He looked at her.

"You talk about her in the past tense," she said gently.

"Insurgents blew up the village. As a statement to the army because we had informants there. I was the one who had befriended most of the villagers, softened them up with food and money in exchange for information." His voice cracked and Alessa reached out to squeeze his hand.

"You are not responsible for her death."

He shook his head. "I was late getting out on patrol that day. If I hadn't been, maybe I would've seen something, been there to stop it…"

"Or gotten blown up with her," Alessa finished for him.

He sighed. "It's not like there was ever going to be a happily ever after for us. She was in love with someone else. A boy from her village who had left for Baghdad to look for work. He'd been gone two years, but she was adamant in her love and loyalty to him. I told her I didn't care, that I had enough love for the two of us but she said it didn't work that way." Why was he telling Alessa all this? He'd mentioned Nazneen to others, more as a way to keep her alive in his own mind, but he never went into the details.

"She was right, you know," Alessa said. "Love is a two-way street. No matter how much you love someone, you can't be happy knowing their heart isn't with you."

Once again, he wondered whether she was talking about Aidan. "Were you ever close to falling in love?"

She bit her lip and her eyes grew distant, as if it was her turn to live in a different place. He knew if he said Aidan's name, she would tell him what was in her heart, but he wanted it to come from her.

"It's not important," she muttered and he felt another painful squeeze in his chest. He let his arm drop from around her. There was a difference between true feelings and the adrenaline-fueled emotions that being in the sandbox generated. It was hard not to reach out for human connection after seeing the devastation that war caused, both literally and figuratively. In a world where every person had a story that took one's heart and ripped it out of their chest, it was only natural to seek comfort in someone close by.

It wasn't just a phenomenon of war. His mother had sought that back home when she was all alone and needed someone to share her soul with.

Luke had learned the hard way how short-term such connections were. It was how short his connection to Alessa would be.

CHAPTER FOURTEEN

NIGHTFALL ON THE Khyber brought an icy wind. They were at over three thousand feet in elevation in the middle of the Spin Ghar Mountains. Known as the Silk Road, the Khyber Pass had been a strategic military route for centuries. Yet one wouldn't know it from looking at the punishing terrain and awe-inspiring beauty.

Ali had parked the pickup in a small camp and hidden it under a camouflaged net covered with leaves and twigs. The camp was made up of three small tents, the kind Boy Scouts might take to a campout. A communal fire roared in the center.

"What is this place?" Luke asked.

"Rest stop for our passengers. Brothers who do this work create this." Ali sounded proud, as if he really were a tour guide showing off a state-of-the-art rest area. "You go warm yourselves by the fire, I'll make tea for us."

Alessa didn't know what to expect from the other "passengers" crowded around the fire pit. No one introduced themselves but they gave each other polite nods. There were two obvious Westerners, a woman with red hair tucked underneath a loosely draped scarf and a thin, brown-haired man with lines etched into his forehead.

"Fantastic view right over there, but be careful where you walk." The redheaded woman was British. In the darkness, the light from the fire flickered across her face, giving it an orange glow.

Amine and Reza stepped in the direction indicated by the redhead so Luke and Alessa followed. There was almost a collective gasp. Both Amine and Alessa lifted their veils so they could get a proper look. They were on a precipice that dropped into a valley between the arid slopes. The full moon reflected off the rock face, outlining the vast mountains around them and the narrow, serpentine road that cut, impossibly, between them.

"Kipling's sword cut through the mountains," Reza said.

"Rudyard Kipling?" Alessa clarified.

He nodded, turning toward her, and for the first time, Alessa got a full look at him. He was nearly six feet tall, his dark eyes accentuated by long black lashes. He had a mop of curly hair and an easy smile that did little to hide the terror that was plain in his eyes.

He didn't seem to mind that Alessa's veil was off, so she didn't bother to lower it.

"Yes, he described the Khyber that way."

"An apt description."

"For centuries now, armies have used this Silk Road to conquer more territory and land. Each one takes something for themselves but leaves us with nothing."

The despair in his low voice tore at her. She didn't want to get into an argument about politics with Reza, but she understood what he was trying to say.

"I hear you are an architect?"

He nodded. "I came home to help with the rebuilding. I came to make a better Afghanistan." He sounded weary and defeated. Alessa wanted to find words to give him hope and comfort. But Luke cut in before she had a chance.

"We're going to have to climb upward to get to Londi Kotwal, and then go across the mountain." His voice was businesslike, and irrationally, Alessa missed the deep warmth it had held when they were sitting in the back of the pickup.

She'd thought about opening up and telling him about Aidan, but hadn't been able to bring herself to say the words out loud. How could she explain that she had fallen for a married man? After what Luke had shared about his family life. While she didn't sense any malice toward his mother, the deep disappointment had been clear in his eyes. Alessa didn't want him to judge her.

It wasn't as if she'd never thought about Aidan's wife, but Aidan had shown her the divorce papers she'd sent. It was perhaps the moment when Alessa and Aidan had truly gotten close, sitting together on a moonless night at a lookout post. It was the first time Alessa had shared a connection with someone, talked about her own past and let another human being comfort her. But how could she explain that to Luke without coming across as a home-wrecker?

"What about the old railway?" Reza asked. There was a railway track that the British had built in the 1920s to ensure efficient transportation to India.

"It flooded about a decade ago and is in bad shape. Besides, it's so heavily used now that we might as well invite someone to come kidnap or rob us," Luke explained.

Alessa had looked at the satellite pictures of the railway. It was still used by smugglers and human traffickers. The latest intelligence was that the track was passable, but when Luke had asked Ali about it, Ali had insisted that recent rockfalls were blocking sections. The track would have been the easy way across, dropping them into a valley near Londi Kot-wal, the border town to Pakistan. Alessa wasn't sure whether Ali was steering them to, or away from, the safer path.

"So are you two CIA or military?" Reza's tone was matter-of-fact. Alessa couldn't fully see Luke's face but pictured him raising his brow. But they were away from Ali, out of ear-shot of anyone but the four of them. Luke answered in the predictable way. "What makes you think we're CIA or military?"

"Your accent slips in and out and your English is too good. We don't speak like you do. What do you Americans call it...like the local way of saying something."

"Slang?" Alessa supplied, then shut her mouth.

"Exactly. See, these are words that don't come easily to our lips." Reza smiled broadly. "You don't have to tell me. To be telling the truth, I hope you are what you call those..." He waved his hands in a Karate Kid wax on, wax off move. "That way you can protect us if something happens."

All of them laughed, desperate to ease the tension. "I do not know if we can trust Ali. He seems like a good person but you never know of a person's circumstance," Reza said.

They all nodded. Even if Ali's intentions

were good, any number of things could change his perspective. If he were faced with being hurt or killed, his priority would likely be to save himself, not to protect any of his "passengers."

"I don't know the pass. Once we get into Pakistan, I can be more helpful." Luke said. Alessa smiled at him. It was hard to know who to trust, but in this moment, the four of them were allies and it was best to know where everyone stood.

"I need to sit," Amine said suddenly and all three of them went to grab her. Alessa and Reza helped her to a rock.

"It's all right, I think it's just the baby kicking, nothing to be concerned with."

Reza locked eyes with Alessa, the plea clear in his big brown eyes. "Don't worry." Alessa said. "We will get her across."

Reza peeled back Amine's burka sleeves and the sleeves of the shirt she was wearing underneath. Amine shook his head at him but he continued undeterred. Alessa's stomach dropped and a knife-like pain twisted inside her gut. Amine's arms were covered in bruises and the telltale circular wounds of cigarette burns. Some had barely scabbed over.

Reza peeled back the top of her burka veil so more of her hair was showing, then turned her head. Alessa couldn't help the gasp that escaped her lips. Despite the cold mountain air, her entire body heated. It wasn't the first time she'd seen such a bad burn behind the ear but it had been a while since she'd come face-to-face with one.

"Her husband and father-in-law did this to her. That's what we're running away from." Reza said with barely suppressed anger.

Amine was studying her hands, her lashes wet.

"You know you don't deserve this," Alessa told her. "There is nothing you've ever done or will ever do in your life to deserve this." Amine continued to look down so Alessa kneeled in front of her and clasped her hands in her own. "Amine, you must believe me—the men who do these things, they are weak men. That's why they do it in places where they don't have to look at the harm they've caused." She knew that was why Amine's face was unmarred. Alessa's mother wore long sleeves and full pants, even on hot days, but her face was always perfect.

"I try so hard, every day, to do it right." Amine sobbed.

Alessa put an arm around her. "You could've been the perfect human being and nothing would have changed what they did. This is about their weakness, not yours. Trust me, I know."

Amine raised her eyes to Alessa's and once again the two women held hands. Alessa made a silent promise that she would get this woman to safety, no matter the cost.

"You are brave to leave them," Alessa said.

Amine shook her head. "It wasn't me. My brother tricked me."

Alessa glanced at Reza, who stared at his feet. "What was I to do? Leave her there until they murdered her? She would not come with me."

Amine let go of Alessa's hand and muttered, "It is my fate to be in that household, and now that I am cursed like that, it is my duty to honor my husband and family."

Alessa's breath stuck in her throat. The words were different, but the sentiment was the same one she'd heard from her mother. A sense of obligation to stay, a misguided notion that things would get better. Perhaps even a sense that she somehow deserved it. This was a conversation she'd had so many times in her life that her chest hurt just looking at Amine. She stood.

"It'll never happen to you again," Luke whispered softly, but his words cut through her. While she knew he was right, a part of her irrationally feared her mother's life. She was terrified of ending up in the same situation as Amine, unable to see when it was a bad situation. It had almost happened with Aidan.

Reza crouched down and cupped his sister's face. He spoke to her in a dialect that Alessa didn't understand but she could translate the desperation in his voice. The shine of Amine's tears reflected the moonlight. She murmured something to her brother, then he shook his head and stood.

"There is no use. She thinks because I studied in America that I have become too Western in my thinking, but that is not true. This is wrong."

He stepped away from Amine, who sobbed quietly. Alessa shot him an encouraging look. She admired his courage in trying to get his sister out. That he had studied abroad accounted for his lack of concern about the women not being veiled, and the physical affection he showed his sister.

Luke let go of Alessa and approached Reza. "You're doing the right thing. If she were my sister, I'd get her as far away as I could, then make sure the man who did this pays." Luke's menacing tone reminded her of when he'd interviewed her for the unit. He'd asked if she needed help with her father.

Amine continued to cry. Alessa didn't move to comfort her. What was the point? She had once tricked her mother into visiting her, then presented her with a plane ticket to Italy. Alessa had spent everything, all the money she'd saved, to put down the deposit for an apartment and pay for the flight. Her mother had flatly refused. Alessa's internet research, which proclaimed that once you got the victim away from the abuser, they could think more clearly, was flawed. It hadn't worked with her mother. She'd offered up a way out and her mother had flatly refused. She understood all too well what Reza was trying to do, but it wouldn't work with Amine. And the situation presented yet another problem for them: Amine's cooperation.

As if he'd read her thoughts, Luke tugged on her arm and they stepped out of earshot of the siblings. He spoke quietly through the comms system.

"We have to let Reza handle this. I'm going to check on the rest of the team. Cover for me."

Luke couldn't exactly pull out his fancy satellite phone. While many people had smartphones, no one would have a cell signal here and the light from the phone would attract a lot of attention. Feigning a call of nature, Luke walked into the brush.

After a while, Reza left Amine and came and

sat beside Alessa. Sensing he needed something else to focus on, Alessa turned to him. "Where did you study?"

Reza brightened at the question. "Ohio University. I got a scholarship to go there for four years to do my studies in architecture. It was the best time of my life. I wish I could have stayed."

"But your student visa expired?"

He nodded. "Yes, I could not find a job to sponsor an H1 visa for me. Besides, it was time to come home. I was a married man and my wife was waiting. My father needed me to earn money for food and to pay his debts."

"Is that why he married Amine to that awful man?"

Reza nodded. "She was married to him when I was in America. She was only fifteen, but my father owed her husband and father-in-law too much money. Her husband..." Reza shook his head in disgust. "The man was forty years old. She was just a child."

"Your father is also to blame in this." Alessa couldn't help it. This was a story she'd heard many times, and in every version, the father of the girl was couched as a victim.

"I agree. I cut off ties with my father when I returned and first went to visit Amine. They would not even let me see her, saying that it was improper for us to meet. I am her brother! But I was not going to be turned away. I got the help of a female cousin, who arranged a secret meeting. That time, Amine pretended she was happy and everything was well. It was my cousin who pushed her sleeves up and showed me her arms, and that is when I knew." He paused, as if to compose himself. "I went to talk to her husband. He said Amine was making things up, then sent some men to beat me. They warned me to stay away from Amine. I have always respected my father, but he told me we must consider Amine a sacrifice. Tell me, would you ever sacrifice your own flesh and blood? Your own sister?"

The words burned through Alessa's ears and ones uttered years ago, when she first joined the army, came back to her.

"Lessi, you're going to leave me all alone?"

"Julia, it's temporary—as soon as I make enough money in the army, I'll come get you out and then we will live together and you'll never have to come home."

Julia had been fifteen when Alessa joined up. At the time, all Alessa wanted was to get as far away from her father as soon as she possibly could. He hadn't touched her since she was fourteen, since she'd taken up martial arts, but that hadn't stopped him from taking out his anger on her mother in front of Alessa. It was a show of power, to demonstrate to her that while she could defend herself, she couldn't protect her mother. Alessa had felt guilty leaving Julia behind, but as a minor herself, she'd had no choice.

After her first two years in the army, Alessa had gone back for Julia, with an offer to petition to adopt her, but Julia wanted none of it. She was seventeen and had plans of her own for when she turned eighteen. So Alessa had done what came easy; she'd agreed to pay for Julia's college, a way to assuage her guilt and not think about what had happened to her baby sister in her absence.

"I think this is a tough situation," Alessa said noncommittally when she realized Reza was waiting for a response. She could plainly see the anguish in the young man's expression and wanted to tell him not to blame himself, to be happy that nothing worse had happened to his sister, that he'd gotten her out in time. But she couldn't say any of those things. They were not out of harm's way.

LUKE FOUND AN outcropping in the rock and sat down. The mountains rose up behind him; the precipitous valley below was mostly dark with a few twinkling lights. The road through the mountains wasn't very wide, barely enough to let two cars pass in some spots. There was no guardrail on the other side, just the dark abyss, shadowed in the moonlight. He leaned against the smooth side of the rock he'd found to hide him from the camp and powered up his phone. A voice startled him.

"Hey!"

"Rodgers! What're you doing here?" Luke couldn't see him well so he turned his cell-phone to shine the light on Rodgers. The man was dressed in local clothes, dirty and a little torn just like Luke's.

"Boots and I ran into some trouble and got separated. I was cutting across Khyber on my own hoping to run into you."

Luke's stomach hardened. This was not good news. Rodgers was the most senior operative on the team and Boots was very good. Even if they had run into trouble and lost each other, there were ways of reconnecting, including tracking the other team member on their GPS.

As if reading his mind, Rodgers whispered, "Boots's GPS has him at a stationary location, but he's not there. I looked for the phone and watch but couldn't find them and didn't want to spend too much time loitering."

It was a neat explanation. Too neat. But what choice did Luke have? He didn't know if it was

Boots he couldn't trust or Rodgers. Ali was ready with glasses of tea when they got back to the campfire. He admonished them for wandering so far away and proclaimed their tea cold and possibly ruined for drinking. Luke insisted on taking the glass from the man anyway and took a sip. The tea was nice and warm, a perfect drinking temperature. There was a tendency for tea to be served boiling hot in the region. If it wasn't hot enough to burn one's tongue, it was too cold.

"Who are you?" Ali studied Rodgers.

Luke explained that he was a wanderer they'd found on their walk. "He wants to make a deal with you to join our group."

Ali pulled Rodgers aside and negotiated a fee. Luke heard the entire conversation through the comms. Rodgers protested, bargained, then finally settled on a fee that was slightly higher than what Luke had paid. Ali scuttled off to make Rodgers some tea. Reza and Amine had taken a seat by the fire. Their conversation looked intense, so Luke, Rodgers and Alessa took a seat a few yards from the blaze. Alessa had her veil back on and turned her back to them. Luke and Rodgers positioned themselves so it looked like they were just hanging out, not necessarily talking to each other. Luke explained Rodgers's appearance to Alessa.

"I don't see Boots on the GPS, but Dan, Steele and Dimples are across." Alessa had pulled out the phone under the cover of the burka.

"What should we do, boss? I can go back and try to find Boots."

Luke wished the right answer would magically appear. His gut told him he should send Rodgers back for Boots, but what if he then put Rodgers in even more danger? What if Boots was a traitor and that's why he was missing? His brain was firing a number of scenarios at him, none of which amounted to sending Rodgers back. But something told him Boots wasn't in trouble. Either Rodgers had ditched him or Boots had separated himself. If Boots had been captured, he'd have found a way to get them a message.

"No, until he gets in touch, we continue."

The panic button on Boots's phone would send a signal to a server back in the States, which would then send an automated message to the team's phones. If the members were out of range, the message would come when they reconnected. If Boots had lost his phone, there was a backup protocol he could use from a payphone. That was assuming Boots was alive and hadn't lost his phone.

"What's the play?" Rodgers asked.

Luke took a breath. "We stay with Ali but the first sign that he's turned, we break and go our own way."

They sat in silence, Luke wondering whether any of these were the right call. He was going with his gut on Ali. He had to. He didn't have enough information on the guy to make a strategic decision. Luke had to decide based on their brief meeting whether Ali would stab them in the back and get them killed. To Luke, the guy seemed as honest as a human smuggler could be.

"I'm not sure about Ali." Alessa said softly after a while. Luke swallowed and waited, let the silence hang between them.

"He's been extra chummy with the other guides at the camp here."

"That's normal," Luke replied evenly. "The camp is set up by a group—they need to coordinate logistics, make sure they all take different routes."

"Or gang up on the rest of us." This time Rodgers spoke up. Luke stopped himself from taking a sharp breath. When the comms were on, you could hear every inhale and he didn't want the team to know he was sweating this. What was the answer? He may have already lost Boots; he couldn't lose more of his team. Especially not Alessa. *What's the right call here?*

"We continue with the plan. Like I said, stay vigilant and first sign of trouble, we bail." His voice was firm. Feelings for Alessa couldn't play into any decision he made. She was a soldier in his command; that was all.

Ali came toward them, motioning with his hands that they had to go. They all hurried behind him. Reza and Amine seemed to have reached some sort of understanding. He held his sister's elbow, a little awkwardly through the cloth. She wasn't resisting, although Luke didn't expect her to. He thought about the way Alessa had stiffened like a steel plate when Reza first showed them Amine's bruises, the way she'd backed away as if just by being close to them, her own wounds were opening. He thought about the man that had done that to Alessa and a rage unlike any he'd ever felt heated his blood. She was walking behind him and he resisted the urge to look back and make sure she was okay. *A soldier in my command. Nothing more.*

They would be trekking through arid, mountainous terrain. Biting cold air mixed with dust stung his face. So far the walk was easy, but he knew it would get treacherous as they made their way toward the Khyber Pass.

He toggled the comms on his watch so he

could talk to Alessa privately. "Just you and me. You okay?"

"Are you seriously asking me again?"

"How's your shoulder?"

There was a long pause. "I'm fine," she said tightly.

"I'm going to find an opening when we can ditch the group."

"Why?"

"I think we'll be safer on our own." It was a gut feeling and he was going to trust it.

"Shouldn't Rodgers be in on this conversation?"

"I don't want to give him a heads-up."

"You don't trust him?" she said incredulously.

"Would you?"

"Yes! Rodgers wouldn't betray us."

Luke bit his lips and tamped down on the flare of jealousy that burned in his chest. Alessa and Rodgers had gotten close working together; had she developed feelings for him?

As if reading his mind, Alessa's voice came through reassuringly. "Rodgers is like a brother to me. I know him well enough to know he's a good man, and he's loyal to the unit."

"I see some flashlights around the bend, maybe two clicks from us." Rodgers's voice was crisp on the comms.

Luke kept his eyes peeled and toggled his comms back so he could talk to everyone.

"I see them." Alessa's voice came through at the same second he saw the lights. They kept moving, Luke surreptitiously keeping track of their progress on his watch. The uneven, winding terrain made it difficult to count steps.

The lights were stationary. That meant they were walking into a trap. Luke took inventory of the weapons he was carrying and began formulating a plan. Lights were highly suspicious, especially in an area that was well known for not having a reliable electrical grid. They weren't car headlights, and if people had money for oil or battery-operated lamps, they were likely too rich to be domiciling in a harsh mountain cave.

They inched closer to the lights. By now the whole group had seen them and Luke noticed Reza and Amine slow their steps. Ali on the other hand seemed to quicken his pace.

Luke knew now that his gut was nothing to go on. He'd obviously been wrong to trust Ali. As they approached, the smuggler waved, no doubt letting whoever was waiting know that he'd brought fresh targets.

Luke didn't need to check with Alessa and Rodgers to know they'd be ready to fight.

The team had trained for this scenario—even Alessa.

Just as they rounded the corner which would bring them face-to-face with whoever held the lights, Alessa's scream came through on the comms. She had tripped and was about to plummet to her death.

CHAPTER FIFTEEN

ALESSA DANGLED OFF the rock face. She had managed to catch the edge of a cliff as she fell. Searching, she found a foothold. This is going to hurt. She pushed off and hoisted herself with her arms, ignoring the screaming pain in her shoulder. Just as she got her knee onto the edge of the cliff, not an easy feat in the burka, a pair of hands gripped her under the arms. *Rodgers.* He pulled her the rest of the way until she could scramble back onto the road.

"Are you okay?" Luke nearly pushed Rodgers off the cliff in his rush to get to her. Less than a minute had passed since she'd tripped, likely catching the edge of the burka on a jagged piece of rock.

She nodded. "I'm fine."

"Sorry," Rodgers muttered and both Alessa and Luke looked up at him. "I was following too closely. I think I stepped on your skirt."

Even in the darkness, Alessa could see the murder in Luke's eyes. He moved toward Rodgers, then seemed to think better of it. There was something animalistic about him and it scared her a little.

"No worries, nothing I couldn't handle," she said, standing up and dusting loose pebbles off her burka.

A small crowd was approaching, including newcomers with lanterns. Alessa, Luke and Rodgers went on alert, ready to fight if it came to that. Each of them had a gun and a knife readily available.

Ali came toward them. "You okay?"

They all nodded. The men with the lanterns stood back. "These are my brothers, they have shelter, we take rest here." The men were already leading Amine and Reza through the opening of the cave. Alessa, Luke and Rodgers reluctantly followed but felt better once they saw that the cave held nothing but a steel drum with a fire and a *charpai*. There were no visible weapons and the men were placing a kettle on the flames.

"You all rest, we will continue when the light breaks." Ali announced. It was a good idea. It had gotten windier and colder and the little bit of moonlight had disappeared.

"I'll take the first shift," Alessa said quietly. They didn't need any discussion to know that one of them would stand watch while the other two slept.

Luke put a hand on her good shoulder. "Rodgers and I don't think any less of you for needing to rest. You could've…" His voice cracked.

Luke locked eyes with her and his expression was firm. She sighed and nodded. Her shoulder was killing her. Ali gestured for her and Amine to take the *charpai*. Alessa let Amine have it and took a seat on the rock floor, finding a smooth surface to lean against. Luke sat down beside her. Rodgers sat a few feet away from them, pretending to sleep. He had the first shift.

"You're holding your arm against your chest. Does it hurt?"

She shouldn't have been surprised that he noticed. Her shoulder was in serious pain and holding it in that position, the way the doctor had put it in the sling after her dislocation, seemed to help. Her impulse was to claim it was okay, but she didn't want to lie to him.

"My shoulder's bugging me. When we get out of here, it might help to put it back in the sling for a little bit, give it a rest."

For some insane reason, she felt safe with Luke. Showing weakness was not something she did. It was a lesson she'd learned early in life, the first time she'd begged her father not to hit her mother and covered her mother's body with her own. Since that day, there was only one other time she'd let her guard down and that hadn't worked out so well, either.

"Why won't you let someone take care of you?" he whispered. She only heard him through the comms system. She checked the unit on her wrist to make sure they were in private mode. She didn't need Rodgers hearing this conversation.

"Because there's only been one person in my life who has ever offered to take care of me and when I let him, he betrayed me."

"Aidan Connors."

She wasn't surprised that he knew. There was probably more in her file than she realized. She might as well give him the story since he seemed to be able to read her like an open book.

"We were out on patrol together—I barely knew him. I made a mistake and accidentally discharged my weapon. I injured him. Not badly, but enough that he needed some serious stitches. He should have written me up, but he covered for me."

It was the first time she'd made such a mistake and she still wasn't sure how it had happened. She'd checked her weapon before they'd started the patrol. Regardless, it would have been a serious reprimand in her file but Aidan had told her to keep it quiet. It was the first secret they'd shared.

"I'll take care of it, Alessa. I'll protect you."

"Why would you do that, Aidan?"

"Because you need a break and I consider you a friend."

"A friend?"

"I don't have many, but I feel like we have a connection. Maybe we can look out for each other in this strange country?"

That was how it had all started.

"So that's why you did it," Luke said.

She nodded. "I owed him one. So, I covered for him." *The incident.*

One night, some local kids had decided to dare each other to try to get over the fence. Someone had fired a shot, killing one of the kids. It had happened in the dead of night and it wasn't clear exactly who had pulled the trigger. The kids had come armed and the initial story was that patrols had fired warning shots but then someone else got into the mix and started shooting, too. The kids then fired back, and one of them caught a stray round.

There was no autopsy, so the bullet hadn't been identified. There had, of course, been an internal inquiry and every soldier was asked to account for his or her whereabouts. Alessa had been alone in the female sleeping quarters. The only other enlisted female soldier on camp at the time had been out on patrol. Aidan had told her he'd been off camp without permission, trying to clear his head after a bad fight with his wife over the divorce. He'd begged her to serve as his alibi since another officer had knocked on his door and knew Aidan hadn't been in his quarters. He was the only one unaccounted for.

"Were you ever with him that night?"

It was a question she'd never honestly answered; she'd always stuck to the story she and Aidan had agreed to. But she shook her head now.

"Let me guess—he was with a superior officer."

Alessa looked up at him. How could he possibly know that?

"There have been rumors of him having relationships that are too close to be professional with certain superior officers," he explained.

"This stays between us," she said and he nodded.

She told him how Aidan had asked her to be his alibi. It had been months later when she'd finally found out that he'd been with another officer that night—one who was married and had two kids at home. She was also Aidan's commanding officer.

"He shouldn't have asked that of you." Luke looked like he wanted to say more but stopped.

There was more to the story but what was she supposed to say? When Aidan asked her to be his alibi, he had sworn to protect both their careers by saying that they were discussing a recent patrol. Not that anyone bought the story that she and Aidan were just talking business. Apparently, he'd thought it would be easier for him to withstand rumors of inappropriate contact with an enlisted than with a married superior officer who was doing his evaluation. But adultery was punishable by the Uniform Code of Military Justice. If someone admitted to an affair, then they'd both be court-martialed. Yet Aidan and Alessa's insistence that there was nothing between them had just fueled more rumors.

So much so that the officer that Aidan had been having the affair with had come to Alessa to warn her that he was bad news and to tell Alessa exactly where Aidan had been that night.

That was how she'd found out and it all made sense to her then. She'd been asked to be the scapegoat so Aidan's promotion wouldn't be jeopardized. Word had gotten around that she had pursued him and he'd put her in her place. She hadn't done anything to counter those rumors because she'd been under the impression that Aidan was her friend, and perhaps they could have something special together when she got promoted and they were in different units.

Even after she found out about his betrayal, she'd covered for him and continued the lie. To this day she couldn't say why. Partly because she had feelings for him, and perhaps out of some misguided sense of obligation that she owed him something because he'd once covered for her. She'd never told him that she knew the truth about him and the other officer. He'd continued lying to her until the day she left Kuwait.

"I made a mistake trusting him."

Luke nodded. "He took advantage of you." He didn't have to say the rest. *Because I told him about my father. I showed him my Achilles heel. Just like I've shown Luke.*

"I am not the same man he is, Alessa. I'll take care of you." His words were so soft that for a second she thought she'd imagined them. She closed her eyes to clear the thoughts of Aidan from her mind.

Luke reached across and found her hand. *I want to believe that things will be different this time.* But given how badly she'd misjudged Aidan, could she even trust her feelings for Luke? She savored the feel of his thumb moving in careful strokes across her palm. The caress seemed to telegraph a message she was desperate to believe. *I've got you*.

Exhaling, she closed her eyes again. The hushed sounds of men talking, the wind howling outside and the crackle of the fire soothed her. Even if it was just for a minute, it felt nice not to be on guard, to let someone else take care of her. Her body felt weightless, like she was floating on air, and she let herself get pulled into the welcome darkness of sleep.

LUKE WATCHED ALESSA'S eyes flutter, then close. He saw Rodgers look toward them and retracted his hand.

"Status?" Rodgers said through the comms so only Luke would hear.

"All quiet." Luke hesitated. "I need cover."

Rodgers nodded.

Luke looked at Alessa, her face covered with the veil. He needed to go outside to use the sat phone. Alessa was just another soldier. If it were Boots or Dan, he wouldn't even think twice. He was the leader; his job was to check on his team. To keep them safe. All of them. Alessa was a special woman, but was her life worth more than the others under his command? Or Ethan's? And what if he made a decision, like he had with his mom or with Nazneen, that ended up getting her killed?

"The best thing you can do for all of us is stay focused on the mission." It was an insolent comment from Rodgers, one that would get him reprimanded in any unit other than this one.

"Stay alert," Luke said curtly. He motioned to the men by the fire that he had to answer the call of nature so they wouldn't wonder why he was wandering off.

The wind bit into him as he stepped outside. In the hour or so they'd been inside the cave, the temperature had dropped considerably. He had layered two sweaters on top of his *kameez* and wrapped a shawl around his neck. While warm, these items did nothing to keep the wind out and he wished he could have his army-issued gear, as much as he had complained about its poor quality during his last deployment.

He walked carefully down the path they'd be taking to Londi Kotwal to get a glimpse at what lay ahead. The moon was partially hidden behind some clouds so he used his phone to throw light on the twisty path and keep from falling to his death.

A few minutes later, he found an boulder that was out of the line of sight of the cave. The satellite signal wasn't great, but it worked. Dan, Steele and Dimples were already at the safe house and had sent him a coded message that it was okay. Boots's tracker was still stationary. Luke checked the latest intelligence reports for the area. Lucky for them, insurgent activity was low. His phone pinged with an urgent message and his pulse quickened. It was a text from Boots.

StinkySocks. I'm safe. Watch your back.

Luke responded immediately asking for details. "StinkySocks" was Boots's safe word to let them know that he was not sending the message under duress.

There was no response. He stared at the phone, willing it to light up with another message. The silence was not unusual. Boots could have sent the text when he had a signal and it was possible Luke had just received it now because he'd gotten into range.

He consulted his watch. Seventeen minutes had passed since he'd left Alessa. It wasn't a long time and she wasn't in immediate danger. His chest squeezed and he tapped his foot as he scrolled through his phone, the words swimming before his eyes. He took a breath and stared out at the darkness. He needed to go through the intelligence reports again, really read them to make sure he wasn't missing anything. It was critical. A single line in one of hundreds of pages could mean the difference between his mission being a success or failure. Luke couldn't let Alessa distract him. This mission was too important. Deservedly or not, the unit had been entrusted to him, and his soldiers were counting on him to get them through.

He scrolled through the reports, his mind laser focused on the words. He was halfway through a document when an item made him freeze. He clicked back to a previous report and realized what he was seeing. The analysts hadn't connected the reports because they weren't looking at the issue with the same lens he was. His heart raced. There was a real possibility he could find Ethan.

Standing, he scrambled back up the path. It didn't matter what Alessa's condition was; they needed to make their way into Pakistan now. *Time to get the mission back on track.*

When he returned to the cave, things were quiet. He had been gone for more than an hour. Aside from Rodgers, everyone was asleep. Ali, Reza and three villagers—were stretched out on the floor or leaning against a wall, huddled underneath threadbare shawls.

Luke met Rodgers's eyes and the other man stood and nodded as if he sensed what was coming. A pang of guilt swept through him for keeping Rodgers in the dark about ditching Ali. Luke stepped over lifted Alessa off the ground, putting her over his shoulder in a fireman's carry. She stirred, but he and Rodgers were out of the cave before she fully wakened. Rodgers walked ahead of him, shining the flashlight on his phone to light the way and clear the path for Luke. Alessa struggled against him.

"Shhhh…" he admonished into the comms. To her credit, she expressed her frustration silently, punching him lightly in the shoulder to let him know she wanted to be set down.

He waited until they'd rounded the corner and were out of eyesight of the cave before putting her on the ground. The wind shrieked around them and he knew it was unlikely anyone would hear them. Still, he kept his voice low as he spoke into the comms, talking to both Alessa and Rodgers.

"I got a message from Boots using the safe word saying he's okay but nothing else. Dan, Steele and Dimples are across and I have new intel on our mission. We need to make it into Pakistan before daybreak."

"What about Reza and Amine?" Alessa asked.

"They're on their own," he said firmly.

"Luke, we need to take them with us. I don't know if they'll be safe with Ali." The pleading in her voice ripped at his soul but he couldn't give in. There was too much at stake.

"We've already wasted too much time."

"But…" Alessa protested.

"Parrino, you're enough of a liability, I don't need another." His stomach hardened as he heard her take a sharp breath. He didn't need to see her face to know he'd just stabbed her in the gut. Under normal circumstances he would've done everything he could to help Reza and Amine, but his priority had to be the people he was responsible for. It was time to think and act like Ethan. Alessa was a soldier in his command and despite the unorthodox way the unit operated, there was a time when orders had to be obeyed. If any of the other guys had questioned him standing on a dangerous mountain in the middle of Afghanistan, he would've been much harsher.

Rodgers picked up his pace and Alessa followed, keeping up. Luke put his hand on her arm. When she stopped and turned, he toggled the comms so only she could hear.

"I need you to hold on to me. I can't risk you falling."

"Why not? If I fall to my death, you'll be able to proceed much faster, one less *liability* to worry about."

He knew the words were said in anger but the

thought of Alessa even considering that death was an option hit him so hard that his mouth soured. Had his mother thought that way? That dying was easier than facing her life?

"Just do as I say, Parrino. You just told me your shoulder's not right. I'm responsible for your safety." His tone and words were much harsher than he intended. What he longed to do more than anything was to take her in his arms and carry her the rest of the hike, making sure she stayed safe.

She turned and he tightened his grip on her good arm so he could catch her if she fell.

The crisp air stung at their faces but they kept going. They stopped once at an outcropping to drink water from their canteens and eat a few power bars that Alessa had stowed in the backpack she kept under her burka. The men carried locally made bags; she was the only one who could carry gear. Luke had forgotten she had that additional burden. He took the backpack from her once the break was done.

"I can carry it," she said stiffly.

He didn't answer her, just slung it over his shoulder and continued the trek.

They made it to the border near Londi Kotwal just before daybreak. They needed to cross over a stream in order to avoid the fenced area of the official checkpoint. The stream looked to be about four feet deep and would be treacherous for all of them, but Alessa in particular. She was much shorter than both men, and the burka would hamper her movement.

They put all of their sacks and the backpack into a waterproof bag, which Rodgers carried over his head. He continued to lead with Alessa in the middle and Luke keeping an eye on their backs.

The water was ice-cold as they stepped into it and Luke heard Alessa's slight moan of pain as she got knee-deep into it. He stopped and faced her.

"It's okay, I just hit my knee on a rock."

He bent down, water lapping at his waist and lifted her burka. Her white *salwar* was red underneath. A jagged piece of wood protruded from her shin. He pulled it out and she cried involuntarily. Something exploded inside him and he didn't stop and think or wait for permission. He lifted her and threw her over his shoulder again.

"Luke, no! I'm fine."

"Be quiet, Alessa. I'm not taking no for an answer. You can either continue struggling and make it more difficult for me or cooperate and we'll both get through this a little easier."

That silenced her. He carried her across the stream, his legs protesting as various pieces of debris rammed against them. Ahead of him Rodgers was having the same problem, doing his best to dodge driftwood and small rocks. The man grunted painfully as a sharp piece of wood caught him on the hip. He yelled in pain as he pulled it out.

The river was several yards wide and the water raced past Luke's chest now, the cold chilling his bones so deeply, he couldn't imagine ever getting warm again. Alessa had stilled and he did his best to keep most of her body out of the water but it was getting harder and harder as they got to the middle of the river where the footing also became more precarious. He stumbled more than a few times, nearly losing his balance. Light though she was, it was hard to push his own weight and hers through the flow.

"You need to put me down, Luke." Alessa's voice was calm but the anger was clear in her tone.

"I'm fine. We're almost across." Luke said. He couldn't have her hurt again and at her height, she'd almost be swimming. That wouldn't be good for her shoulder.

They finally made it to the bank. "Now I know why even the smugglers won't use this route." Rogers quipped. He was shorter than Luke so he'd been soaked nearly to the neck.

They took a second to find cover to change

their clothes and bandage the scratches and cuts they'd gotten from the crossing. Rodgers and Luke were behind a rock. Rodgers turned off the comms system and faced him.

"Listen man, whatever's going on between you and Parrino, it's got to end."

"Excuse me?" Luke glared at the other man. They were both shivering in their wet clothes but Rodgers didn't back down.

"I'm not an idiot. What you did back there… I don't know what that was, but it wasn't professional. She's a soldier, that woman's kicked me down, she could've handled it. If you think she couldn't, you should have made her stay home."

"She's injured. If your sorry behind was hurt, I'd have dragged you, too."

Rodgers shook his head. "Hey, that line isn't working with her, and it isn't working with me. I didn't see you offer to carry me when one of those shards cut me up." He pointed to his thigh where blood was still oozing out of his wound. Taking a breath, Luke forced himself to maintain eye contact. Rodgers was right, of course. Luke gotten several bumps and bruises along the journey and so had Rodgers. Soldiers were expected to get hurt during operations and he knew, logically, that Alessa could handle it. As Rodgers had pointed out, she was stronger than his men.

"Look, I get it, you've got a thing for her. But you're unit command and my life depends on you being focused."

"You're wrong, Rodgers. There's nothing going on between us." Luke's words sounded hollow even to him.

"Maybe not physically—" he tapped his chest "—but in here, you're totally messed up."

Rodgers spun away and began stripping his clothes. Luke did the same. His hands were shaking and it wasn't entirely from the cold.

They met up with Alessa, who didn't have a second burka. Thankfully, hers was only wet from the hips down.

Luke toggled the comms so only she could hear as they continued trekking their way into Pakistan. "See, aren't you glad I carried you?" He meant for his tone to be light but it came out clipped.

"Luke, don't ever, I mean ever, touch me like that again. It is not okay to handle me without my permission."

This time he knew it wasn't the cold that iced his veins. He had crossed a line.

CHAPTER SIXTEEN

CROSSING THE BORDER seemed far easier than it should have been. They simply walked across and only had to go another mile before encountering a rickshaw stand. They squeezed into the back of the bicycle-drawn carriage that delivered them four blocks from their safe house.

All told, it was the most exciting mission Alessa had ever been on, but she knew without a doubt that this would be her last time with the unit. She loved the team, and she would never experience a more interesting army deployment without making it into Special Forces, but she would much rather go back and face Aidan than deal with Luke. Despite all that had transpired between her and Aidan, he had never touched her against her will. *How dare Luke think he can take liberties with me?* Of all the people she had worked with, Luke should have respected her boundaries.

"Okay, Rodgers, you're the journalist and I—"

"Oh, come on." Alessa knew *she* was probably crossing boundaries now, but there was no way she could pretend to be Luke's wife.

"Parrino, this is not up for discussion. You are my wife and Rodgers is the journalist."

"You don't look Azerbaijani," she said. Though they had dyed Luke's golden locks and eyebrows to a dark brown and given him brown contacts, he didn't have the right look. That's why he'd been given the cover she had chosen for him. Why was he being so pigheaded? He was jeopardizing the mission, and for what?

"I'll be fine. I'll make a joke about how I resemble an American."

"Luke…" Rodgers tried to interject but Luke cut him off. "That's the way it'll be." Luke said shortly. Rodgers agreed to roam the streets for a few hours so they wouldn't show up together.

The building looked like any other in the surrounding neighborhood. A U-shaped midrise with apartments that overlooked a courtyard. There were six stories and Alessa counted eleven apartments per floor. Each floor could be accessed through an external staircase and the apartments were connected by long balconies. It reminded Alessa of cheap motels in the United States. The short, skinny business manager confirmed that each unit had its own "wet" bathroom, which meant it had a shower and toilet. The entire space couldn't have been more than six hundred square feet and consisted of a galley kitchen, living room and small bedroom with one double bed. Alessa tried not to stare at the bed as the manager proudly showed them the roach-infested apartment as if he were giving them a tour of the Taj Mahal.

Luke thanked him in Urdu and closed the door behind him. Alessa took off the burka, which had mostly dried off but was still damp. Looking at the local women on their way here, she knew she could get away with just wearing a hijab that covered her hair and neck but left her face exposed.

Before she could formulate the words to let him know just how bad an idea it was for them to share a room. He turned to her. "Listen, I am sorry for what happened at the creek. I didn't mean to... I mean I shouldn't have... I was just..." He shuffled on his feet, unable to meet her eyes.

"You do not have permission to touch me in any way," she said flatly.

He nodded. "I respect that."

"I don't like these arrangements."

He straightened. "I'll sleep on the floor in the living room. You can have the bedroom to yourself. I need you with me because I have some intelligence that could help us find Ethan."

That drew her attention away from wondering how she was going to avoid him in the tiny apartment.

"I didn't ask to change assignments with Rodgers because of what's happening between..." At the glare she gave him he stopped and changed tact. "I changed the assignments because you and I are going to have to sneak out of here without the team knowing and go rescue Ethan."

Now her interest was piqued.

"You have his location? How? When?"

He shook his head. "I'm not discussing anything until we have you checked out by a doctor. I need to know you're okay."

She rolled her eyes but couldn't argue with him. Only she knew how she'd managed to complete the trek. While she hated that Luke had carried her across the stream, she had to admit that she might not have made it to Peshawar on her own. She had been dizzy with pain ever since they left the cave, and it was only Luke's hand on her arm, constantly steadying her, that had given her the courage to keep going.

"It's highly unnecessary, but let's get it over with just to make you feel better." She was done showing him her Achilles heel. He was no different than any other man she'd ever encountered. He was kind until it suited him and then he used whatever information he had about her to his benefit. Not to mention making the most of the physical advantage he had.

"I had Dan scope one out. The doctor seems legit and in it for the money. He has a small hospital a couple clicks away. Get dressed. I'll check in with the rest of the team and then we'll go."

The hospital was a glorified clinic. This particular doctor claimed to be an orthopedist, and they sat in his waiting room under the watchful eye of a white-clad nurse, Luke paced the room to silently show his irritation to the young nurse, who seemed to not notice. Two hours went by. This was also not uncommon.

Alessa beckoned to her side. "Why don't you go back to the safe house and I'll meet you there," she said in hushed tones.

Luke had spent most of the time looking at his phone, no doubt taking care of details for the mission. He shook his head. "I gave the guys some surveillance work—they're checking in via texts."

"I don't need a babysitter," she said angrily. She also knew that if Luke identified himself as her husband, he would have the right to be present in the room during her examination and make medical decisions for her.

"I have the right to my privacy," she said more firmly. He frowned but nodded. "Yes, of course, I'll leave the room when the doctor is looking you over, but as your commander, I have a right to know whether you're fit for duty."

So we're back to that.

She pressed her lips together. There was no reason she had to tell the doctor exactly what her symptoms were. The pain wasn't that bad. Another hour slowly ticked by before the nurse finally led them to the doctor's office. Dr. Abdul was of medium height, medium build with a medium-brown complexion. He spoke with a surprisingly light accent. Diplomas hung on his wall, and Alessa was comforted by the fact that in addition to having gone to Rawalpindi Medical College on the eastern side of Pakistan, he'd also completed a fellowship program at the University of Toronto in Canada.

They all agreed to speak in English once it was established that Luke and Alessa were from Azerbaijan and did not speak much Urdu.

"Kind sir, you are welcome to stay here with your wife, but I find it is most helpful if you could wait outside while I talk to her. Then you can be here for any tests I administer." Luke looked like he might protest, so the doctor went on melodiously. "I will not examine her or touch her without you being present, and you can stand right outside the door so she can call for you if necessary."

Alessa silently encouraged Luke to leave and after a curt nod, he exited the room.

"Yes, Mrs. Rashida, tell me why you are coming here today."

"I fell and hurt my shoulder."

"Okay," he said. "How did you fall?"

"I was doing some house cleaning and slipped on the stairs." It took Alessa a second to realize that it was an excuse her mother often used. How easily it had come rolling off her tongue.

"I see." Dr. Abdul's voice was neutral, but the not-so-subtle shake of his head told her he didn't buy it. However, she knew he wouldn't believe if she said that she'd dislocated it while hanging off a cliff on the Khyber pass.

"What are your symptoms?"

"Some pain, but otherwise I'm okay. Local doctor popped the shoulder back into place." Alessa had thought about it and not indicating that anything was wrong would raise even more suspicion.

"Anything else? Any other injuries?"

Alessa suddenly realized this was not the first time she'd heard this conversation. It was how all her mother's medical appointments went. The doctors would probe and try to get her to admit that she was being beaten. Her mother would provide short answers in clipped tones. Everything was always okay and there was always an explanation for her inexplicable injuries. Alessa had never understood why her mother lied. Why, not once, had she leaned forward to say, "Doctor, my husband is beating me." Perhaps for the same reasons Alessa had continued to cover for Aidan. Why she'd taken the blow to her career that he deserved. *I'm trained, all my life I've been taught to take the hits.*

"If that is all you want to tell me, I'll tell your husband to come back in." The doctor stood and paused, but when she didn't react, he opened the door. If Luke was surprised at the brevity, he didn't show it.

Dr. Abdul had Alessa lie on the table and pull off her hijab. He examined her shoulder and arm.

"I will do X-rays, but I am also thinking you should get an MRI. I have one here but it will be expensive." He paused dramatically.

"How much?" Luke said irritably.

"Ten thousand rupees. That's in addition to my fees." Alessa could tell that Luke was trying hard to look serious. He paced the room, then reached into his pocket and pulled out a wad of cash. It was not uncommon in Pakistan to carry around bundles of rupees. The banks often just stapled them together so people didn't have to count hundreds of notes. The American equivalent of the test was a hundred dollars. In the States, you couldn't even pay the doctor's visit for that amount, but for a Pakistani, it was a lot of money.

The doctor looked pleased at the show of cash. "The nurse will get the machine ready."

It took another two hours for the MRI to be completed. The doctor also took care of stitching up her knee, for an extra fee.

When the results came back, Dr. Abdul pulled them back into his office, which now smelled of fragrant cardamom tea. The nurse brought Luke and Alessa a cup, too, and she savored hers, enjoying the sweet, milky liquid.

"I have bad news," Dr. Abdul said. "The scan shows that you have a Hill-Sachs lesion." Luke leaned forward. "I am surprised you are not having more symptoms related to pain like dizziness, maybe nausea. Frankly, I am shocked you are sitting here drinking tea without medicine to numb the pain."

Alessa was feeling quite dizzy right now. Did this mean she couldn't go on with the mission?

"What exactly is a Hill-Sachs? I thought she had a dislocated shoulder."

"That's what the local doctor told us," Alessa

added quickly to make sure Luke didn't accidentally contradict her story.

The doctor pushed a piece of paper forward and drew a bad rendition of a shoulder and arm. "Your local doctor was correct. You dislocated your shoulder, meaning the normal structures that hold the ball at the end of the arm bone inside the shoulder socket are damaged." He looked pointedly at Luke. "I would guess this is not the first time you have dislocated."

Alessa took a sip of her tea. The doctor went on when neither of them responded. He pointed to the little ball he had drawn on his picture. "As this ball dislocates from the shoulder joint, it strikes the edge of the socket like this…" He slapped his hands together with force.

He lifted an MRI image and pointed to a little marking. "This is a compression fracture on that ball."

"What do we need to do?" Luke asked.

"You are lucky, madam." Dr. Abdul looked directly at Alessa. "It's not that big, so I don't have to operate. It will heal on its own." Both Alessa and Luke took a breath.

The doctor held up a finger. "But you need to be careful. Any more falling down stairs and your shoulder could separate or that fracture could get bigger." He stood and retrieved a bottle from a shelf, handing it to Alessa. "These are painkillers. No more than three a day."

Alessa didn't recognize the name of the drug on the bottle and had no plans to take the painkillers, but she thanked him anyway.

The doctor let them go after one more lecture and some more instructions. Once again Alessa was struck by how similar his speech sounded to the ones her mother's doctors used to give her.

"Don't worry, Doctor, I will take care of her." Luke said quietly.

Alessa wondered how she would deal with Luke if he followed through on that promise.

CHAPTER SEVENTEEN

ALESSA, RODGERS AND STEELE stopped at a *chai-wallah,* a roadside vendor selling fragrant tea from a pushcart. He had a kerosene stove for boiling water and a steel container full of loose leaf tea. Cardamom pods were scattered on the cart and he grabbed a few and ground them with a stone, then threw them into the boiling water. He added milk and sugar to the pot and let it simmer to the top until it nearly overflowed, then picked it up. He repeated this a couple of times, then strained the tea into three glasses and handed them out. The brew smelled wonderfully sweet and spicy, mixing with the dewy predawn air.

The dust levels were still tolerable. By late afternoon, the cars and foot traffic would make the street noisy, hot and suffocating. The melodious *azam,* the morning call to prayer, rang out from the mosques.

"Hey, if you close your eyes, I could pretend it's reveille," Steele joked. They had stepped away from the *chaiwallah* after paying him.

Dressed in local clothes, they blended in some but none of them spoke enough of the language to even fake it.

They had been tasked with following their target, a man named Azizi who was fast asleep in his home half a block away. The three of them had started attracting the guard's attention by loitering most of the night, so they'd decided to move out and leave a small camera to record in case the target moved. Alessa had argued with Luke for the better part of an hour to let her go with him to check out the location he suspected Ethan was being held at, but he had insisted she go on the easier surveillance assignment. The doctor had suggested a pain pill that wouldn't make her drowsy when she'd insisted she had too much housework to do. Still, she just took half the dose and it helped a lot. She didn't feel dizzy anymore.

Alessa's phone chimed and she nearly dropped her tea glass. It was her emergency ring. She spilled some hot tea on her hand in her haste to pass the glass to Rodgers. "Hello?"

"Is this Miss Parrino?"

Her heart stopped. This was her operational phone and to reach it, someone would have had to call her US-based emergency number and convince the operator that this was a true emergency. Then that operator would have had to route the call to a non-army operator who would reconfirm details. Only then would her phone ring. She'd set up the system so the guys could be reached if there was an emergency with their families. Especially Dimples, who worried about his kids. She hadn't been expecting her own ringer to go off.

"Who is this?" she asked carefully.

"This is Detective Michaels from the LAPD." Alessa's breath stuck in her chest. Julia went to law school in Los Angeles. Her sister had worked for years as a paralegal after college, then decided to finally get her degree. "Is this about Julia Parrino?" she blurted out.

Both Steele and Rodgers had been staring at her and now Steele walked over to the *chai-wallah* to return their half-drunk glasses while Rodgers led Alessa into an alleyway so she'd have more privacy to talk.

"Yes, ma'am. We've been trying to reach you. There was a student protest on campus that got out of hand. Several students were hurt and fled the scene. Your sister's purse with her ID and keys was found on scene but we haven't been able to locate her. You're listed as her emergency contact with the university."

Alessa forced a breath into her lungs. She needed to think clearly. "Is she hurt?"

"We're not sure, ma'am. As I said, students

were injured in the altercation with our department. She hasn't shown up to her apartment or any of the local hospitals or clinics. That's why we're calling—to ask if you know where she might be."

Alessa was at a loss. She and Julia used to be so close, but now she had no idea who her friends were or where she could have gone for safety. "Have you tried calling her phone?"

"Yes, it's turned off. We've tried to locate it using GPS, but it's not tracking."

"I… I don't know any of her friends. I'll try calling her as well and leave a message."

"Okay, ma'am. Let me give you my personal number. Please call me if you think of anything or hear from her."

Shaking, she put the detective's number into her phone, then clicked off.

Rodgers put his hand on her shoulder in a brotherly gesture. "What's going on, Parrino?"

She told him. He led her to a little brick stoop that belonged to a shuttered storefront. She sat down and buried her face in her hands. "What am I going to do? Should I go to California?"

"It won't do any good." Steele had joined them. "If she was part of the protest, she's likely hiding from the police and you said you don't know her friends or anything."

Tears stung her eyes. This wasn't the first

time she'd thought about the fact that military life hadn't let her keep a close relationship with her sister, but the weight of her complacency choked her.

"I may be able to help." She looked up at Rodgers. He shifted on his feet. "My ex-wife's new guy is a hotshot lawyer in Hollywood. I bet he has a good private eye who can track her down."

A ray of hope bloomed in her chest. Even if she left right this second, it would take her more than a day to get back to LA. Not to mention the possibility that she might compromise the team. And even then, what could she do in LA that the police weren't already doing?

"You'd ask your ex-wife for a favor from me?" She remembered him mentioning how his ex had asked him to stop calling her because she was getting serious with her new guy and needed distance. It wouldn't be easy for him to make the call.

Without another word, Rodgers moved away from them down the block. Alessa and Steele didn't follow. This was the kind of call he needed to make alone. Meanwhile, Alessa pulled up a private internet browser to search the news about the University of California, Los Angeles. Apparently, riots had broken out over the university's treatment of a student who had been attacked on campus by another student. Of course Julia would be in the thick of such a thing. A committee had been reviewing the student's case and when they came out from their meeting and announced that they would stand by their previous decision not to expel the attacker, one protestor had fired a gun at the dean and then everything went awry.

She closed her eyes and wished with everything she had that Julia had gotten away and was just hiding somewhere, afraid of the police questioning her.

Rogers returned, his face so drawn that Alessa felt guilty for putting him through this. "She was with him. He has a really good investigator and will help. They'll call me the minute they have something."

Alessa stood and hugged Rodgers. "Thank you so much!"

"I hate to be indelicate, but we have another problem." Steele said. Alessa turned to him. "You've got to decide whether you go back or stay. If you want to stay, we can't tell Luke. He'll send you stateside."

She hadn't thought about Luke but of course Steele was right. "Let's give it twelve hours. If there's no news, then I'll tell him and go back. You guys okay with that?" She looked at each man. She felt bad asking them to lie to their unit commander for her. If Luke found out, they'd both get a reprimand. They didn't owe her anything and this was a big ask.

Both men nodded. "You're one of us, Parrino, and we protect each other."

She thanked the men, trying to beat back the tears that were forming in her eyes. She wasn't used to anyone going out on a limb for her.

Ten hours later, there was still no word and she was pacing the apartment she shared with Luke. Rodgers and Steele had retreated to their own places to rest. Dan and Dimples had taken over surveillance and Luke was reading intelligence reports.

"What's wrong?" He was seated at the small kitchen table, staring at her.

"Nothing, I'm just going over things in my head, thinking." He stood and approached her. She wanted him to come closer but he kept his distance. She leaned into him, settling her head on his chest. She needed to feel the beat of his heart and the love that flowed through it for her. He kissed the top of her head. "Can I put my arms around you?" he asked nervously. She nodded and he circled her in a hug. She let him carry her weight for a minute, enjoying the momentary calm for her mind and body.

"Hey, is everything really okay?" He leaned back so he could look directly in her eyes.

She blinked back tears, unable to control them. She wanted to tell him all about Julia, but she couldn't. He'd insist on taking her back to California himself and abandon the mission. His lead hadn't panned out so he was back to looking for other clues as to Ethan's whereabouts. If something happened to Ethan because he was helping her, neither one of them could live with it.

"Alessa, what is it? You can talk to me." His voice was soft and she wanted nothing more than to tell him what was going on.

"I'm just not used to being taken care of," she said.

Now he teared up. "Alessa, I don't just want to take care of you—I want to love you."

Did he really mean it? She couldn't hold the tears in any longer, and they began to fall down he cheeks. He cupped her face. "I know it's complicated between us right now, but I want us to be honest with each other. Once this mission is over, we will find a way. Together."

A sob shook her. She needed to tell him about Julia. Her phone pinged and she reluctantly left Luke's arms to extract it from her *kameez* pocket.

Meet me outside

It was from Rodgers. Had he heard something?

"Who is that?"

Alessa looked at him. It felt awful, but she had to lie.

"It's Rodgers. He wants to know if I can come out with him to pick up dinner."

Luke frowned. This wasn't part of their normal operating procedure.

"I think he wants to talk about his ex-wife. I've been giving him a woman's perspective," she said nonchalantly. How easy it was for her to lie. Years of practice were paying off. Except that when she was a child hiding bruises, it was a relief when the teachers believed her. Now, when Luke smiled, a deep, gaping hole opened up in her heart. She wanted to throw up.

"Bring me back some lamb rice—that stuff was good." Luke dropped a kiss on her head.

She grabbed her purse, put on the hijab and rushed out. She and Rodgers had established a meeting spot a block away so someone from the building wouldn't spot them together. Rodgers was already there. He held out his phone and she took it.

"Hello?"

"Lessi?"

"Julia? Oh my God, are you okay?"

"Yes, things got out of hand and someone

snatched my purse, so I walked to a friend's house on campus. When the police came I told her to say I wasn't here. I didn't want to get caught up with those other kids. Lessi, I was only there for a peaceful protest. This random guy decided that…"

"It's okay, Julia," Alessa said reassuringly. "I'm just glad you're not hurt."

"Where are you, Lessi?" Her sister's voice was small and reminded Alessa of when they were kids.

"I'm far away, but I'll come see you soon, okay?" And Alessa meant it. She wasn't going to keep her distance from Julia anymore. She missed her sister.

"I'd like that."

They chatted for a few more minutes, then Julia handed the phone to the investigator who had found her. He promised to call Detective Michaels and smooth things over.

Rodgers was smiling when Alessa passed the phone back to him.

"I know that cost you a lot," she said.

"Nothing I hadn't already lost—the privilege to call the love of my life," Rodgers said sadly. His heartbreak was clear in his eyes and Alessa gave him a hug. She could feel the sobs deep in his chest that he wouldn't let surface.

"I owe you big-time."

"Yeah, you do." Rodgers laughed.

"I don't even know how to thank you."

Rodgers smiled slowly. "Stay away from Luke. I like the guy, but I don't want to see you get hurt."

CHAPTER EIGHTEEN

NOTHING SEEMED TO be going their way. The team had spent the last two days tracking down Boots, but they had no leads. None of them wanted to risk going back into Afghanistan and there was only so much they could do from Pakistan. Everyone was climbing the walls.

"I think we should move forward with the mission," Luke said. "Let's pick up Azizi."

They were all crowded into Luke and Alessa's little apartment. The meeting itself had been risky since they each had to enter the unit without any of the neighbors asking questions, so they had to wait until the balconies were clear. Normally they just talked to each other on the comms system from their own apartments, but Luke felt the team needed to see each other face-to-face.

Dan and Steele had taken up spots on the tiny couch. Alessa and Rodgers were sitting cross-legged on the floor and Dimples and Luke occupied the only two chairs in the apartment.

"I don't know if that's a good idea." Rodgers took a bite of his pizza, chewed a little, then spit it out and frantically motioned for water. "What is that?" he choked out.

"Hot stuff." Steele grinned. They all warily eyed the pizza boxes. Steele had managed to find a Pizza Hut to give them a break from the spicy Pakistani food. "I just brought one to try. Stick with the chicken tikka or the pepperoni," he advised.

Alessa reached for a slice of the pizza Steele had tried. Luke had discovered that she loved spicy food and had been enjoying the local cuisine while the others missed MREs and desperatcly searched for yogurt.

Dan chimed in. "I think Rodgers is right. We need to wait a bit, get the lay of the land, see why Boots went missing. We were compromised last time and may be again."

These were all valid points. Peshawar was one of the breeding grounds for Taliban insurgents. Ethan had been pursuing a lead reported by a CIA asset that one of the Taliban leaders was friendly with someone high up in the army who was feeding him information on US operations. According to the unit members who had been on the mission, they'd identified the Taliban leader and were about to approach him when Ethan got killed. Their current mission was to make the approach the team missed the last time. It would be prudent to take a wait-

and-see approach. But Ethan was here in Peshawar. Between what Alessa had found on the satellite imagery of the house where Ethan had disappeared, and the new intelligence reports, Luke didn't need his gut to tell him Ethan was close.

Their target had a home base that didn't change. The team had already surveilled him the last time and knew him on sight. They knew how many spoons of sugar he put in his tea and what time he liked to go to bed at night. Still, the team had to be on their A game. Azizi was the prime suspect in Ethan's murder, and if he was holding Ethan, Luke needed the man's cooperation.

But other than Alessa, the team didn't know Ethan might be alive. He felt Alessa's eyes on him and refused to look in her direction. They'd discussed it last night and she firmly believed they should read the team in on the clues she and Luke were following to find Ethan. She trusted the men, but Luke didn't. He felt in his gut that the leak was coming from the team. It also made logical sense.

"If Boots doesn't contact us again, we need to go to Afghanistan to find him and I don't want us to return without completing this mission," Luke said.

"I say we go in guns blazing," Steele said

through a mouthful of pizza. He finished chewing and leaned forward. "Look, if someone did pick up Boots, they would expect us to sit back and wait, analyze and reanalyze, giving them time to warn off the target or whatever they're planning to do to counteract."

Steele's statement sank in.

"Okay, so what would Colonel McBride tell us to do?" Dimples asked.

"He'd tell us we're a bunch of screwups—in not so nice language—and order us to come home, then blame Luke for everything," Steele said without hesitation.

They all burst out laughing. "Luke is right, we keep moving forward, the un-army way, and hope Boots is okay," Rodgers said.

They made plans for the next day, then each unit member snuck out of the apartment with prep instructions.

Alessa was tasked with analyzing the latest satellite images and she wasted no time in pulling them up on the rugged tablet computer, tucking her legs underneath her on the couch. She was still wearing traditional Pakistani clothing: black harem-like pants and a bright pink *kameez* that came to her knees. They had bought the outfit at a local bazaar and while she bristled at the richly colored fabric, Luke loved the way it brought out the hint of color in her cheeks and lips, and contrasted with her pale golden skin and dark hair. He had his own homework to do for the mission, but he couldn't pull his eyes away from the long lashes shadowing her cheeks in the glow of the computer screen.

As if sensing his gaze on her, she glanced up and met his eyes. He looked away and busied himself with the reports he was supposed to be reading, trying to focus on the mission. Now that the team was on board, he was responsible for making sure he hadn't led them astray. Luke should have felt a sense of relief that everyone agreed about moving forward but all he felt was fear. What if he was wrong? He hadn't exactly made stellar decisions so far. If he hadn't insisted on having Alessa by his side, he would've been with Boots. He couldn't deny that his feelings for her had affected his decision. But what had he been thinking? The army was the only thing Alessa had; he couldn't jeopardize that by exploring his feelings for her. Relationships between officers and enlisted weren't tolerated. The reprisals were worse when the individuals were in the same chain of command. Even the hint of something with Luke would ruin Alessa's career and get them both court-martialed. For what? He couldn't make any promises to her. He didn't even know what his future held next month. Would he continue commanding the unit? If the command was taken away from him, what would he do? Leave the army? And then what? Could he just turn the unit over to Ethan and walk away?

It had been easy to fall for Nazneen. She was unavailable. He knew that going in. No promises needed to be made. But that wasn't the case with Alessa. Even if he left the military, could he really be with her? Was he ready to be a family man? Live the life of an army spouse the way his mother had? Just the thought of waiting at home wondering if Alessa was safe made him shudder.

His phone vibrated against his hip and he was thankful for something other than Alessa to focus on. Adrenaline shot through his fuzzy brain when he saw the text.

Your brother is alive. StinkySocks.

It wasn't exactly news to him, but he felt reassured by the fact that Boots had sent the message. It meant Boots was okay and someone else had confirmation that his brother was indeed alive.

Where are you? How do you know?

A quick response pinged on his phone. Our target is holding him.

How do you know?

He wanted to make sure Boots wasn't the leak and that Luke wasn't being set up to walk into a trap.

Maddeningly, there was no response. The fact that Boots was communicating with him was a good sign. That his text messages were intermittent could mean that he was in a rural area—or that he was playing with Luke. All signs pointed to the latter. Boots had enough of a signal to send one quick string of messages. But he could have drafted a longer communication when he was offline and sent it to Luke when he had a connection. His gut told him Boots was loyal, that he was working to figure out what had happened to the team, but things weren't adding up. Why had he ditched Rodgers? And why wouldn't he send Luke a full report?

Once again he thought about what Ethan would do and the answer became clearer. He needed to treat Boots as potentially compromised. He wouldn't ignore Boots's intelligence but he would move with extreme caution.

It was well past midnight when he checked in with Dan, who had been surveilling the target.

"What's the update on Azizi?"

"He's at home watching TV, like clockwork, nothing exciting." It was unusual to find a target with such a predictable schedule, but Azizi was in friendly territory and obviously felt safe. It was human nature to fall into routines.

"Can you do a thermal scan on the house and tell me how many people are in there?"

He waited for Dan to complete the scan.

"Nine right now. One hasn't moved since yesterday—they're in a room in the southwest corner of the house. The rest are mobile."

Luke smiled. His brother had picked good men. They didn't need to be told how to do their jobs.

"How does it compare to the surveillance from the last mission?"

Dan paused. He was most likely checking the old reports. "We are plus one for stationary and plus five for mobile."

Luke clicked off. That scenario was completely consistent with Ethan being held there. Luke and Alessa had visited the site of the previous safe house and, as expected, found a tunnel underneath the depression she'd seen on the satellite images. Ethan was alive and if he was being held at Azizi's house, there was no telling how much longer he might be there. In these situations, even the slightest threat could make their target move Ethan to a new location—or worse. If that happened they might never find him.

"You're thinking we should pick up Azizi tonight, not even wait until tomorrow." Alessa's voice broke through his reverie.

"I think I should check out the situation."

She stood, setting the tablet on the rickety coffee table. "I'll get ready."

He shook his head. "I need to go alone."

The look on her face told him that this would be a battle. He stepped into her personal space and she put her hands on her hips.

"Luke, you need backup. You can't go in alone. Wasn't that the whole point of your switching apartments?"

"No, the point was for you to cover for me when I need to slip out, like I do now. Besides, you know what the doctor said, any strenuous activity and your shoulder could get worse. You could do permanent damage."

She stepped toward him, coming within touching distance. "What's the real reason you don't want me to go with you?"

"Excuse me?"

She took another step, now just inches from him, her chin tilted stubbornly. Her brown eyes blazed and there was a hint of color in the freckles on her nose. His heart drummed so loudly he was sure she could hear it. She placed her hand on his chest, and the contact made it hard to breathe. He put his arm on her good shoulder, mostly to stop her from coming any closer. As it was, he was having a hard time focusing on their discussion.

"Why are you hell-bent on protecting me when I don't need it? Or do you have another secret mission you don't want me to know about?"

She moved her hand from his chest and put a finger to his lips, her eyes as dark as a moonless night. He grabbed her hand. If she kept it there, he'd lose all sense of reason.

"I thought I told you not to touch me without permission." Her voice was soft and teasing but he released her hand and began to step back but she was faster. She grabbed him by the shirt and pulled him to her, then planted her lips on his.

That was when all conscious thought left his mind. All he could do was feel. The softness of her lips against his, the smoothness of her arms as they circled his neck. He felt her strength, the power in the small woman before him. She was a partner who could stand by his side, one he'd fallen hard for. Wrapping an arm around her waist, he pulled her even closer, and a whimper of protest escaped her mouth.

"Oh, God, did I hurt you?" he breathed, his voice thick.

She shook her head. "You just caught me by surprise."

She's lying. He could tell by the way she shifted her shoulder. He closed his eyes and stepped back from her. What was he doing rough-handling her again? And kissing her? *I could, and probably should, be court-martialed for this.*

"I'm sorry…" he muttered, opening his eyes to find her staring unblinkingly at him.

"What for? I kissed you."

Right. So she did. But I'm her commander.

"I shouldn't have let it happen."

"I felt like we needed to get it out of the way," she said matter-of-factly, her face maddeningly neutral save for the tinge of pink on her cheeks, neck and ears and the rapid rise and fall of her chest.

"I didn't realize it was on our to do list."

"Neither one of us can deny the attraction between us, and that's why you're behaving so erratically, wanting me close to you, then pushing me away. We can't go on like this."

She was right. There was too much at stake and he was having a hard enough time figuring out what to do to deal with the added distraction of his feelings for Alessa.

He held up his hands in a conciliatory gesture. "What do you propose we do?"

"I propose we admit that that was the most incredible kiss of our lives and we owe it to ourselves to see if it happens again."

She's serious! He was not going to ignore an invitation like that.

ALESSA HAD NEVER been so brazen with a man. At least not in a romantic way. She'd punched, kicked and dropped many men to the ground, but never had she demanded a kiss. In fact, she and Aidan had only kissed once. An awkward, fumbling moment reminiscent of a high school first date. Never had she experienced such soul-burning intensity. A feeling she'd never truly experienced. Love. It was intoxicating, and she wanted more. She was done with rational thinking. A fire burned through her, screaming at her to grab hold of this feeling while she could.

Luke closed the distance between them and cupped her face. His mouth met hers with the lightness of a feather. He was still asking permission, making sure it was what she wanted, and she responded by wrapping her arms around his neck, hardly noticing the protest of her shoulder. She weaved her fingers into his hair, letting the soft strands caress her fingers. Pressing closer to him, she deepened the kiss and the fire that burned inside her intensified. Apparently Luke felt the same way because she couldn't tell whether she broke the contact or he did. She had hoped that the second kiss would be like a wet cloth to cool her soul, but it had only stoked the flames.

"We can't," he said. "It's not that I don't want to…"

"But now is not the time," she agreed. "Let's get through this mission, then we'll figure out what we have and what to do."

They both nodded in unison. She didn't want to emerge from the warm cocoon she was in, savoring the lingering feel of his five o'clock shadow on her cheeks. But she had to. Once this mission was over and they found Ethan, Luke wouldn't be unit commander any more. He could leave the army and they could be together without any risk. It was just a matter of time. She'd waited thirty-five years for something resembling love; she could wait a little longer for the real thing.

'Luke, trust me to tell you what I'm up for. I'm strong. I can handle a little injury."

"I'm sorry, Alessa, but you can't come."

CHAPTER NINETEEN

IT HADN'T TAKEN long to organize all of the pieces. The team knew what they were doing and the stakes were high. As far as the unit was concerned, Ethan had died for this mission and they were going to complete it.

"I feel like Parrino should be here, being a pain in all our behinds." Rodgers said into the comms system. Dan and Dimples muttered their agreement and Luke's chest warmed. He was like a teenage boy; even the mention of Alessa made his heart flutter.

"You know I couldn't risk it with her shoulder." There were sounds of agreement. In truth, it had been a hard sell to get Alessa to stay behind, but she'd finally agreed. His concern for Alessa's shoulder was real; he didn't want to risk exacerbating her fracture. More importantly, there was a good chance the team was walking into an ambush. She'd fought him, but he'd convinced her that he needed someone to mount a rescue if anything went down. She was the designated survivor. Last night, they'd come to this house and surveilled it. Luke hadn't gleaned any new information but hoped that the stationary person they were seeing in the southwest room was Ethan. It was the only room that didn't have any windows. If Luke were keeping someone prisoner, he'd put them in that room.

His phone pinged. It was Boots.

I am in the tree eighty degrees clockwise from you. I see all of you. StinkySocks.

It took all of Luke's self-discipline not to whirl around and to continue to do a visual sweep as he would have if Boots hadn't called attention to himself. Even though he was staring right at him, it took Luke a second to spot Boots. He was well hidden.

Think Ethan is the stationary in there.

Adrenaline was already coursing through him but the news electrified every sense in his body. Could he trust Boots? Luke had a lot of questions for him but his gut told him to trust Boots for the moment.

Why are you hiding from the team?

The answer was instant and Luke went cold.

I think we have a leak.

Who?

He knew it was a fruitless question even as
he asked it.

There was a pause, then his phone buzzed.

The only thing I know for sure is that it's not me,
and it's not you.

The only thing *Luke* knew for sure was that it
wasn't him and it wasn't Alessa. While he had
every reason to mistrust his team, he couldn't
believe it was any of those guys, either. Including Boots. There had to be another explanation.

"Five more tangos than we had yesterday."
Rodgers's voice crackled in his ear.

This was not a rescue mission for Ethan but
a snatch-and-grab of the target. If someone shot
at them, they would shoot back. Had they been
compromised? The surge in guards was not a
good sign. Should he order a retreat? Ethan had
walked into the safe house alone. Luke was taking his entire team in. He was doubly glad he'd
forced Alessa to stay behind.

"Looks like we may need to shoot through the

house. Collateral damage is likely." Rodgers came through again. He was supposed to lead them inside.

The team needed to know that Ethan was in there. His instincts had gotten him this far.

"I have intel that the stationary person inside is Ethan." He had toggled the comms so the entire team could hear. There was a beat, then everyone began talking at once.

"No time to explain, just be careful who you shoot." He was about to tell them about Boots but something held him back.

"Okay, let's go." Rodgers got into position to kick down the door. Luke would bring up the rear.

"Guys, don't go into the house." Alessa's voice screamed into the comms.

"Stand down." Luke ordered. "Petaldust, where are you?" he said, using Parrino's code word. She must be nearby, because the comms system had a limited range, but she was supposed to be well, well outside that range.

"To your ten o'clock, Leopard," came her reply. He spotted her and strode over. She was hiding behind a giant banyan tree, its branches elegantly reaching out under dark green leaves.

"You're supposed to be in the apartment." They had talked about this half the night. *Why is she so stubborn?*

"Look." She pulled up her tablet and showed him a satellite map of the house, zooming in on a fuzzy corner of the house that was hidden under tree branches and leaves. "These are pictures from late last night, after we did our surveillance."

"What am I looking at?"

She zoomed in some more. "Look more carefully now." That's when he saw it.

"Something was moved into the house yesterday."

She nodded. "We'd need an expert to tell us what it is. My skills aren't that good."

"This is no reason to stop us going in. It could be anything— groceries, alcohol…"

"Yes, but look at pictures from about an hour before you got here."

His blood ran cold. It was a clear image of the target getting into a car and new men entering the house. According to the meticulously consistent schedule Azizi kept, he shouldn't even be awake.

"This is a setup."

Alessa nodded. He looked back at the house, then slammed his fist into the tree trunk in frustration. His instincts had been wrong. He'd been about to get his entire team killed.

"You couldn't have known."

Then he remembered. He spun toward the tree Boots had been hanging out in. He was gone.

"How long have you known Ethan is alive?" Steele glared at Luke. They were back at Luke and Alessa's apartment, squeezed into the tiny living room. Luke was in the hot seat on the couch. No one had taken the spot next to him, despite the prime sitting real estate. Most of the team were standing. Alessa was the only one seated on one of the chairs from the dinette, her hands flying over satellite images.

"I *don't* know if Ethan is alive. It's a theory," Luke answered wearily. They'd gone over the mission and the team disagreed as to whether they should have gone in. Luke shared the evidence he'd given Alessa. It was time to come clean with the team.

"Why did Parrino get to decide that we abort?" Dimples asked quietly. Luke saw Alessa sit up straighter.

"She didn't. I did. I made a field call based on her intel. It gave me enough cause to abort."

"For what it's worth, I think he made the right decision," Alessa chimed in.

"You would," Rodgers muttered under his breath.

"Okay, look, we need to focus on our next

step. After what happened to Ethan, it's good to be cautious. I don't want us compromised," Luke said firmly. He needed to pull the team together and channel their energy toward a shared goal.

"We need new intel before we take a next step. Parrino, I want you to keep on those satellite images. Rodgers and Dimples, I want you to pound the pavement, go around to known associates and see if you can spot the target." He barked out orders to the rest of the team and dismissed them. Some of it was busywork until better intelligence came around, but these were army men; they needed to keep working, especially since they were all hyped up on mission adrenaline.

The team snuck out of the apartment but Rodgers hung back. "Any word from Boots?" Luke and Alessa shared a glance. Alessa knew about Boots's contact. Luke shook his head; he wasn't ready to tell Rodgers about Boots. Not yet.

When Rodgers had left, Luke let out a long breath.

"For what it's worth, you made the right call." Alessa said softly.

"Which call? The one to walk into an ambush or the one to let you stop it?"

"Both, technically. The call to go in was

made based on the best intelligence you had and the call to stop it was the same."

"That's nice of you to say." He rubbed the back of his neck and she sat down beside him.

He lifted her hand and kissed it. *How does she make it feel all okay?* She put her head on his shoulder. He slipped his arm around her and the two of them sat there just enjoying the warmth and comfort of each other.

"I'm going to need your help," he said.

"Whatever you need."

"You set up everyone's phones and emails. I need you to go over all the text messages, phone calls and emails they've sent over the last month. If any of the operational details for this mission have been compromised, it would have happened in that time frame."

She took a sharp breath. As team lead, he had every right to review those communications. But it still felt like a breach of trust.

"I really don't think any one of them is betraying us."

"After today, I'm almost positive the leak is coming from the team. It can be nothing else. Azizi hasn't changed his schedule in months and then suddenly…"

"If the guys find out I'm spying on them…"

"Then I'll tell them I ordered you to do it."

She bit her lip. "There's something I have to tell you," she said softly.

He frowned. A couple of days ago, he'd sensed something was going on with Alessa but she'd hadn't said anything so he'd let it go.

She took a breath, then began telling him about Julia's disappearance and how Rodgers had helped. He clenched his fists. Why had she kept such a thing from him? Just when she needed him, she'd turned to Rodgers. His chest burned. He would've left and gone to California to help her, turned the entire state upside-down to find her sister. Yet she hadn't trusted him enough to tell him about it.

He wanted to tell her all of these things and ask her why she hadn't told him. Instead, he stood and went to the kitchen and took out a bottle of water from the refrigerator. He took a big swig, hoping the cold water would calm the fire inside him, then turned to Alessa.

"Look over those emails, and this time I'm ordering you to tell me what you find. Do not to lie to me. Think you can do that?" His tone was much harsher than he intended and he could tell by the look on Alessa's face that he'd just broken her heart.

CHAPTER TWENTY

"I CAME TO tell you that I'm on your side." Luke was back at the target's house on surveillance duty trying to see if there was anything that would give him a clue as to Azizi's whereabouts. He turned to find Boots beside him.

Luke put a hand on the soldier's shoulder to make sure he wasn't just imagining him. The sun had begun to set, illuminating the dust in the air. Boots looked around before speaking. There was enough ambient noise between honking horns, sputtering car engines and random merchants that there was little chance of anyone overhearing them in the street.

"Listen, I know you don't trust me, but I'm asking you to give me a day to show you what I've been working on. Don't make any decisions until then."

"That won't work for me, Boots. If you're on my side, you need to read me in or you're off the unit." Luke had never taken such a hard line with one of his men, but he was dead serious this time. Boots raised a brow, probably just as surprised as Luke was.

The soldier blew out a breath. "The last time we were here, Ethan shared with me that he suspects someone from the unit is leaking information. Even before the safe house was blown up, we had tried to get to the target twice and each time he eluded us, as if he knew we were coming. You see how regimented this guy is—how come he disrupts his routine at the exact time we try to snatch him?"

That fact had been bothering Luke, too, which was why he'd asked Alessa to look into the team's phone calls, texts and emails. There was no way anyone outside the unit would have known their operational details. Decisions were made on a daily basis and other than Luke, no one was allowed to communicate with the Pentagon. He knew he hadn't talked with anyone in Washington; it was time to find out who had.

Boots kicked at some pebbles on the sidewalk. "Ethan asked me to keep an eye on the other guys."

Luke tried not to smile. Maybe he and Ethan weren't as different as he thought. That had been his first priority, to find a spy within.

"So what have you figured out?"

"I ditched Rodgers in Afghanistan and made it here before everyone else. I've been watching the target. I managed to plant a bug on his driver. They don't sweep the driver like they do Azizi."

Luke raised a brow. It was a great idea, one he had considered but then dismissed because it was unlikely to yield useful information.

"The driver was in range when the target was talking on the phone. He said, 'Don't worry, your boy Ethan is safe, I keep him close to me.'"

Luke's blood ran cold. While it was great to hear that Ethan was alive, that he was being held like that meant that they planned to use him as collateral for something. He needed to get to his brother.

"I followed Azizi and I'm near certain I saw Ethan in the house where we almost got ambushed. That's why I sent you the text." A tide of relief washed over Luke. He wasn't crazy; Ethan really was alive. But unease also tugged at him.

Boots kicked at another pebble. "There's one more thing." He swallowed. "I saw Alessa and Rodgers together a couple of days ago. They looked close. Be careful what you tell her—I think she's on his side."

Luke's chest burned. He wasn't a jealous man by nature, but he hadn't stopped wondering why Alessa had waited so long to tell him about Julia being missing and Rodgers's involvement. Luke thought they finally had trust and rapport between them, yet she'd kept something important to her from him. It wasn't the first time a woman had chosen another man over him, so why was his heart in such a twist? Had he finally let himself dream of a having a family? He knew there was nothing romantic between Alessa and Rodgers—she herself described him as a brother—but Rodgers had something Luke didn't: Alessa's faith and trust.

"You need to come back into the team."

Boots frowned. "But…"

"You can just say that it took you a while to get across the border. The rest of this stays between us. I need you to keep an eye on everyone from the inside. Including Parrino. I'll start compartmentalizing information."

An hour later his phone buzzed. It was Alessa calling. He didn't pick up but responded with a text.

Boots is back with the team.

Good. Keep an eye on him.

Right now, Luke didn't know who he could trust.

THE SATELLITE IMAGES floated in front of her eyes. Luke's face when she told him about what happened with Julia kept blocking them out. He'd been hurt that she had turned to Rodgers instead of him, but what choice did she have?

Once again, she wondered whether she should have allowed herself to get close to Luke. After what had gone down with Aidan, any leaks of what had happened between her and Luke would be devastating. He wasn't worth the risk. Was he?

She thought about their kiss and the moment he'd admitted that he wanted to be with her. He made her feel something she'd never felt in her entire life. Safe. Loved. That moment was the first time she'd understood what love was. Her mother claimed to love her father, but Alessa knew that was just fear. While Aidan had never proclaimed love, he had intimated that he cared for her deeply. At the time, the words had meant something to her, but when she'd found how he'd been using her, her affection had turned to anger. With Luke it was a whole new level. It wasn't just the way he said the words, or the look in his eyes when he said them. When he touched her hand, she felt connected to him at a cellular level.

But something had changed between them. She'd seen it in his eyes when she told him about Julia. She shook her head to bring things into focus. She was looking at images taken earlier this morning at various houses Azizi had been known to frequent to see if she could detect activity in any of them. Her pulse kicked up a notch as she zoomed in on a particular picture. She stared at it for several minutes to make sure she wasn't seeing things. *Yep, that's Azizi.* The time stamp was from six hours ago, which meant there was a good chance he was still there.

She called Luke, who was surveilling the house they'd almost broken into yesterday.

"Stay at the apartment, I'll mobilize the guys and we'll gear up."

"I'm ready to go and your bag is ready, too." She had been packing as she talked to him. They couldn't exactly roam the streets with guns and bombs in their arms so everyone would have to come back to the safe house to gear up for an assault. "I'll go ahead and do recon on the location. It hasn't been on our list. I'll have info for you when you get there."

"Alessa, I don't want you going alone."

"I can handle it," she said dismissively and hung up. She wasn't going to waste precious time arguing with him and risk losing Azizi. The sooner they wrapped up this mission, the faster she and Luke could uncomplicate their relationship.

She took a rickshaw to the house in the satellite picture. On the way, she thought about what it would mean if they found Azizi and Ethan in that house. The mission would be over, Ethan would regain command of the unit and Luke would leave the army. The two of them could finally be together.

She asked the rickshaw driver to drop her off a block from the house. It was on a busy road but had a long driveway that led to a secluded area covered by brush and trees. The house was surrounded by a five-foot-tall concrete wall and there were houses on either side. The only way in was through the front door. There was no guard at the gate and when she walked up to it, she opened it easily.

She had a cover story in case someone questioned her. Her backpack held some gear, but she was dressed in a *salwar kameez*. Sometimes the best option was the most direct one. She got all the way to the front door before encountering a guard. He yelled at her and she stopped, then in halting Urdu said, "I'm coming to ask if they have a job. For a maid."

The guy shook his head but she kept insisting and begging, repeating the same phrases. "Please, I am very good. I need money to feed my children. Let me talk to the woman of the house."

Alessa wanted to make a fuss to draw out

the other guards, but only the one guy remained. He eventually got frustrated with her and came close, grabbing her by the elbow to escort her off the property. She whirled and delivered a blow to his head, knocking him unconscious. Then she made her way to the front door, keeping an eye out for any other guards. Seeing none, she knocked, but there was no answer. The door was locked. It was a heavy wood door; she wasn't going to be able to kick it open, so she opted for a walk around the periphery.

The house seemed deserted. Then she heard it, a footfall behind her. She turned to find a man pointing a gun at her.

CHAPTER TWENTY-ONE

LUKE'S PHONE BUZZED and he wanted to ignore it. Maybe even throw it into oncoming traffic. The only thing he could think about was finding Alessa. They'd arrived at the new house to find one guard lying unconscious by the front door and Alessa's backpack on the ground. Tire treads and fresh footprints indicated that a bunch of people had driven away in a hurry. The team had spread out to find her, and Luke had decided to stay close to the house in case she was nearby.

He fished out the phone to see that an unknown number was calling him. He frowned. The only people who had this number were his teammates. He had a separate phone to call and communicate with Washington. A phone that was well hidden inside the seams of the mattress in the safe house with the SIM card in Luke's pocket. One advantage of the unit was that he chose when to call the Pentagon. They couldn't reach him for status updates. That was

Ethan's design, to let the unit operate without influence or interference.

He hit the answer button, needing to know who had managed to breach unit security.

The voice that greeted him on the other made him stop dead. "Luke, m'boy."

"Dad?"

"I'm callin' to see how you're getting along."

His father was originally from Georgia and had never lost his Southern twang.

"How did you get this number?"

"Oh, you know, I got my ways."

"No, really, Dad. This is a matter of operational security. How did you get this number?"

"I'm a four-star in the army, son. Now, assuming you're in the thick of things and don't have time to grill your dad, how 'bout I get to the point."

Luke resumed walking, eyes peeled for Alessa. His dad was infamous for charmingly dodging questions. It was part of the reason he'd risen through the army ranks so well. The brass knew they could put him in front of a congressional committee and his father would give away nothing, yet leave the inquirers smiling at the end.

"Now, I realize I'm not supposed to know what your mission is, but y'know, I helped Ethan start the unit. If you're thinkin' like your brother, I got a pretty good guess where you're at. I have a lead I'm running down at the Pentagon and I need you to tell me if you got your target."

Luke sighed. The package he'd sent his father wasn't supposed to be delivered for another week. That meant his father had figured it out on his own. He wasn't surprised that he'd put two and two together, but that meant others would, too. The intelligence agencies weren't officially aware of the unit, but stuff like this didn't need official channels to become well-known.

"No, Dad, we haven't, but we're close."

Or so he hoped. He was running out of time. Every minute the unit stayed in the country, their lives were even more in jeopardy.

Where are you, Alessa?

The thought of her possibly being kidnapped gripped his heart so tightly that he could barely breathe. He missed what his father said next.

"Sorry Dad, I lost you for a second. What did you say?"

"I said you be careful, m'boy. More than a few people know where you are now. I lost one son to this mission—I don't want to lose another. I suggest you give up on this and come on home."

His father disconnected and Luke stared at

the phone in his hands. It was no secret that Ethan was the golden child where his father was concerned. Ethan had dragged Luke kicking and screaming to West Point. Ethan had progressed up the army career ladder the way their father wanted. Ethan was the one who spent evenings drinking whiskey and discussing army matters with their dad when they were both in town. Luke, on the other hand, had never connected with his father. The general always joked that he'd been too much of a mama's boy. Maybe that was true. Luke had felt his mother's pain in a way Ethan never seemed to.

He passed by a park and stopped, then turned back. If she wanted to hide, the park would be a good location. As he scanned for Alessa, a boy with ragged, dirty clothes came up to him and tapped his arm. He looked down at the boy and reached into his pocket for some bills. It was a bad idea to hand out money in situations like this and especially notes rather than coins because it didn't take long to get swarmed by a dozen kids. But something in the boy's eyes tugged at Luke's heart.

The boy took the notes than tapped Luke again and motioned for him to follow. Luke frowned but decided to trail the boy anyway. The boy turned a corner and Luke's heart leapt into his throat. Alessa was sitting at the bottom of a tree, holding a brown scarf to her head which was obviously bleeding. He raced over to her and nearly collapsed with relief when she looked up at him with clear eyes.

"Luke!"

She sat up a little straighter. "Ow." She rubbed her head.

"What happened?" he asked.

"Back at the house, a guard held a gun to me and forced me into a car. When we got out onto the road, I got the better of him and rolled out while the car was moving. I hit my head on the sidewalk." She pointed to a corner a few feet away. "Right around there. I was a little dizzy so thought it best to come and rest."

"What were you thinking coming to the house on your own? You could've been hurt or killed."

She blinked at him, her eyes wide. "I wanted so badly to find Azizi and to confirm Ethan is alive. One way or another, we need to finish this mission." He already knew Ethan was alive from what Boots had said. He was so close to telling her. Then she added, "So we can be together. I want us to be together…"

The words were whispered with such softness, her face so open and inviting that his heart went wild. All thought left his brain as he bent his head and brought his lips down on hers. She put her good arm around his neck and she tilted her head upward, giving him full access to her lips. Everything he had tried to push away came crashing down on him; the kick-ass way she'd caught his attention, the strength and character that made her fight for herself. Alessa was the woman he'd been looking for all his life, and she was his. In this moment, in the here and now, she was his. She'd be his equal in every sense of the word. She'd be able to handle everything life threw her way. But was he going to be able to deal with what she wanted from life?

She was the one to break the kiss. Eyes shimmering, her lips were slightly swollen and a rosy pink tinged her cheeks. He placed a light kiss on her forehead.

A small tear escaped from her long lashes. He kissed it, letting the salty drop wet his lips.

"Thank you for that. I need your love." Her lips trembled and her voice was so hoarse, it cracked.

The depth of pain in her tone squeezed his heart so hard, he thought it would shatter into a million pieces.

"I love you more than anything in this world, Alessa." He meant every word, and he knew he could count on her.

Another tear rolled down her cheek, her eyes telling him that she believed what he said and felt it right back. She leaned forward and he didn't hesitate to kiss her again. More gently this time, letting her feel the love in his heart.

"Can we work things out?" she whispered. This time her eyes were so full of sadness that a sharp pain cut through his chest. He wanted nothing more than to spend the rest of his life making her happy. He could be an army husband, couldn't he? For her?

"After this mission, I'll resign from the army."

She smiled. "Are you sure you want to give up the unit?" Her tone was teasing but Luke paused. Was he? Luke had never enjoyed being in the army. Until now. The unit felt like the right fit. But it didn't belong to him. And the only thing he knew for sure was that he loved Alessa. Her eyes widened slightly, the panic so clear that he shook his head vehemently.

"I was going to leave the army before Ethan died. I want to spend my life doing something more meaningful. I was thinking of working with an NGO."

"You want to save the world." His father had said the same words to him, but there was no sarcasm in her voice, just awe and hope.

He smiled. "Something like that. I want to

wake up in the morning and know that I've done something to better the world."

"You know we're saving lives in the army, too."

He knew what she meant, but he didn't agree. Having served in Iraq and Afghanistan, he wasn't convinced that he was doing any good. But this was not the time to get into a philosophical argument about US defense policy. This was a moment they'd remember for the rest of their lives, the time when they'd discovered true love.

The sound of laughter pulled their attention to the homeless kid who began dancing and blowing them kisses. He'd been standing there watching the entire time and Luke realized just how exposed they were, sitting in the park like that. They were in a relatively secluded area surrounded by tall trees. There weren't any other people around. It was early afternoon, a time when almost everyone was at work. Yet Luke should have been more careful, a little more aware. The second he'd seen Alessa, all other thoughts became secondary. He hadn't done a proper sweep of the area.

He stood and held out his hand for her. She took it and stumbled slightly.

"You okay?"

She nodded. "Just a little dizzy from the

bump. I guess I'm not completely back to normal." She adjusted the scarf so it covered her head.

"Let's get you to the doctor and have you checked out."

She shook her head. "I'm okay."

Luke didn't like it but he knew better than to argue with her now. He'd watch her carefully. They began walking and Luke noticed the homeless kid following them. He turned and pulled out a packet of stapled notes. The little boy's eyes became saucers. Luke held out the notes but the boy stood frozen. It was probably more money than he'd ever seen in his life. From the country briefings, he knew that gangs of adults ran little kids as beggars as a moneymaking racket. There was strict protocol not to give out money, which could encourage further exploitation of kids and pose a security risk. But Luke was pretty sure the kid had pulled Alessa away from the road where she'd tripped, and there was always the small hope that he would take the money and use it to run away, start a new life.

Alessa put a hand on the boy's shoulder and nodded. He held up a hand in a "wait" gesture, then took off at a run. Luke and Alessa looked at each other in confusion. Luke put the money away. They watched as the boy went to an overflowing garbage can and rummaged through it before racing back holding a filthy plastic bag. When he saw Luke's empty hands, his face fell. Luke brought out the stack of notes again. This time, the boy snatched the notes from Luke, put the wad to his nose, thumbed through the stack, then put it in the plastic bag. He grinned at Alessa and Luke, then darted away.

Shaking his head, Luke offered Alessa his arm and she took it. They made their way to the street and hailed a rickshaw.

"You think we were compromised again?" Alessa asked when they dismounted a few blocks from the apartment.

He nodded. "It's highly suspicious that they reacted so violently to you. The house isn't that secluded—I'm sure people walk up to the front door to sell stuff all the time. The fact that the guy pulled a gun on you right away makes me wonder whether Azizi was in the process of escaping when you showed up. It has to be one of our guys. You find anything in the phones or emails?"

She shook her head, her face neutral. He frowned. "Alessa, if you found something, don't protect the team. If anything, today should be proof enough that one of them is the leak."

She sighed. "Okay, there's one thing I need to check out. I'll let you know if it's real."

He raised his brows. "Alessa."

"Just give me until tonight," she insisted. "I'll look into it when I'm on surveillance."

Luke shook his head. "No surveillance shift for you tonight. I want you safe and recovering. You need to rest."

"You'd better be kidding."

He winced at the determination in her voice. This was not going to be easy.

"Alessa, I need to know you're okay. How am I supposed to focus on the mission if I'm worrying about you?"

She took a sharp breath. "You have to get used to it, Luke. I'm a soldier on a mission. I'll get dinged up. Yeah, my shoulder's fractured, but I haven't been through any worse than the other guys. If you can get out combat with just a few bumps and bruises, that's a good outcome. You know this." She took a breath, then softened her tone. "Even after you quit the army, I'll still be inside. This is what our life will be like. You won't be around to force me to rest or stay off a mission. I can't have you strong-arming me anymore. You have to let me take care of myself."

A deep ache settled into his chest. She was going to stay in the army, and he'd be home wondering whether she'd return. Just like his mother had all her life.

CHAPTER TWENTY-TWO

THEY ENTERED THE APARTMENT, and suddenly it seemed a little too small for the both of them. Apparently, Luke felt it, too. They didn't know how to move around without bumping into each other. They had both decided to put their relationship on hold until the mission was completed.

Luke got a call. He'd already let the rest of the team know he'd found Alessa and instructed them to go back to their scheduled surveillance assignments. "I'm on my way," he said.

"Rodgers needs me to check something out," he told Alessa. "Stay here until I get back."

"Yes, *sir*." He walked out and she sank into the hard loveseat, closing her eyes. Luke's expression when they'd talked about him leaving the army came back to her. He'd said the right words but there was clear doubt in his eyes. Did she really have a chance at a normal life? A house where she wouldn't be afraid all the time. Where her life wouldn't be filled with uncertainty. *Is Daddy going to be in a bad mood when he comes home? Are those foot-steps outside my room Mommy's or Daddy's? Are we staying home from school today because Mommy is in the hospital?*

The army structure, the certainty of the day's routine, had been so comforting. What if she couldn't have both Luke and the army? She touched her lips, still full from when he'd kissed her. *It's worth it, for him.* Things would be different once the mission ended. Wouldn't they? It was hard now, with Luke as her commanding officer. He wouldn't be ordering her around when she wasn't reporting to him. Right? Or was she weaving herself a fairy tale again, like she had with Aidan? The way her mother had all her life?

She cleaned herself up and changed into fresh clothes, glad she had bought a couple of additional local outfits. Touching the pink outfit, she appreciated the softness of the cloth. She'd never been much of a girly-girl, choosing jeans and hoodies over dresses or skirts; that's why she loved the army uniform. It was an equalizer. She was not the outcast because of her thrift store clothing.

Alessa had assumed that Luke would quit after this mission like he'd been planning, but that look in his eyes when she'd asked about him leaving the army was troubling her. She'd believed him when he said he was willing to become a civilian for her, but what if he wanted to stay? Was it fair for her to ask him to leave? Was she willing to do the same for him? The answer to that question frightened her.

As tired as she had been this morning, she was wide-awake now. Pacing the apartment, she tried to figure out how she could be helpful. They needed to rescue Ethan and finish the mission. Only then could things be settled between her and Luke and she could finally have some peace with what was happening between them.

A knock on the door startled her. She picked up her scarf and wrapped it around her head in case it was a neighbor. She looked through the peephole and sighed. Opening the door, she tried to paste an easy smile on her face.

"Did Luke send you to check on me?"

Boots grinned. "Of course he did. You're the loose cannon of the team." The amusement in his voice made Alessa smile.

He entered and she motioned for him to grab a seat. "Want something to drink?"

"I think I'm supposed to be making you tea."

Alessa plopped herself on the couch. "By all means, then—a cup of tea sounds great."

Boots began boiling water in a pan. That was how tea was made in Pakistan. They had watched a YouTube video in case a neighbor showed up and they actually had to be social.

"So how's it going?" She stood in the doorway kitchen so they wouldn't have to talk too loudly.

"Well, we're throwing darts until we hit the target. We just need a break."

Boots added loose tea to the boiling water plus milk and sugar.

They chatted about the details for a few minutes. Boots poured the liquid into cups, using a strainer to catch the loose tea. "We haven't been here long, but I'm seriously craving a real cup of coffee." Instant coffee was everywhere here, and the unit members had found it preferable to switch to tea than drink the freeze-dried stuff.

Alessa smiled. "We were worried about you. What happened?"

"Luke didn't tell you?"

Alessa shook her head, feeling awful for lying to him, but she figured that Luke had sent Boots to her for a reason. For her to gather intelligence. To do the job he'd hired her to do. She realized with a start that he'd found a way to make her feel useful while still protecting her.

"I got separated from Rodgers and made my way across."

It was the story he'd told the rest of the team, so she tried another tack.

"Just as well you didn't have to suffer traveling with Luke. I don't know how he got command of this unit."

That got Boots. He smiled. "I like the guy, but he's not Ethan."

"Yeah? I love the unit, but I'm not sure I can deal with Luke." Her stomach churned as she said the words but she kept her tone light.

"Give him a chance. I felt the same way, but I'm coming around."

"How so?"

"Don't get me wrong—I don't agree with all the decisions he's made, but he's got good instincts and I'm not sure Ethan would have done it better."

Alessa's heart swelled. She too had noticed that Luke seemed to be a natural at taking command. Which brought up another issue for her. Did she want to be with a man who was used to being in charge?

"I'm not so sure. Maybe he got lucky. He seems to be convinced Ethan is still alive." She let that hang in the air.

"Ethan is alive."

She scoffed. "Based on what? Luke's gut?"

"I saw him with my own eyes."

"What? When? How?" Alessa's surprise was genuine. Luke hadn't told her about this.

Boots seemed to realize that he might have said too much. He took a sip of his tea. "When I was waiting for the unit to get here. I didn't just want to show up at the safe house without making sure everything was okay, so I surveilled the target and saw Ethan."

"Does Luke know this?" Her stomach churned. While she was a natural at it, she hated lying. It was yet another thing she enjoyed about army life; all she had to do was follow the rules and she never had to lie about who she was or what she was doing. Until Aidan. It seemed her and Luke's relationship was also full of half-truths. Was that what their permanent relationship would be like? If there was a relationship beyond this mission. If their feelings survived whatever it would take to complete this mission.

"Of course Luke knows." Boots's reply refocused her attention. All this time she'd been obsessing over finding out whether Ethan was alive so they wouldn't be on a wild goose chase, and Luke had kept her in the dark?

"You trust him, then? I mean, after what happened to Ethan…" She left the thought hanging in the air.

Boots jumped in. "He wasn't part of the unit when we got ambushed the last time, and neither were you. The three of us are the only people I trust."

Alessa widened her eyes and raised her brows. "You think there are traitors in the unit?" Boots shifted on his feet. "You do, don't you?" Alessa almost marveled at her own acting skills.

"I've said too much."

"Come on, you said yourself that Luke and I are the only ones who definitely had nothing to do with the last mission. You need someone to talk to." Boots seem to mull this over.

"You can trust me." Alessa said softly.

Boots sighed. "This has to stay between us. You can't even tell Rodgers."

Why was Boots singling out Rodgers? Alessa nodded, even as her stomach twisted.

"I haven't told Luke because, you know…"

"He has to act on anything you tell him. I'll keep this between us. Maybe I can help you bounce around ideas."

Boots seemed to warm to this idea. Alessa motioned for them to go into the living room. Alessa sat on the loveseat and Boots pulled one of the chairs over so he could sit across from her. His large frame dwarfed the seat.

"Okay, the whole point of the unit is to investigate leaks, right? So, no one can know where we are exactly. We made some mistakes with logistics last time. Rodgers admits it—he's beaten himself up over using army assets to find the safe house. But even if someone knew where we were staying, it shouldn't have been that easy to identify the mission and the target. There are at least a dozen possible things we could have been doing at the border. We even talked about doing two different missions and prepped for both. The only way for anyone to have known exactly what we were doing and the exact second we were doing it is if one of the unit members talked."

"I see the logic in that. But who would do that—and why?" She bit her lip. She had thought about the problem quite a bit and had had trouble coming up with a motivation for any of the unit members.

"Dan is up for promotion. He wants to get into Special Forces. Badly."

Alessa knew this. She and Dan had talked about it. "After his work here, he'll more than make it, but if he gets caught being a traitor, he'll be kicked out."

"Unless he's talking to someone who's promised him the promotion."

"Yeah, but Rodgers is also up for promotion and he also tried out for Delta."

"He's also on my list."

"So you've ruled out Dimples?"

Boots shook his head. "He has three kids back home. I hear his wife's having trouble making ends meet. He could be turned with money."

Alessa held up her hands. "You've been keeping an eye on the entire unit. You have to be leaning toward someone."

Again, Boots looked uncomfortable. "I don't have hard evidence."

"But you have a feeling…" She watched his face carefully. "Or you've noticed something unusual that by itself doesn't mean much but when you put it in context with the mission going belly-up, it's something." His face twitched and she knew she had him.

"I've relived that last mission for months. Let me tell you what I saw without telling you who it was, and you tell me if it sounds suspicious."

Alessa leaned forward, and Boots continued. "The last time we were here, before Ethan was killed, I saw one of our teammates talking on a cell that wasn't one of the mission phones."

"He could have had a phone to talk to someone back home, a loved one he needed to check on," Alessa suggested.

"That was my initial thought, but then I saw the same guy poking around Ethan's office— now Luke's—back on post. He didn't think anyone was in the training center, but I had left something in the locker room and had gone back for it. I noticed this on my way out. At that point Luke hadn't taken over unit command so I had no one to report it to aside from Colonel Black Tag, and I didn't want him to fly off the handle."

"Maybe he was doing the same thing you were—retrieving something he left there or looking into what went wrong on the mission."

Boots shrugged. "That's why I haven't said anything. Individually, it's not a big deal. Even together it could be totally innocent."

"What motivation does this team member have?"

"Promotion. You know how it is. Brown-nosing is a good way to move up."

Alessa chewed on that. "That makes sense. Whoever is jeopardizing army operations in Afghanistan found out about the unit and some-how got a unit member to spy for them. When they found out the mission was to expose the very guy, they took Ethan out."

"Except they didn't, which makes this all the more mysterious." Boots countered.

"They kidnapped him hoping for more information, maybe?"

Boots nodded. "And I think whoever the traitor is, he's high up in the army. That's the only way he could influence one of the unit members."

"The only thing I don't get is why one of our unit would betray our country. None of the guys strike me as someone disenchanted or upset," Alessa said.

"Me neither. Maybe they don't think they are betraying us."

A thought struck Alessa. "When you guys went to the house I sent you to, where I got accosted, and saw it was deserted, did anyone react differently? I expect all of you were upset that we missed the target again, but was one of the guys a little off?"

Boots scratched his chin, stood and paced the room. Alessa watched him for several moments, holding the now-cold teacup in her hand.

"Only one. And he was the same one I saw snooping in Ethan's office."

"Who?" Alessa's heart was in her toes. She had a feeling she knew the name even before Boots said it.

"Rodgers."

Then there was a loud banging on the door.

CHAPTER TWENTY-THREE

BOOTS WAS ON his feet in a flash and went to the bedroom. Alessa adjusted her scarf and peered through the peephole.

"It's okay!" she shouted and opened the door to Rodgers, who stood there with bags of food in his hand.

"Luke sent me to take a break so I thought I'd pick up some food for you guys." Rodgers said.

Boots grinned. "Nice! Chinese."

"Before you get too excited, it's something called Manchurian chicken and Hakka noodles." Rodgers said.

Alessa took the containers and opened them. "Close enough to General Tso's and lo mein for me." She tried to keep her voice light but it sounded strained. Rodgers couldn't be the leak. She wanted to ask him, to confirm what he did or did not know. What was she going to tell Luke? And how could she betray Rodgers after he'd helped her with Julia?

They dug into the food, eating right out of the boxes.

"So you okay, or what?" Rodgers said, eying her.

"No more dinged up than you are," Alessa responded.

They all laughed. Rodgers gave them an update on the surveillance. "That guard you knocked out woke up and Luke convinced him to tell us where he was supposed to collect his payment. The rest of the team is checking out that new location. I tell you, that guy can sell underwear to a nudist."

"That's why the ladies love him," said Boots. "I can't even get a date when I'm showing off my six-pack, and all that guy has to do is smile and women swoon. Parrino, how have you resisted his charm?"

Alessa didn't miss the look Rodgers gave her. "Maybe I'm even better at charming than he is," she said easily. Boots laughed but Rodgers's tight smile told her that he didn't believe it for a second. Her own smile disappeared.

They chatted easily while eating but Alessa sensed there was a tension between the two men. Maybe it had to do with Boots ditching Rodgers in Afghanistan. Surely Rodgers was smart enough to figure out Boots's subterfuge.

The guys couldn't leave at the same time. They had each taken great pains to make sure no one saw them and had to leave the same way. Boots left first, after sneaking a camera underneath the door to make sure no one was in the hallway or watching from across the street. This was no easy feat in a busy apartment complex. He had to wait several minutes before making the move.

Alessa and Rodgers sat in uncomfortable silence. They usually had an easy rapport, especially after he had helped her with Julia, but things seemed different now. He cleared his throat. "Parrino, I've been meaning to say something."

Alessa stiffened. His tone and the fact that he wouldn't meet her eyes told her she wasn't going to like what he had to say.

"I'm not judging, and I don't mean to get in your business, but I think you should stay away from Luke."

Her face reddened. "You're right. It is none of your business."

He held up his hands. "I'm not going to say anything to anyone about it. I'm only thinking of your career. I thought we had an understanding stateside."

"Rodgers, you know my career is the only thing I have. I'm not going to jeopardize it. For anything." She meant it and he must have heard the sincerity in her voice because he nodded.

"That's all I needed to hear. Luke is not totally himself around you, and we need him focused on this mission. Especially now."

"What're you trying to say?"

"I'm saying it's obvious he has feelings for you and I worry that his judgment is off when he's around you."

Alessa crossed her arms. "I think he's done a good job as commander, given the circumstances."

"Yeah, but...look, Parrino, it's not just me that sees it. The guys were saying he's different around you."

"So the whole team is talking about me now?" Her mouth soured.

"We're looking out for you. This is going to stay within the unit. I just... Well, the guys wanted me to say something before things got out of hand. At the end of the day, he's the unit commander, we do what he says and there's no scenario where this is a good thing. We're just looking out for you. You know how it is in the army, it's never the commanders who get reprimanded."

Alessa knew discussing this further would just make her madder. The guys were talking about her and Luke and making it seem like she was responsible for anything between them. This was how it had started with Aidan, too. A few people saw them together and that was how the rumors had started. And she'd been the one to suffer the consequences. The guys were right about that: if her relationship with Luke became public, despite his reputation, she'd bear the brunt of the reprisals.

Rodgers began checking the balcony so he could make his exit. Alessa didn't blame him. This was the most awkward conversation they'd ever had. How was she supposed to look any of them in the eyes now?

She stayed up for a little while longer reviewing reports, then gave up waiting for Luke and went to bed in the early morning hours.

She woke to Luke stroking her cheek.

"What are you looking at?" she asked, smiling. It was nice waking up to him.

"I want to see you every morning" he said.

She didn't hesitate. "Me, too. But Luke..." Sitting up, she bit her lip. "Rodgers warned me against getting too close to you."

Luke took a sharp breath. "When?"

"Yesterday."

"We'll be careful. In a few weeks, all this won't matter. I think we're getting close with the target. We have a new location from that guard you took out."

"But what happens when we get back home?" she asked.

"Then we think about how we want to live

our lives," he said easily. "For example, we can decide if we want children."

She froze. "Children? Do you want kids?"

"I'm not sure."

She leaned forward and kissed him on the cheek. "Oh, thank God! Neither am I. I was afraid you were going to say you want a dozen."

"I've never really thought about it seriously, but you know what? I might not mind a brat or two. Maybe a little brown-eyed girl like you?" he said.

She smiled, "Hmm, brown is boring. Maybe a little blue-eyed boy." The thought of having a son who looked like Luke warmed her heart and once again she considered what it might be like to have a family with Luke. To have a home to call her own, a family to love, a safe place to live.

"I guess we'll just have to experiment to find out," he murmured, nuzzling her neck. She savored the feel of his warm breath across her skin.

"Well, don't start making too many plans. If I stay with the unit, I can't exactly take a lot of time off for maternity leave. I may be gone a lot. You sure you want to stay at home changing diapers?"

He stilled, then lifted his head. She turned so she was looking right into his eyes. "It's a hard life for a kid, having a parent away all the time." He swallowed and dropped his eyes. "Would you ever consider leaving the army?" he asked.

Would I? She'd never thought about the prospect of Luke at home with children while she was out in combat. What was the point of having a family if she didn't get to spend time with them? She'd seen other men and women in combat who had young children. Their hearts were always at home. *Do I really want a family enough to give up everything I've worked for?*

"No. The army is the only thing I've ever known that makes sense. Right now, this seems like such a beautiful dream, but it's not real. I can't picture the day-to-day."

Luke took her hand and kissed her palm. Every nerve in her body sent delicious flutters up and down her spine. This had never happened with Aidan. While Aidan had made her feel warm and fuzzy, Luke made her feel... loved. He made her feel safe and secure. Like she could drop her guard and just be free to enjoy the moment.

"How about we take it one day at a time. The only decision we need to make right now is whether we make tea or try the instant coffee."

She smiled at him. "Definitely tea."

"I'll make it. You stay here."

She threw the covers off. "Actually, I think I'm going to get dressed. I feel really good today—I'll come with you."

She swung her legs over the bed and stood.

"Parrino."

His tone made her stop. She turned.

"Oh, come on. You're going to bench me again today?"

"You hit your head on top of a shoulder fracture. Take a day off."

"I would if I were in an office job sitting and typing away at a computer. But we're in theatre. I can't afford to sit on my thumbs." Before he could say anything, she went on. "Besides, I'm not seriously injured—no worse than coming back from a rough patrol. Dimples got hit by a cyclist the other day. Soldiers get roughed up. It's part of the job."

Luke seemed like he was about to protest, then thought better of it. "Fine, but you stick close to me." He stood and pulled her into his arms. Her face flamed at the intense look he gave her.

"I won't have anything happen to you. Just promise me you won't take any unnecessary risks. I've already lost the two women I've ever loved in my life. I can't afford to lose you, too."

Tears stung her eyes at the pain and raw love in his voice.

He bent his head and kissed her. A slow kiss that filled her so completely that it made her want to believe in happily ever after.

He groaned as his phone vibrated in his pocket, startling both of them. It was his burner phone, which he used when he needed to give his number to a local. Frowning, he clicked the answer button and listened for a few minutes.

"Okay, where are you?"

Alessa strained her ears but couldn't hear who was on the other end.

"Stay there. I'm on my way."

He stabbed the end button, then looked at Alessa. "That was Reza."

Luke could have bowled her over with a feather, but once she processed his words, it all made sense. "You gave him your number in case he needed help." It had bothered her that he'd been so quick to abandon Reza and Amine.

"I left it on a slip of paper in his hand."

"Where are they?"

"Not far. Amine's family has found them and he's freaking out. I think it's best I go alone."

Alessa shook her head. She was already moving toward the bathroom. Her clothes were rumpled but clean; all she needed to do was wash her face and pin a scarf over her hair. "I'm coming with you," she yelled over her shoulder.

She came out less than two minutes later, but Luke was already gone.

Standing in the middle of the room, she spun on her heels, as if expecting him to pop out of a corner. She was stunned. How could he just leave her like that without any discussion? Then it hit her. He could do what he wanted; he was the commanding officer, a man who gave orders. And she was the subordinate who was supposed to follow them. How could she expect to have any kind of partnership with him when he was used to bossing her around, ignoring what she had to say?

The answer was she couldn't.

CHAPTER TWENTY-FOUR

LUKE FELT TERRIBLE leaving Alessa behind like that, but he had no idea what he might find with Reza and Amine and he didn't want Alessa to take any more risks than necessary. He knew she had a connection to Amine, so he didn't want to bring her in until he had a better sense of what was going on. He knew he should have talked to her rather than just leaving, but he suspected she would have talked him into bringing her along.

The place was close enough that he walked rather than take the motorcycles the team had purchased to get around town. It was an apartment complex with the same design as the one the team was staying at. He found the number Reza had given him and knocked. A small boy wearing a *salwar kameez* and vest opened the door. Luke blinked, trying to formulate the words to ask for Reza, when the man appeared. Reza shooed the boy away, then extended his hand. Luke went to shake Reza's hand but he pulled Luke into a half hug. Luke smiled.

"I am so glad you came, my friend—I did not know who else to call." Reza's face was etched with worry lines.

"Tell me what's going on. Is Amine okay?"

Reza nodded. "This apartment belongs to a childhood friend. He was here years ago, before the Taliban took over in Afghanistan." He looked around, and noticing the little boy standing in the corner, told him to go make tea. "That's their son. They're not home right now—Amine went with them to buy necessities." Reza lowered his voice. "My friends are good people but they do not want trouble."

"What happened?"

"Some men showed up at the door yesterday. By God's grace Amine and I were in the market helping my friend's wife with the shopping. These men came barging in and searched his house looking for me and Amine, then told my friend to call them if we showed up. I think they threatened him."

"Who were they?"

"The best I can tell from asking around is that they are hired goons. They work for whoever pays them money. It is probably the uncle of Amine's husband. He lives in the area." Reza's expression was pleading. "We need a safe place to stay."

It wasn't that Luke couldn't find a safe house

for them. It didn't have to meet operational standards, just needed to be something Amine's family wouldn't connect them to. But he didn't need yet another complication on this mission. He had to focus on finding Ethan and keeping the team safe.

"I'll see what I can do. In the meantime, stay here. They're probably going to every single relative's house. Since they've already been here, it'll be a day or two before they come around to check again."

"I will try to convince my friend of this. He is too gracious to ask us to leave, but I do not wish to impose on his friendship."

"You have no choice," Luke said dryly. He'd do his best to help Reza but he needed a day to find him a safe house.

The little boy came into the room carrying two steaming glasses of tea. Luke was about to take the cups when the sound of screams broke through the usual city noises. Luke was at the door a second before Reza. The apartment complex was in a familiar U shape with a balcony on each floor facing into a courtyard. A crowd had gathered around a car in the courtyard below, and Luke watched two men stuff a burka-clad woman into the back seat. From her size and shape, Luke was sure it was

Amine. He raced down the stairs with Reza close on his heels.

The car screeched out of the courtyard. Luke had walked over and regretted not bringing his motorcycle. He ran behind the car, which had tinted windows and no license plate, looking for something he could use for transportation. Despite nearly running people over, the car wasn't able to go more than a few miles per hour through the traffic-logged streets, and Luke was able to keep it in sight as he ran. But once they hit the main road, the car picked up speed. The gap between them increased.

"I've got them!" came a shout and Luke turned to see Alessa on a motorcycle whizzing past him in a blur of pink.

A fresh shot of adrenaline propelled him to run faster, but it was no use. Once the car got up to speed, he quickly lost them. Heart racing, he turned to see Reza had kept up. Huffing, the young man leaned over, putting his hands on his hips.

"Did you recognize any of those men?"

Reza shook his head. He coughed out each word. "Never…seen…them."

Think, Luke. Think. He should've known Alessa wouldn't just sit back at the apartment and do nothing, but this was too much. Regardless of their personal relationship, he was still her commanding officer. It wasn't safe for her to be out in the open chasing criminals; she was on a covert mission. He loved Alessa's courage and strength, but he was once again left wondering what life would be like for them. Could he deal with her constantly putting her life in danger? He sighed. That was exactly how things would work if she stayed in the army. He'd be at home each night worrying about whether she was safe, and *if,* not when, she'd make it back to him. It was the life his mother had led. Was he prepared to do the same?

How did she even know how to find us? Then it hit him.

He brought out his phone and looked at the GPS tracker on hers. He hailed a three-wheeled, motorized rickshaw and got into the open back seat. Reza jumped in after him and Luke didn't bother to kick him out. The determination was clear in the man's eyes and depending on the situation, it might be useful to have another set of hands. He directed the driver, following Alessa's GPS. She was a good distance ahead of them and still moving.

He called the team but it would take them at least twenty minutes to mobilize. Way too late to help.

The driver slammed on the brake and Luke sucked in a breath. The street ahead was jammed. A cart had overturned, spilling bricks across the road. It had happened seconds ahead of them. Bricks were still tumbling from the wagon. He checked the screen. Alessa had stopped moving and was two clicks ahead of him.

He threw money at the driver and hopped out. He broke into a run. On a good day, he could do a five-minute mile but he knew he would be slower dodging cars and people. Still, he ran as fast as he could, legs burning as he tore through the city toward Alessa. If the kidnappers had reached their destination, Alessa wouldn't just sit still, even knowing that Luke was right on her tail.

The best chance at rescuing Amine was when they brought her out of the car, while she was still mobile with no physical barriers aside from the guards between them. Alessa would try to rescue Amine immediately, he knew without a doubt she wouldn't think twice about taking on a bunch of thugs by herself.

He turned down a side street, consulting the map on his phone. The path was clearer and he increased his pace. He didn't bother to check on Reza; he could hear the man's footsteps and labored breathing behind him. When he got within a few hundred feet of Alessa, he slowed, needing to assess the area. Reza had fallen a little behind but caught up to him, his panting loud enough to be heard over the relative quiet of the street they were on. It looked like an industrial section of the city with warehouse-like structures. The usual sounds of the city—horns, birds, people—were muted. Luke turned and put a finger to his lips. Reza understood and put a hand to his mouth, trying to calm his rapid breathing.

Then he saw it. A bike. He couldn't be sure it was the one Alessa had been riding—he'd only seen it in a flash and it was a generic gray and black that were a dime a dozen in the city—but he bet it was hers. It lay in the middle of the street, as if the rider had carelessly thrown it or had been plucked off. Luke's chest tightened but he forced himself to stay focused. He couldn't rescue Alessa or Amine if he let his emotions get the better of him.

He didn't see any security but he moved slowly. It wouldn't do any of them any good for him to walk into an ambush. His heart leaped into his throat as he heard a series of thumps and groans and the soft sound of someone crying. He couldn't take it anymore.

He whipped around the corner, a knife in one hand and the pistol he kept hidden in his pant leg in the other.

"About time you showed up. I had to do all the hard work myself."

He shouldn't have been surprised. Alessa stood with Amine, an arm around the sobbing woman. Three men lay on the ground, moaning in pain. The car that had taken Amine was parked, its passenger door open. Alessa's clothes were dirty and her hijab was askew, but other than that she looked fine. Amine was distraught, but she seemed to be physically okay.

Reza whistled. "I know my sister didn't do this." Luke tried not to bristle at the admiring look Reza gave Alessa.

That's my woman.

Reza went to his sister's side to check on her. Luke wanted to glare at Alessa, silently tell her just how mad he was at her for putting her life in danger like that, but all he managed to do was mouth *I love you.* She was safe, and she'd done quite a job of neutralizing the threat. Wasn't that all that mattered? He thought about when his mother's sister had died and she couldn't go to the funeral. She'd been so upset, ready to leave his father and the army life. But then there had been casualties on an operation her father was leading and when he returned, his mother greeted the general with relief and love, forgetting all about anger. Now he understood why. And the thought made his chest burn. Life was always tentative in the army, and he'd never stop worrying about Alessa.

Luke got to work looking through the car for something to secure the men. He found some rope in the trunk and hog-tied the two men to each other, then hauled them into warehouse. It turned out to be more of a storage unit. He threw the men inside, then closed the door. They made an anonymous phone call to the police.

By unsaid agreement, they all piled into the kidnappers' car, leaving the motorcycle on the street with the keys next to it. It would be stolen in seconds once they left. Reza sat in the front and Amine and Alessa sat in the back. Luke started driving to get them out of the area, they needed to be far away when the police arrived, but he had to think about where they could go.

"Our apartment," Alessa said without hesitation, as if she'd read his mind.

Luke shook his head. The entire unit was staying in the same building. They couldn't compromise their location. He motored the car toward the safe house where they had planned to hold the target. It was a huge risk, but he didn't have a choice. They couldn't arrange for another safe house with such little notice and they didn't have the target yet, anyway.

"So *are* you CIA?" Reza asked with a gleam in his eyes.

"Let's just say something like that." The less he shared the safer they would be, but he couldn't exactly keep pretending he and Alessa were just civilians. "You can't tell anyone." He added, taking a second to look Reza in the eyes. "You tell someone and we'll die."

Reza nodded. "Do not worry, if there is one thing we know how to do, it's keep our mouths shut."

Amine sniffed in the backseat and Luke glanced in the rearview mirror to see Alessa putting an arm around her.

"I can't protect you for long. What do you plan to do?" Luke asked Reza.

He sighed. "I don't know. I thought maybe we would make our way to the other side, to Rawalpindi, or go to the American consulate and ask for asylum. Is there anything you can do?"

Luke shook his head. He had absolutely no contacts in the State Department and asylum applications were impossible in the current political climate in Washington, DC. "I think your best bet is to get to India. There's less of a Taliban influence there and you'll be well hidden."

Reza rubbed his head. "I only have so much money. It's hard to find jobs in India."

"It's not that easy in the United States," Alessa noted.

"It is when you have a degree and an education," Reza said matter-of-factly and Luke saw Alessa sit up straighter. He wondered if going to college was something she'd ever considered. He had been ready to go into an ROTC program to experience regular college life, but at the last minute, Ethan and his father had leaned hard enough on him and he'd accepted his admission to West Point. He knew there were kids who staked their entire lives on getting into West Point, but he often wondered whether he'd have continued with the army if he'd experienced an existence outside the army family.

"Think about it. I still believe India is your best option. You speak English, so you'll be fine there."

He looked sideways at Reza and the man appeared pensive.

"You'll be safe at the house I'm taking you to, but I need you to stay inside and not make any phone calls or tell anyone where you are." He was taking a big risk using the safe house where they planned to hold Azizi, but he had no other options. Luke wanted to make sure Reza and Amine understood the parameters so they didn't inadvertently risk his unit's lives.

"Like prisoners," Reza said.

"Yes." Luke's tone was hard. He wanted there to be no confusion on this point. "I can drop you off somewhere else if this is not agreeable, but if you come with us, we need to keep you locked up for everyone's safety."

Reza seemed to consider this and Luke turned onto a street that would take him a circuitous way to the safe house. He hadn't seen anyone following them but it was hard to tell in the chaotic traffic.

"I trust you," Reza said softly and the words were like a punch to the gut. He didn't deserve Reza's trust. He had left the young man and his pregnant sister on a dangerous mountain in an effort to complete his mission. More than that, he had no idea whether he could truly protect them. Just like he couldn't protect Alessa.

When they arrived at the house, Luke quickly ushered them inside. While they'd selected the house because it offered a high cement fence and vegetation, it wasn't completely private. Luke had called Boots and Dan, and he introduced them now by their cover names.

Luke took Amine and Reza to one of the spare bedrooms.

"We'll bring you supplies in a little bit." Alessa said thoughtfully. She went to the kitchen and brought back two glasses and a jug of water.

Luke left the siblings and called the team together so they could talk. They gathered in the living room with Rodgers and Steele on the phone. It was time to wrap things up. Luke didn't want this mission to drag on and get more complicated than it already was.

He asked the team for ideas on where the target could be. They bandied it about, discussing various options until everyone was out of steam. Dan offered to go arrange for food. Boots and Dimples were patrolling the outside of the house. Rodgers and Steele were still back at the safe house. Luke pulled Alessa aside.

"Do you have any ideas on who the leak might be?" Luke asked.

Alessa shrugged. "I'm working on it."

Luke rubbed his neck. Alessa was hiding something. But he couldn't imagine Rodgers or Dan or any of the other guys, for that matter, betraying the unit. Not on purpose. Then it hit him.

"Boots told me Ethan asked him to keep an eye on the unit. Do you know if he was also monitoring Colonel McBride?"

Alessa nodded. "I assume so. The colonel was my prime suspect initially."

"So after Ethan disappeared, who did Boots report his suspicions to?"

"Nobody."

"But what if another unit member had been tasked with the same assignment by Colonel McBride? To keep an eye on the unit. What if they are under direct orders to keep tabs on me? Maybe the leak isn't coming from one of the guys but Colonel McBride."

Alessa sighed. "That would explain it."

"Explain what?"

"Give me a day to check something out."

"Alessa!"

"Tomorrow, Luke. Before I betray a friend, I want to be sure."

He clenched his jaw. There was a lot he wanted to say, but knew by the tide of anger rushing through him that now was not the time. Alessa was supposed to be on his side.

Luke went outside to find Boots, who was patrolling the grounds. Darkness had settled into the city but the sound of horns and the general populous moving around still screamed strong.

"Go ahead and bar the windows from the inside so someone can't get in." Luke said after he'd reviewed the perimeter security. Boots nodded.

"You know, you're pretty good at this." Boots said.

Luke laughed. "That's nice of you to say."

"No, I mean it. This isn't an easy job. Ethan

struggled with it, too, but I don't think he could quite think outside the box like you can. Even though he encouraged us to break from the army mold, he had trouble doing it himself."

That didn't surprise Luke. Ethan ate, slept and breathed the army. Luke often joked that he should really go into recruitment. The way he talked about the army, one would think joining up was the equivalent of winning the lottery.

Boots slapped him on the shoulder. "I hope you stay."

Luke turned from the doorway. "What?"

"I hope you keep command of the unit. I think we can do good work here. Together. This is a solid team, and you're the right guy to lead it."

Luke was never one to seek praise, but Boots's words shot a bolt of excitement through him. Truth was, he had been enjoying the work with the unit—perhaps because it wasn't the typical deployment. He was allowed to think for himself. He had a knack for this, and for the first time in his life, he was figuring out how to use his instincts to make strategic decisions. He wasn't just doing things by the seat of his pants, but he also wasn't overthinking every single move.

Maybe the unit was the right place for him. It wasn't as if he'd figured out some other dream career. What if this was where he was meant to stay? But it wasn't an option for him. Not if he wanted Alessa.

CHAPTER TWENTY-FIVE

ALESSA KNEW IT was no use. As tired as she'd been the last few days, she'd figured sleep would descend as soon as she closed her eyes. Instead, she lay wide-awake blinking into the darkness of the cold house. She was thankful for a break from Luke so she could think about their relationship without his distracting presence. She had offered to take the night shift at the house with Rodgers. Luke had initially refused but she'd reminded him that with Amine there, it would be advantageous to have another woman just in case she went into labor and needed help before they could get a doctor or midwife. She looked over at the pregnant woman now and saw her hands moving over her belly.

"You okay?" Alessa asked.

"Yes," came the small reply.

"What's wrong?"

"I am thinking about what kind of life I will give my child."

Alessa didn't hesitate. "A better one than you

had," she said softly and meant it. A conversation she once had with her mother flitted back to her.

He's not perfect, but he's given us a better life than what he had—and what I had—as a child.

While her mother hadn't shared a lot about her childhood, Alessa knew she'd grown up poor and had often gone to bed hungry. Alessa's father had reminded them every night to be thankful for food on the table. She hadn't really grasped the meaning of that until she'd run away from home when she was twelve years old.

She'd taken a hundred dollars with her, money she had carefully saved from babysitting, and had grand plans to find a job and support herself. Then she'd discovered that not only could she not get a job even if she lied about her age, but that the money would get her a night at a motel and not much else. She'd survived for a week by barely eating and sleeping on a park bench, until someone stole her cash. It was the only time in her life she'd actually been glad to come home and have dinner. Yet food and shelter weren't the only things a child needed. Her parents hadn't realized it, and all her life she'd wondered whether she had enough love in her heart for a husband and children.

She didn't wonder anymore. Luke had thawed her heart.

"I did not want this child. But now that I know he or she is coming, I want nothing more than to be a mother. I want to give love like it should be given."

Tears stung her eyes. Alessa knew exactly what Amine meant. She'd thought a lot about why Aidan had been able to take advantage of her like he had. It was because he had given her a glimpse of what it might be like to love and be loved.

"How will you manage?" Alessa hadn't meant to ask the question that way. When the other soldiers in the barracks talked about babies, it was always something they planned to do after they left the army. She'd only met a few who had children, and they spent their entire deployment counting the minutes until they could go home. They looked longingly at the birthday pictures, missing the cake they didn't get to eat, reliving the first time their kid walked or scored a goal through videos. A never-ending litany of missed moments. It was partly why Alessa had never considered kids as something that could ever be a part of her life.

"I am not knowing where you are from. But in my country, everybody takes care of a child.

The whole village. All I have to do is provide the love. Allah will take care of the rest."

Alessa closed her eyes, wondering what it would be like if she had a child. The army would give her a housing allowance or a home on post. Once you had a family, you didn't have to stay in the barracks. There were daycare facilities. Her salary was enough to buy food and necessities from the Post Exchange. There was a school at every post and when she deployed, there were services and programs to find child care stateside. It did take a village to raise a child, but her village was the army.

"I did not go to school," Amine said. "But whether I have a son or a daughter, I will send them to school. I will make sure they know how to read and write."

"Your English is pretty good," Alessa commented.

"Reza taught me. Since he was a little boy, he was into everything English. He learned from one of the foreign aid workers and he says to me, I will walk English and I will talk English and I will only be speaking to you in English."

"It's a good thing he taught you. You will have many more options open to you."

"I don't know. Sometimes knowing puts things in your head. My husband did not like me talking English. I listened to programs on the radio when we had a signal. He caught me once…"

She didn't need to say more for Alessa to understand.

"I heard a story once," Amine continued, "about an Afghan girl who went to America and became a doctor and has a big house and buys everything for herself. She didn't even have a husband."

"That's what education can do. You have a whole new life to look forward to."

Which made Alessa think about her own options. The GI Bill meant she could go to college if she wanted. In high school, a career counselor had told her she could have a great career in the "humanities." Alessa still didn't know what that meant. But one thing was for sure: after this mission, she would go visit the Barden Education Center when they returned to Fort Belvoir and find out what programs were available to her. She couldn't just wait for the army to promote her. She'd always thought her path was to become an officer by being promoted through the enlisted ranks, but maybe she should consider other army careers. Get a degree. Maybe with Luke's commendation, she could get time off to do a course. Then it hit her.

She had assumed that all they had to do

was keep their feelings for each other a secret until Luke left the army after this mission was complete. But Luke's commendation in her file would be a firebrand against her career if they continued their relationship. If he didn't put anything in her file, she'd be tagged as having been demoted to logistics. Most importantly, if she got promoted and someone on the team didn't, they would no longer respect her.

What if it doesn't work out with me and Luke? Her career was real, a way to support herself and Julia. Without it, she'd be left with nothing. *Without Luke, I'm back to where I was. Without the army, I'm nothing.*

THINGS DIDN'T LOOK much better in the morning than they had the night before. Luke had no idea what to do with Reza and Amine—or Alessa, for that matter. So much was being left unsaid between them. And they were no closer to finding their target. He had the one location the guard had given him. Luke hadn't discussed it with the team, unsure of whom he could trust.

Reza, Steele, and Boots were out gathering supplies to replenish their stocks. Reza spoke Urdu fluently and offered to help them navigate the local marketplace. They had discussed it as a team and decided Reza was low risk. He'd given his phone to Luke and the guys would keep a close eye on him. Luke wanted no stone unturned and had instructed the team to continue looking into every lead regarding Azizi's location. Dan and Dimples were surveilling one spot and Rodgers had been on the night shift surveilling another.

Alessa entered the living room and set down two steaming cups of tea on the rickety coffee table.

"How's Amine?" he asked.

"She's sleeping. Didn't get much rest last night." She motioned with her head toward the back of the house. There was a storage room there where they could speak with more privacy.

"Alessa, that location the guard gave us— you, me and Boots are the only ones aware it even exists. Before I launch another raid, I need to know who the leak is. This is our last shot to get the guy. We can't lose it."

The poker face was back. "I don't want to ruin someone's career over a hunch. I need more time."

"We are out of time!" Anger roared through him. After everything that had happened between them, Luke expected Alessa on his side. His team had narrowly escaped two potential ambushes. He couldn't risk taking them into another one. Who was she protecting? And why didn't she trust him? Hadn't he lived up to her expectations as a leader? Did she think he couldn't handle it? He gave her a hard look. "The only reason I let you come on this mission is to gather intelligence on the team. Tell me what you've found, Parrino. I'm not asking."

Her face cracked and his heart crumpled at the pain in her eyes. "Yes, sir."

He knew she meant to sound sarcastic but her voice came out small. He hated himself for taking that tone with her but it's what he would've done if it had been any other team member. Wasn't that what she had been asking of him, to treat her like all the others?

"For what it's worth, I don't think he's doing it maliciously. My guess is he thinks he's doing his patriotic duty. I found some calls to the Pentagon and haven't been able to figure out who they are going to, but I've confirmed they're all being made by one unit member."

Luke's pulse raced. "Who is it?"

Alessa swallowed. "Rodgers."

Luke squeezed the bridge of his nose. That explained why she was so reluctant to tell him anything. "Why didn't you come to me sooner?"

"Because I couldn't figure out what to make of it until you came up with your theory yesterday about someone under orders to spy on the unit and report back."

"Maybe it's because you owe Rodgers."

She had the decency not to deny it.

"Alessa, did you consider that he did you a favor so he could ask for one in return? It's not the first time a guy's used that ploy with you." Fire roared through his veins, making it hard to think.

Her eyes blazed. "Don't lash out at me for keeping things from you when you've been doing the same."

"Excuse me?"

"Boots said he saw Ethan alive."

Luke frowned. "Yeah, so?"

"So why didn't you tell me about it?"

"What?"

"You kept that from me even after I was going on about needing to make sure he was still alive. Why?"

"It must have slipped my mind. I didn't keep it from you purposely. It's not exactly news— all signs pointed to him being here." He meant it. He wasn't sure why he hadn't told Alessa about his brother.

"It must be a relief to know you were right about Ethan." Something in her tone made him look up.

"Of course it is…"

"But Ethan's return means you are done with the unit. Are you ready for that? Are you still willing to leave the army?"

He took a sharp breath. Maybe this was why he hadn't told her. How could he explain what he was thinking without sounding like a complete jerk? It was more than a relief to know that Ethan was alive. Though he'd feel even better once he actually laid eyes on him and confirmed Ethan was okay. But Ethan being alive meant he'd take back command of the unit. Luke had wondered what it would be like to really be the unit commander. To stop focusing on proving himself and finding Ethan and really work on the unit's goals. He wanted to share all of this Alessa, have an open and honest conversation about how they could make things work between them.

"If I wanted to stay, would you be willing to leave so we could be together?"

She stepped back. "That's not fair!"

"Why not?"

"The army is the only thing I've ever had," she said, her voice cracking.

"Same here." Luke said in a softer voice.

She moved closer to him, then stopped, hesitant. He stood and closed the distance between them, taking her in his arms, needing to feel what it was like to be with her, to know that he wasn't just imagining the greatest love of his life. "What'll we do?"

Alarm bells were ringing in his head but he couldn't think of anything other than feeling her heart beat against his. More than anything, he needed to connect to her soul, to know that she still loved him and that nothing else mattered in this world. In the thick of the mission, it was easy to forget that one day the mission would end. And what would he be left with? What did he want to be left with? His hands were around her waist and he moved them up her back, feeling the sharp intake of her breath against his chest. She fit perfectly against him, as if some cosmic universal force had designed them to fit together. Impossibly, destiny had brought them together, and now it was up to him to make sure he found a way forward for them.

He was so lost in that it took a gasp from Alessa, and her quick withdrawal from his embrace, for him to realize something was wrong.

His eyes flew open. Alessa's hand was on her mouth. He whirled to find Boots standing there gaping at them.

CHAPTER TWENTY-SIX

"I KNOW WHERE Ethan is." Boots announced quietly. He looked from Alessa to Luke, his lips pressed together. She wanted to explain, to fix the situation. If Boots said something, her army career was over. But it was clear now was not the time.

Luke went into command mode, getting all the details and issuing orders. Boots had been surveilling one of the locations the team had brainstormed yesterday and happened to see the target. He had then found a high perch and was able to look into some windows and spotted Ethan through a scope.

Luke called the rest of the team and instructed Alessa to get the packs ready.

"Rodgers, you stay here and guard Reza and Amine."

Rodgers protested but Luke remained firm, refusing to discuss the location or any other details. As she was packing their supplies, Rodgers caught Alessa's arm. "It's not fair. I don't understand why I'm being sidelined. Is it because I said something about you and Luke?" He was referring to the conversation they'd had at the apartment.

Alessa's chest tightened. Rodgers had been her friend and Alessa owed it to him. "You're not coming because we know you've been spying on the team."

"What?"

"There's no time to play the back and forth of denial, Rodgers. We know you've been reporting the team's activities to someone high up in the Pentagon. We think that's the traitor and your information is why the team hasn't been able to grab Azizi." Rodgers staggered backward, clearly surprised. Alessa had never believed he was purposely jeopardizing the team and now she was sure of it. "Think about it— our last two attempts at getting the target? No way he got out just in time through sheer luck. Do us all a favor—don't report in today and see what happens."

The look of horror on Rodgers's face told her she'd done the right thing in telling him. He hadn't considered that his contact was the leak.

Once they were in the jeep, Luke explained the operation to the team. He was efficient with his instructions but covered all the bases. Just the way a commander should be. The men nodded, their understanding, respect and awe clear in their eyes.

These types of rescue missions were not done on the fly. They often took hours and days of planning, but the team didn't have that much time. It was possible they were already too late but Alessa could tell from Luke's energy that he was feeling optimistic. The men could feel it, too. There was intense focus in their eyes, their jaws set in firm lines. When they got to the house, they followed in step with Luke, none of them wavering.

He was a natural born leader. She hadn't encountered many of them, but she could see it in Luke's eyes. He loved every second of this. He wanted this. Now that Boots had caught them, they only had one option. Either Alessa or Luke would have to leave the team. There was no other solution. She had always assumed it would be him. But what if he wanted her to go?

THINGS WERE FINALLY going according to plan. They found the house that Boots had been surveilling. Alessa created a diversion that got most of the security people out onto the road so all they had to contend with were a few guards inside. According to the thermal scan, there were two stationary people inside as well.

Luke entered first. He quickly dealt with the first guard he encountered, then made a beeline to the room of Stationary One, as they'd dubbed the lone figure. Boots was in charge of Stationary Two. The door was locked, so he used a crowbar to pry it open. The door was stubborn but Luke was high on adrenaline. Ethan was on the other side of that door. He could feel it. He pushed against the bar until he heard the lock give way, then pushed some more and rushed into the room.

"About time you showed up."

His own face looked back at him. Ethan was on a bed, one hand tied to the metal grate on the window. He had a few days' growth of hair on his face and his eyes were bloodshot but otherwise he looked okay.

Luke grinned. "You know I had better things to do with my time than rescue your sorry behind." He got to work freeing Ethan's hand.

"I've tried loosening the bar, but it won't budge. The best I could do was get the window open hoping that someone would spot me," Ethan said.

Luke had a small axe strapped to his leg and he took it out now and whacked at the chain that connected Ethan to the window. "You did well." Ethan still had a handcuff around his wrist, but that could be cut off later. As soon as the chain was off, Ethan was on his feet in a flash. He stumbled and Luke grabbed hold of him.

"They haven't let me out for a few days." Ethan grumbled.

"I got you," Luke said and Ethan placed an arm around his brother's shoulder, squeezing it tightly. The knot that had twisted inside of his stomach ever since he'd heard about Ethan's death finally loosened.

Alessa met them at the door. "Stationary Two was Azizi. Boots has him but the guards from the road are coming back. We need to go."

They half carried Ethan to the jeep and shoved him in the back. Dan, Dimples and Boots were already inside. The smiles on their faces were the biggest that Luke had ever seen. As Dan careened out into the streets of Peshawar, the guys slapped Ethan on the arms and legs, whatever they could reach, and he did the same.

This was Ethan's unit. Always had been. The guys tolerated Luke because he was a shadow of their leader. He'd been crazy to think he could ever command the unit on a permanent basis.

They all agreed it was better to take Ethan back to the apartment Luke was sharing with Alessa until they dealt with the target. Steele was put in charge of Ethan while the rest of the team secured Azizi. Once they had the name of the army traitor, they'd turn Azizi over to the CIA station chief to deal with.

When they got Azizi back to the safe house where Rodgers had prepared a room, Luke had Dimples lead the interrogation while he watched. He sent Alessa with Boots and Dan to secure what they needed to return home.

It took the better part of the night, but Luke managed to get a lot of information out of Azizi. Except the name of his army contact. Near dawn, he went outside to get some fresh air. A rickshaw pulled to the mouth of the drive-way and Alessa stepped out. Luke's heart leapt into his throat at the sight of her. She was wear-ing the pink *salwar kameez* he liked. The shade brought out the slight color in her cheeks and the golden undertones of her skin. She looked radiant and her eyes were wide with anticipa-tion. Luke walked toward her and she gave him a smile so brilliant that his knees threatened to buckle beneath him.

"I hear you did well." The team had checked in with each other throughout the night. Every-one was in high spirits. They'd accomplished their objective and recovered Ethan. Luke was exhausted and relieved.

"You know the guys are impressed with your

leadership. They plan to tell Ethan how great you are as unit command."

"I know." He smirked. Not that it would make a difference to have the team's recommendation, but it was still nice to have.

"Really?" Her eyes sparkled. "What else do you know?"

"I know more than you think."

She raised a brow. "Like what?"

"I know what the guys call me." He wiggled his eyebrows and felt his heart flutter at the twinkle in her eyes.

"What're you talking about?" she said with a neutral expression.

He had gotten better at reading her poker face. "I guess I shouldn't be that insulted. From what I understand, Fabio is the man of many women's dreams."

She put a hand to her mouth and laughed. "Do not say anything to the guys or they'll think I told you," she whispered fiercely.

He leaned over, unable to resist getting closer to her. "You just did."

She gasped. "You mean…"

"I figured it was the nickname they were most likely to give me. That or Ken after Barbie's boyfriend. It was a toss-up. Glad I guessed right."

"You are horrible."

"Oh, you don't know the half of it." He leaned closer, intending to drop a kiss on her head before he realized where he was and who she was. He straightened and stepped back into the house.

"Where are Reza and Amine?" she asked, following him in.

"They're talking, evaluating their options."

Alessa touched his arm. "We need to help them."

Luke closed his eyes for a second. Alessa was right of course.

"We can only do so much. I'll talk to some contacts I have, see what we figure out."

She didn't bother to hide her disappointment. But it wasn't just about him anymore. Everything he did reflected on the unit, and the guys didn't deserve to have the team dismantled or get stuck with a lousy commander because he'd gone rogue.

When the entire team returned, he pulled them together in the living room. They conferenced Boots in on the mobile phone.

"You want Ethan in on this conversation?" Steele asked.

Luke hesitated. He had a plan for wrapping up this mission and he didn't want his brother second-guessing his every move. The one thing that every unit needed without question was clear chain of command.

"Sure," Luke said. It was his brother's unit, after all; he had just been the temporary keeper. He kept his voice low. The team huddled together. While Dan was between him and Alessa, Luke knew where she was, felt a charge of electricity course through him and irrationally wanted to tell Dan to switch places with him. There was no doubt in his mind that he could never treat Alessa as just another soldier. This was exactly why the military had such strict rules about dating.

He went through his plan for the target and their exit from the country. "It's dangerous to stay on. I've talked to the CIA station chief and he'll continue Azizi's interrogation."

The guys asked a few questions, then they nodded, a signal that they were okay with the plan.

"Ethan, do you have any idea who the target might be?"

His brother's slightly hoarse voice came through the phone. "It's someone I've worked with. That's about as far as I got. When I got to the safe house on our last mission, someone ambushed me and knocked me out. Since then I haven't been able to figure out why they kept me, why they didn't just kill me or try to ransom me right away. My best guess is I'm valuable to whoever the leak is, and they were using me to keep him in line."

Luke's blood went cold as a thought formed in his mind. Rodgers was refusing to give up his contact until they returned stateside and he could consult with an army lawyer. Luke had taken away his phone and was keeping close tabs on him but had chosen not to tell the rest of the unit about the leak. Alessa had convinced him that Rodgers had not purposely betrayed them and could be trusted to keep quiet until they got back home.

He went over the final plans for their departure and was met with more silent nods. "What, you guys aren't going to rip it apart and ask twenty questions?" he joked.

"It's a good plan, Luke." Ethan's voice came through the speaker phone, surprising him. Whether it was what to eat or where to bury their mother, Ethan had never agreed with Luke on anything. Was his brother just patronizing him? Luke dismissed the thought. Ethan wasn't like that and while the hard part of the mission was done, there were still plenty of opportunities to get hurt or worse.

"What about Reza and Amine?" The question came from Alessa.

Luke sighed involuntarily. "We leave them

here with a few weeks' worth of food and supplies. Tell them they can use the house and the jeep. The rent is paid for two more months."

"We need to do more for them," Alessa countered. He could tell by the fact that none of the guys met his eyes or nodded that they disagreed with her.

"That's outside the scope of the mission. We're not risking ourselves for them anymore. Unless someone else wants to argue Parrino's position, we're not discussing it further."

Alessa looked around but couldn't get any of the guys to meet her gaze. She turned to Luke. He thought he'd felt his heart shatter before, but nothing compared to the sharp pain that pierced through him as he took in her hurt and disappointment. He wanted more than anything to be her knight in shining armor.

He shook his head slightly. There was a brief flash in her eyes, then the poker face was back.

"Fine, then," she said.

He gave the command to mobilize. He wanted them out of country and back on home ground as soon as possible. The mission had been completed with more success than he had ever hoped for and he should be on cloud nine, but that bland look on Alessa's face squeezed his heart painfully. He'd let her down.

"I'll go tell them," she said softly.

"No. It's my decision and I'll break it to them."

He issued some more orders for the team. "Parrino and I will sanitize this house. The rest of you can take care of the apartment complex."

They needed to wipe down every place where they'd spent significant time so that if the target escaped, the authorities wouldn't come and catalogue their fingerprints or DNA. While it was doubtful the Pakistanis would accuse the US Army of espionage, they didn't need their information ending up in a database in case they came back in country. Legally or otherwise.

"Luke, might be better for Parrino to do the apartment. It could be strange having one of us go into your unit." Boots looked at him meaningfully and Luke felt his ears go hot. That was something he'd deal with stateside. Things were moving too fast here to talk with Boots about what he'd seen.

"No worries, I'll do it." Ethan said.

"Ethan, you need to rest," Luke said.

"I'm fine, it'll be good to move my muscles, get ready for the trip home."

Boots didn't look happy but Luke wasn't going to let this become an issue. He issued more orders and they all got to work.

When he came back into the living room, he

and Alessa were alone. Her eyes held a thousand questions.

"We don't have time." He said flinching at his own tone. He stepped past her toward the staircase to go talk to Reza and Amine.

"I just have one question."

He stopped but didn't turn.

"Do you want to keep being unit commander?"

He turned and met her gaze. The chances of him keeping his job were slim to none. Ethan was back and in good shape. His brother would take over the unit and Luke would be back where he was before he'd disappeared. The easy thing to do was lie to Alessa. He was already going to lose the unit, why lose her, too?

"Honestly? Yes, I want to keep command. For the first time in my life, I've found something I'm good at. I want to do this. But I also want to be with you."

She nodded. "Me, too. I can transfer out of the unit to another area."

He shook his head. "If you were an officer, we could make it work. But you know how the army is about officers and enlisted mixing. Whoever your next commander is won't put you up for promotion, and if you stay at the current rank any longer, after the combat you've seen…" He didn't need to finish the sentence.

She got it. She'd be labeled and given the worst assignments in an attempt to squeeze her out.

"I don't know any other life. I feel safe in the army." And those words said it all. Why she couldn't leave.

The words were on his lips. To tell her that he would quit. Chances were he didn't have anything to leave, anyway. But even if he did become a civilian again, she wouldn't. Was he willing to live his mother's life? A few days of worrying about Alessa had him growing new gray hairs. How could he do it for a lifetime?

"I'd give up the unit for you, Alessa. Will you give up the army for me?"

She stepped back.

"Why would you ask me to?"

"Because I will lose my mind every time you're deployed. Because I want us to have a life together—not the life my mom had, seeing my dad every few months." He didn't need to explain more. She got it. "We need to go."

THE REST OF the day went by in a blur. The pain in Alessa's eyes haunted him as he told Reza and Amine that they would be abandoned. Reza took it remarkably well, thankful that they had the house to stay in until he figured things out. Luke gave Reza a burner phone and instructed him to keep it on at all times so he could call from time to time and check up on them. Luke pressed some money in his hands, though the young man initially refused to take it. They could hide at the safe house at least until the baby was born.

The rest of the team's exit was smoother than Luke could have hoped. Twenty-six hours later, they were all back at Fort Belvoir. It was late afternoon and Luke had given them the rest of the day off before they had to return to debrief.

Ethan was the first one off the bus that had transported them from the airport. One by one Luke shook hands with each of the unit members as they exited. While he would see them the next day, the moment represented the close of the mission. They were all home safe. Luke thanked each member.

"Thanks for taking care of my unit." Ethan said before Luke could say anything. Ethan's smile matched his own. Months ago, if he'd discussed this scenario in hypotheticals, Luke would have bet his life that he'd return from the mission begging Ethan to take the unit back from him. Now, he wasn't so sure he wanted to give the unit back to this brother. It felt like his.

Dan, Steele and Dimples gave him some variation of "I hope you stick around."

Boots leaned over like he was giving Luke a hug, then whispered in his ear, "I will follow you to the ends of the earth. But you've got to end it with her. Do the right thing." Luke nodded. Boots was right. He didn't deserve Alessa. When had he ever followed through with a woman? Rodgers came out and nodded to him.

Alessa was last. She fumbled with her bag until the rest of the unit was out of earshot. Then she shook his hand like everyone else and looked at him with big brown shining eyes. His chest hurt so much that he would've gladly taken a bullet wound just to distract him from the pain.

"Thank you," she said softly.

The simple words were so loaded that he had to ask, "For what?"

"For letting me feel love."

His throat tightened, and for a moment he couldn't speak. "Goodbye, Alessa."

"Goodbye, Luke."

CHAPTER TWENTY-SEVEN

LUKE ARRIVED AT his office early the next morning to see Ethan sitting behind the desk. "Excuse me, that's my seat."

Ethan looked up in surprise. If there was one lesson Luke had learned during the mission, it was that he had spent far too much time letting other people dictate terms to him.

Luke snapped his fingers impatiently, and Ethan stood slowly, hands up in a conciliatory gesture. "Okay, then. I thought you'd be begging me to file the after-action reports."

"I haven't been relieved of my command," Luke said tightly.

Ethan frowned. "You actually want to keep it?"

Luke met his brother's astonished gaze with an even one. "Turns out, this is what floats my boat."

Ethan laughed and stepped toward his brother, slapping him on the back. The last time they'd talked before Ethan disappeared, Ethan had been upset at him for wanting to leave the army and berated him for not knowing what he wanted to do with his life.

"Thank you for rescuing me. You've earned command of the unit."

Luke raised his brows. He wasn't sure what he'd expected from his brother. Certainly, an argument pointing out all the ways in which Luke was not well-suited to keep the job.

"I picked the best of the best. And they respect you. That's hard to come by," Ethan said.

"What about you? This is your baby."

"You know, being chained to a bed for twenty hours a day gives you a lot of time to think."

Luke smiled. His brother had always been a go-getter. Even as a teenager while Luke slept in, Ethan was out playing tennis or working on a project. He'd never seen Ethan stand still for a minute.

"Did you figure out the cure for cancer?" he quipped.

Ethan rolled his eyes. "Actually, I wasted that entire time thinking about you."

It was Luke's turn to roll his eyes. "Don't tell me, this was all an elaborate plan to make me want to stay in the army. Well, congratulations, it worked."

Ethan laughed. "Now, that would have been something. No, I thought about what you said before I deployed... How you wanted to do something with your life that would energize you. You know, something that floats your boat." His mouth quirked up in a smirk. "To do something you'd chosen rather than been told to do."

"I thought that's exactly what you did."

Ethan shook his head. "I did what Dad told me to do, just like you. Even this unit was his idea. He browbeat me into taking it on. Said the idea came directly from the White House and he wanted someone he could trust."

Luke shook his head. "We are quite a pair. Dad pushed you and you pushed me."

Ethan smiled. "I never thought of it that way. Maybe subconsciously I wanted you by my side. Misery loves company."

Luke extended his arm and hugged his brother. "I'm glad I saved your sorry behind," he whispered to him.

"I'm glad you want the unit. It's a good group of men, and you're the best leader they're going to get."

After Ethan left, it took Luke a few minutes to boot his computer. All his life he had struggled with how to build an identity away from Ethan. Wasn't it ironic that it was now Ethan giving him a path toward something that could be all his own. He knew it wouldn't be long before Colonel McBride came tapping on his door, and there were some important things he needed to take care of. There was a knock on the door. He looked up. Just the person he was expecting to see.

"Sit."

Rodgers scraped the guest chair back and plopped down. The man looked exhausted. "Didn't get much sleep?" Luke asked.

Rodgers shook his head. "The guilt is killing me. I never meant to harm the team."

"I'm pretty sure I know who ordered you to report from the field, but I want to hear you say it. Just you and me, nothing official without your JAG."

Rodgers shifted in the chair. "Okay, first, this has been going on a long time—since before Ethan's disappearance. I was asked to come try out for the unit, with an implicit promise that I'd make it, and that I was marked for a fast-track promotion if I reported on the unit. I promise I never thought my contact was a traitor."

Luke didn't blame Rodgers. In his situation, Luke wouldn't have suspected it, either.

Rodgers sighed, as if he was glad to be relieved of the burden of his secret. "The person who I've been reporting to is General Williams. Your father."

CHAPTER TWENTY-EIGHT

ALESSA TURNED TO GO, then thought better of it. She'd come this far. Closing her fist, she rapped on the door. She didn't know whether to hope for an answer or not. A few moments later, she heard footsteps and kept her feet firmly planted.

The door opened and her sister's eyes widened. "Lessi!" She waved her sister inside.

The two women had not been physically affectionate with each other since they were kids, so a hug would have been awkward. Julia was the same height as Alessa but with softer brown hair and hazel eyes. She was also curvier, having inherited their mother's more voluptuous build.

"Come in. It's a little messy, I wasn't expecting you."

Alessa realized she'd never been to her sister's apartment. It was a studio with a living room that also functioned as a bedroom and a galley kitchen on one end. A nice, cozy place.

"It's not much, but it's mine."

Alessa smiled. "It's lovely." She took a seat on the daybed. "Sorry, I should've called, but I needed to see you."

"Is everything okay?"

Alessa nodded. Luke had put in a glowing commendation for her and said he would make sure she got a decent transfer. Whatever that meant. Something big had gone down with Colonel McBride. She wasn't privy to everything that had happened but the rumors around the post were that Luke was meeting with some heavy hitters at the Pentagon. He'd been officially offered the unit command position, permanently, and he'd accepted. Only a month had passed since they'd returned from the mission but things seemed to be moving quickly.

Boots had promised not to say anything about the kiss he'd witnessed once she announced she was leaving the unit. He was a good man and didn't want to see Alessa or Luke lose their careers over what he saw as an infatuation that had petered out.

Not once had Luke offered to turn down the position that had been offered to him. While she was technically still under his command, she was on detail to another commander at Fort Belvoir running training exercises. Light duty. After their time in Pakistan, she couldn't imagine doing anything other than special operations. She was bored out of her mind so had requested leave to take care of the things that had been bothering her.

Julia sat down beside her. "What is it, sis?"

"There's something I've never said and I want to say it now."

Julia sat up straighter.

"I'm sorry I left you alone with Dad. I escaped when I joined the army, but I left you behind. I know you hate me for it, and you deserve to."

Julia frowned. "I don't hate you, Lessi. I was angry at you for leaving, but that's because I missed you, not because I couldn't deal with Dad. In fact, I learned from you. I watched how you dealt with him and I followed suit. You scared him, so the first time I showed some gumption, he backed off."

Why have I waited so long to have this conversation? She'd carried around the guilt of leaving Julia, too fearful to ever talk with her sister about it.

"You know, you inspired me to work toward college. When you enlisted, you got out and it gave me hope that I could have a different future, too." Julia didn't have to specify that she meant a different future from their mother. Then it struck her. All her life, Alessa had tried to get her mother to leave the only life she knew, and she'd never understood why she refused. But Alessa was doing the same thing with her own unwillingness to leave the army.

They chatted a while about how law school was going for Julia. Alessa smiled as her sister went on and on about what she wanted to do after she passed the bar exam. "I mean, I could get a loan to go do an international fellowship or I could work for a few years and earn enough money…"

"Don't worry about it. I'll pay for the international program. You focus on getting in," Alessa said.

Julia wrapped her in a huge hug, the former awkwardness gone. "You've done so much for me, paying for my undergrad and then law school. But these international programs are really expensive, and I wouldn't be able to work part-time like I am now to pay for housing."

Alessa bit her lip. Even with combat pay, she could only barely afford Julia's tuition. If by some small miracle she got promoted, the pay increase still wouldn't be enough to cover her living expenses on top of the program fees.

"It's okay, sis, I'll figure something out," Julia said.

"We'll think of something together," Alessa said firmly.

"You know, it's not too late for you." Julia said.

"What?"

"College." Julia explained.

Alessa scoffed. "I'd be the oldest student in the class."

Julia shook her head, her soft brown curls falling over her shoulder. "Not these days. I have people who are like Mom and Dad's age in my classes. Didn't you once tell me you wanted to be a lawyer?"

Alessa smiled. "I think what I said was that I wanted to help women like mom who were trying to get out of a bad relationship but needed legal assistance to do that."

"So like a social worker."

Alessa blinked.

Julia continued, unaware of the sudden thumping in Alessa's chest. "Legal social workers help people navigate support services. Like battered women or abused children. They're like the child services people that came and talked to us every time Mom went to the hospital."

It sounded like exactly the kind of thing she'd be interested in. Except her solution would be more than just social services for the woman and child. It might also involve a certain physical lesson for the perpetrator. It was just as well to stick with the army. There was less of a chance she'd get into trouble.

"I'll think about it," she said noncommittally. Julia looked like she was going to press the issue, so Alessa changed the topic.

"So do you have anyone special in your life?"

Julia shook her head. "The guys here are so immature. All they think about is what they want. What about you?"

Alessa thought about Luke. Was he in her life? Certainly not, given the way he'd been avoiding her. She wanted to tell Julia about Luke but she couldn't formulate the words to describe their relationship. *It's complicated* didn't even come close.

She said her goodbyes to Julia with a genuine promise that she'd visit more often. Julia begged her to stay for a few days but Alessa only had ten days leave and she had another important task that would take her considerably more time.

She touched Julia's cheek. "It'll be different between us from now on," Alessa promised.

"Are you sure you aren't seeing someone, sis?" Julia squinted at her.

Alessa couldn't stop the heat that rose in her cheeks. "Why do you say that?"

"Because, I don't know, you seem different. More open. When we were growing up, you were always so standoffish, like 'don't come near me.' But now…" Julia didn't have the words so she just gave Alessa a hug. Alessa returned the gesture, holding on to her sister tightly. What she thought Julia was trying to say was that she seemed more open to receiving love—apparently not just from Luke.

Maybe love wasn't the only thing she was more open to. She just hoped she wasn't too late.

CHAPTER TWENTY-NINE

IT HAD TAKEN longer than Alessa had hoped to get here, but as she surveilled the house she realized she'd made a lot of assumptions. She was hiding behind a tree trying to get a look inside. There were several signs that someone else was in the house. First, there were two jeeps in the driveway. They'd left one of them for Reza. Who did the second belong to? It could be a doctor or another worker Reza had called. Or maybe Reza and Amine were long gone and there were squatters in the house.

"I should've known you'd show up."

She whirled to find Luke standing behind her.

"What are you doing here?"

"Same thing you are," he replied easily, shaking his head as if he couldn't believe that she was really here. Alessa stared at him expectantly, hoping he'd take her into his arms and tell her he had ached for her as much as she had for him. That he was willing to let it all go for her. Because that was important. She needed to know that there would be equality in their relationship. If they had a relationship.

"Come on. Reza and Amine are inside, and I want you to meet someone… She's very special to me."

Her heart skipped a beat. Who could be that important to him? It had only been two months since they'd last been in Pakistan. Had he already found someone new? *Fabio*, an inner voice said jealously. He was every woman's dream.

The door opened and a blond woman in jeans and a *kurti*, a shorter version of the *kameez*, stepped out. She had a shawl loosely around her neck, and her hair was neatly tucked into a bun. "Don't tell me this is Alessa." Luke must have nodded behind her because she stepped forward, her arm extended. "I'm Kat Driscoll-Santiago."

"*Congresswoman* Kat Driscoll-Santiago, soon to be Senator Driscoll-Santiago," Luke clarified.

Alessa's eyes widened. Luke had talked about the congresswoman, how he had met her in Iraq before she got elected and how they'd become fast friends.

"Kat's been doing some work with Syrian refugees and she stopped by to see if she can pull any strings with the embassy to get Reza and Amine asylum."

Alessa's heart swelled. She should have known Luke would never leave Reza and Amine to fend for themselves. "How is Amine? Has she had the baby yet?"

Kat shook her head. "Not yet, but any day now. Anna is looking her over." *Anna?*

"Anna Atao is the doctor I told you about, who I met in Guam," Luke explained, anticipating her question.

Reza had come outside to see what the commotion was. When he saw Alessa he stepped up to her and clasped her hands. "*Bhabi-jaan*, thanks be to you and Luke for all you have done for us."

Alessa looked at Luke. *Bhabi-jaan* was a term of endearment used for a brother's wife, or the wife of a good friend. No one else bothered to correct Reza, so Alessa let it go and followed him inside.

Amine was in the bedroom. A woman about Alessa's age, with brown hair tucked back in a ponytail, was bent over her, stethoscope in hand. She smiled when Alessa entered. "Hi, I'm Anna." Amine reached out her hand and Alessa took it.

"I am so thankful to you and Luke for bringing the good doctor here."

"Please, call me Anna." The doctor turned to Alessa. "Luke has told me so much about you. I'm glad we're getting a chance to meet."

Alessa didn't know what to make of all this.

"Okay, I didn't find anyone on the south side of the house." A tall man with dark hair and olive-toned skin entered the room. His eyes connected with Anna's and she smiled and wiggled her eyebrows.

"We found our intruder," Anna said.

"Is this…?"

Anna nodded.

The man stepped forward and extended his hand. "You're all Luke has talked about for months—I'd recognize you anywhere. I'm Nico, Anna's husband." His brown eyes were warm and Alessa shook his hand, bewildered at everyone who was here.

"Is it supposed to be so much pain?" Amine wailed, bringing everyone's attention back to her. Anna patted the woman's hand. "You're only slightly dilated. It'll be a while before the baby comes."

"I will surely die by then." Amine wailed.

Anna smiled sympathetically. "When I had my little girl, Teresa, I thought the same thing."

"How old is your daughter now?" Alessa asked.

"Teresa is two and a half going on twenty."

"She takes after her mother," Nico added, his voice deadpan. Anna punched him playfully.

"Where is she now?"

"We are blessed to have my mother-in-law and sister living close by in the States, so they help me when we need to travel," Anna said.

"Do you do that a lot?" Alessa knew she was being nosy, but she was curious about these people who were special to Luke. While she'd heard of them, she had never expected to actually meet them.

"We will be now. Didn't Luke tell you?"

Tell me what?

Another moan from Amine pulled everyone's attention and then Anna shooed everyone out of the room so Amine could get some rest.

They all gathered in the living room, where Reza had made tea. The scent of cardamom filled the air, and as she sank into the couch, Alessa realized that she was emotionally overwhelmed. She'd been razor-focused when she got here, but she'd never expected to find Luke and his friends. Yet she wasn't surprised.

"You must be Alessa." She looked up to see another man, broad-chested with intense dark eyes, had entered the room. She stood to shake his hand. "I'm Alex Santiago, Kat's husband."

Luke took a seat beside her and she turned to see him grinning at her. "Alex works for a nonprofit that's doing some work here. He's going to help Amine and Reza get to India safely while we wait for their asylum application to be approved."

"Thank you," Alessa said quietly to Luke as everyone talked around them.

"What for?"

"For helping Amine and Reza."

"I'm just sorry I couldn't get here sooner. I was afraid I wouldn't beat you here."

"You knew I'd come?"

"The minute we left them here, I was certain you'd be back."

Alessa had a thousand questions, but the group was getting excited about something and they were all staring at Luke expectantly.

"I haven't run it by her yet," Luke said.

Run what by me?

Luke stood and held his hand out to her. She took it, eager to touch him, to know that what she'd felt between them was not just a figment of her imagination. The fission of heat that flew up her arm was proof that it wasn't.

She followed him outside to the backyard garden. There was a swing there, and he motioned for her to take a seat next to him.

"What is going on?"

He shook his head. "What I'm about to tell you is highly classified. Only one other unit member knows and that's because he is neck deep in this. I wouldn't be court-martialed for telling you this—I'd be sent to Gitmo."

She sat up straight. Of course she'd keep his confidence. That he was telling her such sensitive information warmed her heart. He trusted her.

"My father was the traitor we were trying to find."

Alessa gasped.

"He was the one who asked Rodgers to keep an eye on the unit and report back to him," Luke continued. "Rodgers had no idea he was a traitor. That's why I had to accept the unit command position and promise Boots I'd keep my distance from you. And let me tell you, that guy watched me like a hawk."

She smiled. That sounded like Boots. The two of them had gotten close, like brother and sister. By unspoken agreement, they didn't talk about Luke, but they'd gotten together for lunch and beers a couple of times since the mission.

"I needed the cover of the unit to set a trap for my father and prove he was really a traitor. I caught him hook, line and sinker. Turns out he got into some gambling debts and exploited an opportunity to earn some easy cash when he was in Afghanistan by stealing a few bars of gold from the national treasury. Our target helped him, and then blackmailed him for information. When it started getting hot, they took Ethan to make sure my father kept the information flowing."

"Why did he start the unit?"

Luke shrugged. "Ethan thinks it was out of some sense of guilt. If he could be turned, so could others. At his core, he's still a patriotic man. He put Ethan, and then me, in charge thinking he could keep an eye on us. It was some sixth sense that got Ethan to pick the very mission that would incriminate our father. Ethan thinks at some level he might've suspected it all along but just couldn't bring himself to admit it."

Alessa could hardly believe any of this. "You turned your father in?" She would have expected nothing less from him. Luke was a man of honor.

"Ethan helped trap him, too. What's wrong is wrong—he doesn't get a free pass just because he's our father. Maybe *especially* not because he's our father. He taught us a code of honor."

"All those meetings at the Pentagon," she murmured. She had assumed he'd been lobbying to get command of the unit, fighting for the very thing that would keep them apart.

"Briefings on the evidence I collected on my father. They want him to go away quietly. The army can't afford a scandal like this. He's a high-profile figure."

"So he gets away with it?"

"I wouldn't say that. He won't get his pension, and he has to live someplace that isn't exactly a tourist destination. And he's lost me and Ethan."

"What will this do to your career?"

"Nothing. I resigned from the army two days ago, right before I came here."

Her heart skipped a beat. "But I thought you liked running the unit."

"Oh, I did. But I can find other things to do with my life. Love, on the other hand, is not something I can find elsewhere." He held her gaze, and her stomach fluttered. He had been swinging them gently but stopped. "Listen, there is something I need to ask you."

Everything stopped. She sucked in a breath and her heart beat wildly in her chest.

"Alex's nonprofit is looking for a company to do some work for them. It's a combination of social work and rescue. They work quite a bit in the Middle East and sometimes need a special-ops-type force to go in and get something done."

"Like bringing Reza and Amine to safety."

He nodded.